YELLOW BRICK

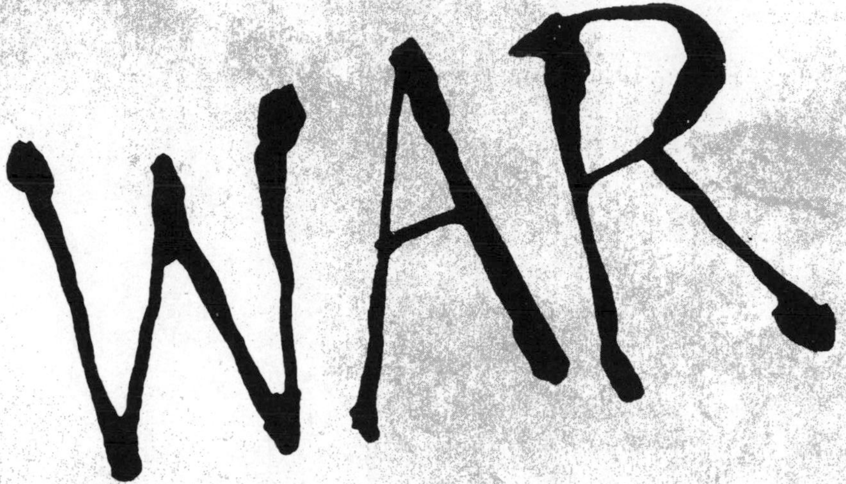

DOROTHY MUST DIE SERIES
BY DANIELLE PAIGE

Novels

Dorothy Must Die

The Wicked Will Rise

Yellow Brick War

Digital Novellas

No Place Like Oz

The Witch Must Burn

The Wizard Returns

Heart of Tin

The Straw King

Ruler of Beasts

Novella Collections

Dorothy Must Die Stories

Dorothy Must Die Stories Volume 2

YELLOW BRICK

WAR

DANIELLE PAIGE

HARPER
An Imprint of HarperCollinsPublishers

Yellow Brick War

For information address HarperCollins Children's Books, a division of HarperCollins Publishers, 195 Broadway, New York, NY 10007. www.epicreads.com

Library of Congress Control Number: 2015959756
ISBN 978-0-06-228073-2 (trade bdg.)
ISBN 978-0-06-245860-5 (special edition)
ISBN 978-0-06-245930-5 (special edition)
ISBN 978-0-06-245842-1 (int. ed.)

Typography by Ray Shappell
Hand lettering by Erin Fitzsimmons

16 17 18 19 20 PC/RRDH 10 9 8 7 6 5 4 3 2 1

First Edition

YELLOW BRICK

The witches were waiting.

The fire blazed behind the three cloaked figures like a scene from *Macbeth*—if *Macbeth* had been set in a bombed-out trailer park. Shadows flickered eerily across the uneven ground. A chilly wind whipped dry dust into tiny cyclones and sent a shiver down my spine. I was standing in the Dusty Acres trailer park—or what was left of Dusty Acres anyway. A fire blazed in the concrete barbecue, the only thing that remained of the place I'd once called home.

Home was nowhere now.

A trio of women faced me, each of them wearing a heavy cloak in a different color: red, gold, and blue. A purple cloak lay on the ground at their feet, glittering with rich gold embroidery. The witch in red was Glamora. The witch in blue was Mombi. And the witch in the gold cloak was hooded so that I couldn't see her features.

"Rise, little witch," Glamora said, picking up the purple cloak. "Take your place among us." I stepped forward. The witches were right. It was time for me to fulfill my destiny. To defeat Dorothy once and for all—with the Revolutionary Order of the Wicked at my back. I took another step forward and reached for the cloak Glamora held out to me.

"You've been training for this your whole life," she said. "You knew we'd ask you to join us. It's time." A second later, her words registered. What did she mean, I'd been training my whole *life*? I'd spent my whole life in this exact trailer park in Kansas, right up until the moment a tornado airlifted me out of Dusty Acres and into a world I thought only existed in books. Then, I'd trained with the Order, learning to fight in the underground network of caves where they housed new recruits, but I'd hardly spent any time at all with them before I'd jumped right into battling Dorothy. Now I realized—Glamora wasn't looking at me—she was looking past me. At someone else.

"I know," a familiar voice said behind me, and Nox stepped forward. "I was hoping it wouldn't be for a while." He met my startled look with a weary smile.

His face was tired and his eyes were sad. He looked exactly as he had when I'd left him, what felt like a thousand years ago. I'd followed Dorothy into the maze behind the Emerald Palace, leaving him behind. I'd found Dorothy—*and* the Wizard. And then the Wizard had opened a portal to Kansas, and Dorothy had killed him and pulled both of us through. *Dorothy*, I thought with a flash of fear. Where was she? If Nox and I had come through the Wizard's portal, she had to be close by. I closed my eyes, reaching for my magic. And . . . nothing. It was gone, like something had scrubbed it out of me.

"You're ready," Mombi said to Nox firmly. She wasn't looking at me either. What was going on?

"I'll never be ready," he said in a low voice. Slowly, painfully, he reached forward and took the cape out of Glamora's outstretched arms, wrapping it around his shoulders. He looked at me. "I'm sorry, Amy," he said.

I opened my mouth to ask him what he was sorry for, and then I realized. The witches didn't want me to take my place among them. They wanted Nox. After everything I'd been through, all my training, they were pushing me aside. "Why did—" I began, but I never got the chance to finish my question.

A huge, booming noise sounded across the gray landscape, and a crackling fork of blue lightning split the sky, landing in the earth in front of Nox with a sizzling noise. Another boom of thunder cracked and echoed, and the cloak began to glow as it swirled around Nox's shoulders. His face was lit with eerie blue light, and magic crackled and sparked around his body. I could feel the charge in the air, like an electric haze radiating from his lean, muscular form. His back stiffened and his mouth fell open. His face twisted as if in pain. "Nox!" I screamed, but the buzz of the magic swirling around him swallowed up his name. The third witch held out a hand to stop me as I lunged toward him.

"He'll be all right," she said. "Stay back until it's done, Amy." Crackling lines of power, like glowing ropes, unfurled from

Nox's body, wrapping themselves around each of the other three witches. I jumped back just in time as power slammed into each of the witches. All four of them rose slowly into the air as magic spun a golden net around them, binding them tightly together. I had no idea what was happening, but it was clearly something big. Something I'd never seen before. Something I didn't even come close to understanding. For one single, shimmering second, the four witches' bodies seemed almost to merge into one huge, flowing form. In the vortex of magic, I could somehow see all the way through to gleaming emerald streets and clear blue skies, and I knew I was looking at Oz. And then with a final, terrifying crack of lightning, the witches split apart and tumbled to the ground. The lines of power snapped back into their bodies like tape zipping back into a tape measure. Nox lay stunned at my feet, wrapped in the purple cloak and gasping for breath. And then I saw the crumpled form lying in the dirt on the far side of the witches. I didn't have to guess who it was: the red shoes, pulsing with a dull throbbing light that hurt my eyes, gave her away. It was Dorothy. Her checked dress was torn and dirty, and her arms and legs were covered in dirt and bloody scratches. But her shoes still glowed with a sickly red light.

"Quickly, now," the hooded witch said urgently. "While she's still weak." She threw back her hood and my jaw dropped.

"Gert?" I gasped. "But you're *dead*!" I had watched her die. I had mourned for her. And now here she was, alive, in front of me.

"No time to explain right now! We'll never have a chance to destroy Dorothy like this again!"

Glamora, Gert, and Mombi joined hands and began to chant, and I recognized the shimmer of magic in the air over their heads. Nox reached for Mombi's free hand, and she took it without interrupting her chant. His voice joined the other witches'.

I tried again to summon my own magic. I was sure this time: there was nothing there. I flexed my fingers, panicking. The magic was gone. My power—all of it. Dorothy was sitting up and looking at her hands in confusion as if she was discovering the same thing. Something had happened to us in that journey through the Wizard's portal—something that hadn't affected Nox and the other witches. And then I knew. Dorothy and I were both from Kansas. I'd never cast a spell in my life before I came to Oz—because whatever magic Kansas supposedly contained, I had no idea how to tap into it—or if I even could. The Wizard had insisted Oz was pulling its magic out of the very dirt of Kansas, but Dorothy and I were out of luck. We were back in a world where we didn't have magic. And if Dorothy was completely powerless, so was I.

"Help us, Amy!" Nox yelled over the other witches' chant.

"I can't!" I said desperately, and his eyes widened in surprise. Dorothy's body was beginning to glow with a pale light that slowly overwhelmed the pulsing from her shoes. But realization suddenly dawned in her eyes.

"We're in Kansas," she said, her voice hoarse and weak. "You brought me back to Kansas. And I *hate* Kansas." She struggled to her feet and the witches' spell dimmed as her shoes began to glow even more fiercely. She flicked her fingers at us and scowled when her magic failed to appear. "I want my palace back," she hissed. "And my power. And my *dresses*." She looked down at the red shoes and they blazed with a brilliant crimson light.

"No!" Gert cried. "Stop her!" But the pale glow of the witches' spell dissolved into a puff of iridescent glitter as Dorothy's shoes radiated light and power. She wobbled a little, clearly exhausted. Her eyes were sunk deep in her skull. Her skin looked dry and stretched over the bones of her face. Her hair was lank and bedraggled.

"Take me home," she whispered feebly. "Please, shoes, take me home." Mombi lunged forward, her own hands radiating the light of a spell, but it was too late. With a flash of red and a sharp pop like a champagne cork shooting out of a bottle, Dorothy vanished.

Dorothy had gone home. And we were stuck in Kansas. For good.

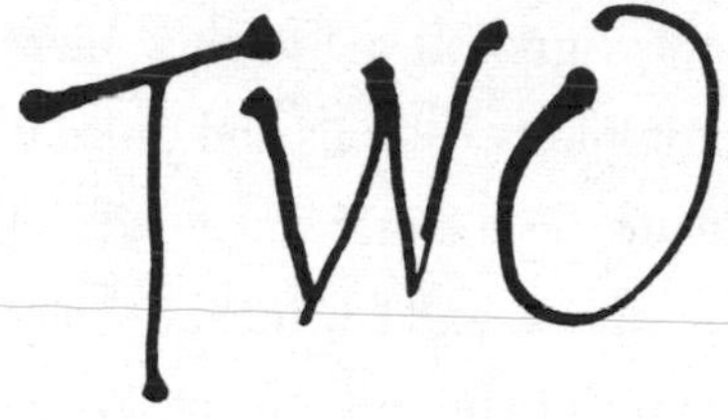

Mombi and Glamora quickly conjured up a silk tent that, fragile as it looked, kept out the dust and the relentless Kansas wind. I hadn't seen much of Glamora lately, and her resemblance to her sister Glinda startled me all over again when I first saw her in the gentle glow of the strands of lights she strung up inside the tent. In a flash, the memory of the time I'd spent with her in the Order's underground caverns came flooding back: her lessons on the art of glamour, her love of beautiful things, and the intense determination in her face when she told me about what Glinda had done to her. She'd nearly lost that first battle with her sister, and I knew how badly she wanted to bring Glinda down. But it still shocked me how close to impossible it was to tell the sisters apart. I'd seen more than enough of Glinda in action for her sister's face to creep me out a little, no matter how much I knew Glamora was on the side of the Wicked. The thing I needed to figure out now, I was realizing, was how much the

Wicked were on the side of *me*.

I tried getting Mombi, Glamora, and Gert to answer my frantic questions, but they ignored me as they bustled around our temporary home plumping cushions and pulling dishes and silverware out of thin air. "What just happened?" I hissed at Nox. He gave me a helpless look, and I wanted to smack him.

"There was too much to tell you, Amy. You know the Order has always had to keep secrets to survive." I shook my head in disgust. When had anyone ever told me the whole truth? I'd thought I could trust Nox at least. Clearly, I'd been wrong. I was furious. More than that, I was hurt. Nox and I weren't just soldiers who fought together anymore. My feelings for him were way more complicated than that—and I'd thought he cared about me.

"Amy, talk to me," he said. "Please."

"Forget it," I snapped.

Glamora being Glamora, she'd also summoned a Pottery Barn's worth of beautiful, soft carpets, heavy throw pillows, decorative tapestries, and a big antique-looking wooden table where the witches were conjuring up a meal. I remembered the handkerchief that Lulu had given me—the one that had created Glinda's version of the same tent. In some ways, the sisters were uncannily alike. Glamora's special touches even included the same votive candles and arrangements of flowers as Glinda's. I wondered, not for the first time, how two people so alike could have possibly turned out so different. Were there other ways the sisters were similar? I'd thought foolishly that I'd been safe in

Glinda's tent. Maybe Glamora's was just as dangerous.

"Amy," Glamora said gently, "why don't you come get something to eat?" I ignored the expression on Nox's face as I turned my back on him and followed her to the table. What did he expect from me? The silk of the tent rustled and I knew he'd slipped outside, which made me even angrier. It was bad enough that he hadn't told me what was going on. But refusing to face me afterward? That was worse.

Mombi, Gert, and Glamora were already sitting around the table over plates of food. I couldn't remember the last time I'd eaten, but I wasn't hungry.

"How can you just sit there?" I exploded. "How is Gert still alive? What just happened back there? What are we doing in Kansas, and how do we get back to Oz? This *is* Kansas, right? Is that why I can't use magic?" Mombi put down her fork and looked at me.

"You can't use magic?"

"No," I said. "Not here. It's just . . . gone, somehow. But that's not the point. You owe me answers."

Gert sighed. "You're right, it's probably time."

"It's way past time," I said.

Gert chuckled. "That's my girl. No beating around the bush, our Amy."

"I'm not anybody's girl," I said. "I'm tired of being jerked around. You obviously know a lot more than I do about what's going on here."

"That's not entirely true," Gert said. "But I do understand

your confusion, and I'm sorry you feel hurt. I know all this has been difficult for you."

"It would be a lot less difficult for me if you would just tell me what the hell is going on!" I yelled. I'd been through so much, and still hadn't managed to kill Dorothy. Tears started to fall and I cried. I cried because Nox, possibly my only friend, probably wasn't such a great friend after all. I cried for poor Polychrome, who'd I'd watched die trying to fight Glinda, and I cried for her dead unicorn. I cried for Star, my mom's pet rat, who the Lion had swallowed whole in front of me. I cried for all the friends I'd lost already in this stupid, senseless, never-ending yellow brick war. And maybe, just maybe, I cried a little for myself, too. When I was done I lifted my tearstained face to find Gert, Glamora, and Mombi looking at me with eyes full of concern. I'd doubted them all, and for good reason. I was more than tired of doing other people's dirty work. But maybe they really did care about me.

"You done?" Mombi asked, gruffly but not unkindly. "Because we have work to do, kid."

"I'm sorry," I said, embarrassment already beginning to replace my outburst of emotion.

Mombi waved a hand at Gert. "Tell her what she wants to know so we can get on with it," she said.

Gert looked at me questioningly, and I nodded. "Okay, let's start with the easy question first. You asked how I'm still alive," she said. "The truth is, I never died."

If that was the easy question, I couldn't *wait* for the hard ones. "But I *saw* you," I said. "I saw you when you died, right in the middle of the first battle I ever fought." I pushed back the gruesome memory of my first meeting with the Lion and his awful animal army. Like a lot of things that had happened to me in Oz, it was something I never wanted to think about again. "I saw you fight the Lion, and lose. It happened right in front of me."

"You did see that," she agreed. "And I did lose, there's no doubt about that either." She shuddered briefly and closed her eyes as if in pain. I wasn't in a mood to be sympathetic to the Order, but it was hard to stay mad at Gert. It was like holding a grudge against your grandmother for accidentally burning your favorite cookies. "But witches are very, very difficult to kill," she went on, opening her eyes again. "Even in a battle like that one. I'm honestly not entirely sure what happened to me when the Lion defeated me. The best guess I can come up with is that Dorothy's magic is weakening the boundaries between your world and ours. When the Lion won, everything went dark for me for a long time. It was as though I was wandering through some kind of shadow country."

"The Darklands?" I interrupted, and Gert looked surprised. I realized that the first time I'd used my magic to find my way into that spooky, desolate parallel universe was after Gert died—or didn't die. Whatever. Gert didn't know I knew about the Darklands.

"She can get there, too," Mombi explained curtly. Gert nodded.

"Your magic has grown considerably since last I saw you,

Amy," Gert said. "Anyway, no—I wasn't in the Darklands, I don't think. There's a lot we don't know about that place. As far as I know I was here, in this clearing, the whole time."

It took me a second to realize she meant Dusty Acres. "You were in the trailer park?" I asked.

Gert looked confused. "I don't know what that is," she said. "But I couldn't leave this area, no. I'd start out in one direction and somehow, without even realizing it, I'd be exactly back where I began, no matter how far I walked. I couldn't touch anything—no matter how far I stretched, everything was just out of reach. I didn't see any other people—not so much as a bird or a beetle." She looked sad and incredibly old. "It was awful," she said gruffly. "It took me a long time to regain any strength, and I'm still much weaker than I was before. But eventually, my magic was strong enough for me to get a message to Mombi and Glamora. They used the breakdown between the worlds to join me here. We had some idea the Wizard would try to use you to open a portal back to Kansas, and we knew the doorway would be in this place, so we came here to wait for you."

"You knew the Wizard wanted to kill me—to use me to open a portal back to Kansas—and you didn't stop him?" I asked angrily.

"Gert was next to useless," Mombi said bluntly. "I'm pretty weak myself. The three of us weren't strong enough to stop the Wizard outright. But we knew if Nox joined us and completed the circle, we'd be powerful enough to defeat him *and* Dorothy."

"Wait, back up," I said. "What circle? Does this have to

do with what happened out there?" And if they were powerful enough to defeat the Wizard and Dorothy with Nox helping them, why had they ever needed *me* in the first place?

"You already know about the balance of power in Oz," Gert said, and I remembered her uncanny trick of reading minds. "Oz depends on magic to survive, and no one person can tap too heavily into it without harming Oz. That balance is part of what the Order was trying to maintain. There have always been four witches—one each in the North, the South, the East, and the West. But that balance has been out of whack since Dorothy's first visit to Oz, and it's even more out of line now. When Dorothy's house killed the Wicked Witch of the East, she opened up a vacuum that no one was strong enough to fill."

"I still don't understand," I said.

"We've been trying to defeat Dorothy by fighting one battle at a time, but that's like trying to put out a forest fire by hauling water in a bucket," Mombi said. "The Order has been scattered across Oz. Half the soldiers you trained with back in the caverns are dead. Others . . ." She shrugged. "We know where some of them are, but we're too spread out to do any good anymore. What we did out there"—she waved vaguely at the ruins of the place where I'd lived since my mom slid into her downward spiral of addiction—"was make Nox into one of us. The Wicked Witch of the East, essentially."

"By restoring the Quadrant, we're finally strong enough to kill Dorothy," Glamora said. "We had all our hopes pinned on you—"

"But I can't kill Dorothy," I said slowly. "Because we're

linked somehow. So you have to do it yourselves."

Mombi nodded.

"Not to mention the fact that Dorothy just teleported herself back to Oz and we're stuck here."

Mombi nodded again.

I sighed and put my head in my hands. I was getting *really* sick of witches. "If you knew all along that you could make Nox into one of you, why didn't you do it sooner? Why didn't you *tell* me?"

"Because once Nox is bound to the Quadrant, he's in for life," Gert said. "There's no hope for him to ever be anything else. We didn't tell you—he didn't tell you—because we hoped it would never come to this. We're older than you can imagine, Amy, and for us the sacrifice is—well, it's done. There's no going back for any of us. But this is a terrible fate to wish on someone as young as Nox."

"He can never live a normal life," Glamora said quietly. "Like us, he's responsible now for the future of Oz. He can never have a family. Grow old like an ordinary person."

"Fall in love," Mombi added, with a significant look at me.

"He can fall in love," Gert corrected. "He just can't do anything about it." She paused. "Of course you still have a place with us, if you want it. But we're in Kansas, Amy. We'll find a way to get back to Oz. And once we're there, we can defeat Dorothy without you. You can go home."

Home. I could go home. It struck me suddenly that I was in Kansas—and I could stay here.

Home was something I hadn't thought about in a long time. I didn't know what Oz was to me anymore. When I first got there, I had thought it was a place where I could finally belong. A place where I had found friends. Then it had become something else entirely.

But had Kansas ever been home either? What was I going to go back to? My mom was gone—who knew if she was even alive. I hadn't exactly been Miss Popularity at Dwight D. Eisenhower Senior High. The trailer where I'd lived with my mom wasn't a place I ever wanted to see again—and even if I did, it was long gone. Home might not be Oz, but it sure wasn't the empty, ruined landscape outside the tent the witches had conjured up. And I'd been through so much in Oz, seen so much, that I couldn't even imagine going back to a normal life. I'd learned how to do things I hadn't even known were possible in a completely new world I hadn't known was real. I'd battled some of the most terrifying enemies imaginable. I'd flown with monkeys, hung out with royalty, killed Dorothy's baddest minions. What was I going to do next, get a job at the mall?

"It's up to you, Amy," Gert said, reading my mind again and pulling me back into the moment. "You don't have to decide right now. But you do need to decide if you want to help us get back to Oz."

"Okay," I said slowly. "So we're not stuck here forever? What's your plan?"

Gert sighed. "It's not going to be easy," she said. "Even with Nox as part of the circle now, we're not powerful enough to open a portal back to Oz. The Wizard was only able to do it because he had the magical gifts he'd given to the Lion, the Scarecrow, and the Woodman." I tried not to think about that last, awful glimpse of the Wizard exploding into blood confetti as Dorothy twisted his spell. "But we do have an idea."

Of course they did—yet another top-secret plan they only decided to clue me in on when they felt like it? I sighed, and Gert gave me a sympathetic smile. "Okay, let's hear it," I said, settling back into a pile of Glamora's cushions. They even smelled heavenly—like the way the makeup counter at a mall smells, kind of glamorous and relaxing all at once.

"You remember Dorothy's shoes," Glamora began.

"Yeah, not likely to forget those," I said.

"Not the shoes she has now," Gert said. "Dorothy's *original* shoes."

I stared at them. "Wait, what do you mean her original shoes? Like, the 'no place like home' ones? Those are real, too?" I almost started laughing. What was I thinking? Of course they were real. If Oz was real, why not Dorothy's magic silver shoes?

"The first time Dorothy came to Oz," Glamora explained, "she didn't want to stay for good."

"If only she'd never returned," Gert sighed.

"My sister, Glinda, sent her home with a pair of enchanted silver shoes—the predecessors to the pair that brought her back here a second time. Dorothy always assumed they'd been lost when she crossed the Deadly Desert, and though she tried to find them again, she was never able to." I wasn't sure how to explain to Glamora that all this Ozian history was a series of classic books—not to mention a hit movie—in Kansas, so I didn't bother trying. "But what if the shoes are still here?"

"Here, like Kansas?"

"She means *here* here," Mombi said. "Where Dorothy's farm used to be."

"Dorothy's farm used to be in *Dusty Acres*?" I asked.

"Not exactly," Glamora said. "Dorothy's farm used to be in the exact spot where your school is sitting right now."

"High school," Gert prompted. She looked at me with her eyebrows raised. "Barbaric system, really. Oz's method of apprenticeship is vastly superior."

Were they serious? Dwight D. Eisenhower Senior High had somehow been sheltering the long-lost magic silver shoes of Oz this whole time? It was almost too much. If only Madison Pendleton had known *that* when she'd done her book report on *The Wonderful Wizard of Oz*. Not that she'd have needed anything extra to get her A+. Everybody loved Madison already. Everyone, that is, except for me. "How do you even know the shoes are still magic?" I asked. "What if they don't work anymore? What if they only go one way, from Oz back to the Other—um, back to Kansas?"

Mombi sighed. "You're right. It's a long shot. But it's the only shot we have. We have to take the chance."

"Okay," I said, "so you guys find the shoes. Then what?"

"Amy," Glamora said, "*we're* not going to find the shoes. If you agree to help us, *you* are."

"But I don't understand how," I argued. "I mean, my magic doesn't work here any better than yours does. Why can't you find them without me?"

"Because they're in your high school," Gert said. "It would look a little funny if three old ladies and a teenage boy showed up for class in the middle of the school year, don't you think? Consider it an undercover mission." She beamed. "To tell you the truth, you're our only hope at this point. If you want to help us get back to Oz, you have to go back to high school."

THREE

"No," I said. "No way. Absolutely, positively, no way in hell am I going back to high school. I didn't even want to come back to *Kansas*."

"We don't have a choice," Mombi said.

"Well, I do. I am not a member of the Quadrant."

"Amy," Gert said gently. "We still need you."

"Why don't you just glamour yourselves?" I said, exasperated. I wanted to help them—at the very least, it would distract me from the decision I had to make. But I sure didn't want to help them like *this*.

"Amy, you've already realized how difficult it is for us to use magic here," Glamora said. "We're close to where the Wizard opened the portal, so we still have some connection to Oz. But the farther we get away from Dusty Acres, the weaker we'll probably be. We simply don't know what effect Kansas will have on our power, and we can't risk a long-term glamour spell."

"You don't need me. You can send Nox," I said. "He can be—he can be a foreign exchange student. From, uh, France."

Glamora cocked her head at me quizzically. "From what?"

"It's like a—uh, it's like Quadling Country," I said. "But with baguettes." The witches stared at me blankly, and the stupidity of my own idea hit me. Right. A foreign exchange student with no papers, no parents, and no passport. A foreign exchange student who had never even heard of the country he was supposedly from. Nox would last about five minutes at Dwight D. Eisenhower Senior High, dreamboat hair or no dreamboat hair.

I didn't want to admit it any more than Mombi did, but the witches were right. Whether or not I wanted to go back to Oz myself, they didn't have a chance of finding the shoes without me. And unless I could come up with a better plan—not that theirs was much of one—the shoes were the only chance they had.

"I can't even get extra credit for learning magic," I muttered. "How long have I *been* in Oz anyway? Everyone in Kansas probably thinks I'm dead."

"You know time works differently here than it does in Oz," Gert said. "As far as we can figure out, about a month of your time has passed while you were in Oz."

Only a month? The idea was crazy. So much had happened to me, so much time had passed. I didn't even feel like the same person anymore. The Amy Gumm who'd lived here was a total stranger. I didn't belong here anymore. I wasn't sure I ever had.

"You'll have to find them fast," Mombi added. "There's no

telling what damage Dorothy will be able to do in Oz. We have to get back as soon as we can."

"I haven't even said I'll help!" I said angrily, but I knew Mombi was right. Yet again it was up to me. "Fine. I'll find the stupid shoes. So where am I supposed to live while I'm repeating senior year?"

"Oh," Glamora said cheerfully, "that part at least is easy. We found your mom."

My mom. Just the word brought back a flood of memories, most of them bad. I'd just been dumped back in Kansas, watched Nox take a place among the witches that they hadn't even considered me for despite how hard I'd worked, and I had no idea if it was possible to return to Oz—or if I even wanted to. And now I was going to have to stay with the woman who'd abandoned me to party with her friends while a tornado descended on our house? It was too much.

"I need a minute," I mumbled, and ducked out of the tent. The air was still and cool; overhead, clouds moved quickly across the stars as if a storm was on its way. Like we needed any more of those. One tornado per lifetime had been way more than enough.

I couldn't help but wonder: What if, that afternoon in the trailer, my mom had decided just that once to take care of me? To drive me to safety—somewhere both of us could ride out the storm together? What if she had finally done the right thing? Was what I'd gained in Oz—strength, power, respect, self-reliance—worth what I'd lost? Without Nox, what did I even have to go back for? Being with him was the closest I'd come to happiness in Oz, but if his duties to the witches meant we could never even try to have a relationship, I didn't relish the idea of returning to Oz just to be the Quadrant's servant.

I wondered what would have happened if my mom had kept me safe and I'd never been airlifted into Oz at all. I knew that somewhere inside the mom who'd abandoned me that day was the mom who'd once loved me as though I was the greatest treasure in her life. But Kansas had a way of stripping the good out of anything, like the harsh prairie winds that peeled pretty paint from siding until all the houses were the same peeling, hopeless gray. And who was I kidding—my life here, in Kansas, had basically been hell.

After my dad bailed, I'd watched my mom's downward spiral: slow at first, circling the drain faster and faster as pills and booze took away anything that resembled the happy, cheerful, loving mom I'd once known. By the time the tornado picked me up out of Dusty Acres, my mom was a couch-hugging wreck who only got up long enough to stagger down to the nearest bar with her best friend, Tawny. And the day the tornado had hit she'd cussed me out for getting suspended—as if über-pregnant tyrant Madison Pendleton's picking a fight with me had been my fault—before abandoning me to the mercy of the storm in order to hit up a tornado party. I remembered what she'd looked like the last time I'd seen her: caked in drugstore makeup, her cheap skirt not much longer than a belt, her boobs racked up to her chin with a push-up bra. Trashy, bitchy, angry, and mean: like a trailer-park version of the Seven Dwarfs. I could've died, easily, because she'd left me that day. And now I was supposed to go back to her? To pretend everything was fine? The witches had asked a lot from me during my time in Oz, but this was something else.

"Amy?" It was Nox. I could barely make out his silhouette where he perched on a crumbling cement foundation. Somehow, he was the person I most *and* least wanted to see at the same time. What comfort was he going to be to me now? He'd made his choice. We could never be together. "Amy, I'm really sorry," he said. I hesitated, and then sat down next to him. He put an arm around me, and I flinched. Hastily, he pulled away.

"Why didn't you just tell me?" I asked. "Why did you even let me hope we could—" I broke off, grateful he couldn't see my cheeks flush in the dark. I was sixteen and I'd only known him for—well, for a month, apparently. It's not like we were engaged, I thought bitterly. Except it had felt like so much *more* than that. I guess Oz did that. Made everything feel larger than life.

The edges of the sky were turning purple, suggesting that sunrise wasn't far off. I couldn't help myself—in spite of all my hurt and anger, I looked up. Kansas didn't have much to offer, but the night sky was something else. The clouds had cleared, and the entire length of the Milky Way spilled across the heavens, blazing with stars. When my dad was around, he'd take me out at night sometimes with a pair of binoculars and point out all the constellations. I could still remember some of them—a lot better than I remembered my dad.

Nox and I were sitting literally on top of where my old trailer had been before the fateful tornado that picked me up and dragged me out of the only world I'd ever known. Being back here was unthinkable. But the Milky Way made me feel for the first time that maybe I had a home here, too. I hadn't missed anything about my world, but seeing the constellations overhead made me reconsider. And if I couldn't be with Nox in Oz, the list of reasons to return had just gotten a lot shorter.

"I'm so sorry," Nox said again. "It's not how I wanted this—" He took a deep breath and started again. "Look, it's normal to have feelings for someone in the heat of battle. Emotions are intense. It's happened before."

Right—how could I forget. Melindra, the half-tin girl I'd trained with when I first came to Oz. She had wasted no time in telling me that she and Nox had been an item. When he took me to the top of Mount Gillikin to see the sprawling, beautiful landscape of Oz and told me I was special, it was the same routine he'd used on her. Now his words stung like crazy. How many girls had he shown that view? How many girls had fallen for his sad orphan shtick? Nox was straight out of Central Casting: Tortured Revolutionary Dreamboat—Are *You* the Girl Who'll Finally Capture His Wounded Heart?

"Oh, great," I snapped. "So I don't mean anything to you."

"Will you let me finish, Amy?" Now he sounded exasperated. "I knew you were different—that's what I'm trying to tell you. From the very beginning. I haven't had a lot of family in my life," he added quietly. "Gert, Mombi, Glamora—as bad as they can be, they were all I had. Until you came along. I didn't tell you because I knew they could call me in at any minute and I'd have to leave yet another thing I cared about. I guess I was dumb enough to think that ignoring the possibility would make it go away. Obviously, I was wrong."

"Can't I help you? Can't I become part of the circle somehow, too?"

"Amy, I don't think you can handle Oz's magic much longer," he said.

"What's that supposed to mean?" I asked angrily. "You think I can't handle myself? Why do you just do everything they tell you?" A sudden thought hit me. "You're *jealous*," I said. "You're jealous of my power, and the fact that I *could* be strong enough to take down Dorothy. You know you need me and you don't want to admit it—because that would be telling the Order that brave, perfect Nox can't do it all on his own."

"Listen to yourself, Amy," he said quietly. "You accused me of doing the same thing when we first met. Remember?"

I didn't want to think about it, but I knew exactly what he was talking about. The night when I was still training with the Wicked. When Gert had first provoked me into using magic, and I'd gotten so angry I couldn't even think. Nox had whisked me away to show me the stars and calm me down. I'd yelled at him for always doing what the Order told him without thinking, and he'd told me how Dorothy and Glinda had killed his family and destroyed his village. He'd opened up to me for the first time, and I'd seen the depths of what haunted him. Of what

Dorothy had taken from him. Compared to Nox, I'd lost hardly anything at all. And now here we were again, under a different set of stars, having the same fight.

"I remember," I said. "But everything was different then." Everything was simpler, I wanted to add.

"Do you really think I'm jealous of you?" Nox said. "How could I be? I've *seen* what Oz's magic is doing to you. It's tearing you apart. I can't let that happen to you. I won't. You know you can't kill Dorothy. You're bound to her somehow. And we know Dorothy has been hopelessly corrupted by Oz's magic—and probably the Wizard, too. When he first came to Oz, he wasn't evil—just bumbling. Every time you try to use your power you turn into a monster. If Oz's magic doesn't twist you into something unrecognizable, it'll—" He stopped short.

"You think it'll kill me."

"I think there's a strong possibility," he said. "You can't use Oz's magic, Amy. Not now, not ever again."

"It hasn't killed Dorothy. Anyway, I can't use magic at *all* here," I said, throwing my hands up in the air. "So it's kind of a moot point for the time being. But if my magic returns somehow, or if we get back to Oz—using magic is my choice to make. Not Gert's. Not Mombi's or Glamora's. Not yours."

"It isn't just your choice, Amy," he said, looking deep into my eyes. "I can't just think about you. I have to think about all of Oz. If you turn into something like Dorothy . . ." He trailed off, tugging helplessly at the Quadrant cloak. "This is so much bigger than just us." I knew what he meant; he didn't have to say it out loud. If Oz's magic made me into anoth[e] he'd have to kill me, too. But being told what to do s my throat. Especially after Nox had refused to tell m truth for all this time.

"You care about Oz more than you care about me," I snapped, hurt and angry. I wanted to take the words back as soon as they were out of my mouth. Of course Nox cared more about Oz than he did about me. Oz was his country, his home, the only world he'd ever known. Oz was his entire life. I was a bitchy, needy teenager who'd crashed the party at the eleventh hour and learned how to be an assassin. If Oz's magic corrupted me, it would be my own fault. Dorothy'd had no idea what the shoes would do to her. But me? I knew all too well the dangers of using magic in Oz.

"You know that's not true," he said. The reproach in his voice was gentle but unmistakable. I wondered how much damage I'd just done acting like a spoiled little kid. I could feel a new distance, like someone had hung a curtain between us.

"I'm sorry," I said quietly. My throat hurt like I'd swallowed a pincushion, but I was sick of crying. For some crazy reason, in that moment I thought of Dustin. Good old Dustin of Dusty Acres, my old high school enemy Madison Pendleton's trusty sidekick. Like me, Dustin had wanted out of this dump. I wondered if he'd gotten it. I wondered if Madison had had the baby that had been threatening to pop out when the tornado hit. I wondered if going back to high school meant I'd have to see her—see both of them—again.

"I wish things were different," Nox said. His voice was tight with some emotion I couldn't pinpoint. Anger? Sadness? Probably he was regretting spending any time with me in the first place. This was war, like everybody kept telling me. Feelings only got in the way. And I was only getting in Nox's. I owed it to him to give him distance. He had to save the world and he didn't need me holding him back.

"Yeah, well, so do I," I said, making my voice cold and hard as I stood up. "But they aren't. So I guess I'd better get to work, since I'm the one trying to save all your asses."

"Amy—" This time there was no mistaking the hurt in his voice, but I turned my back on him. It took all the strength I had not to look back at him as he watched me walk away.

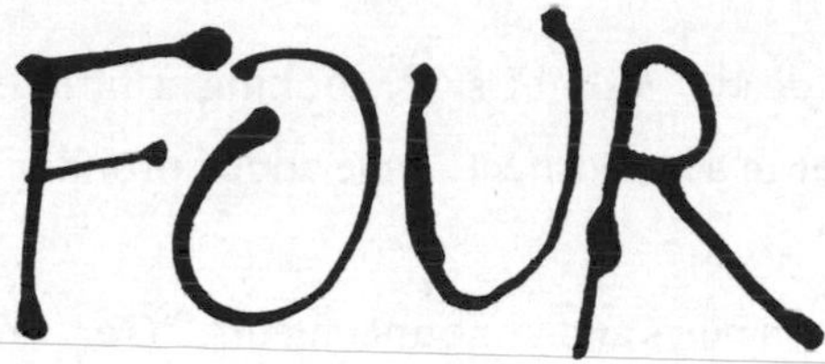

FOUR

"All right," I snapped, pushing my way back into the tent. Gert looked up, startled. "Let's get this done. The last time I saw my mom she was a hot mess. Where'd she end up? How did you find her?"

"Not the last time, Amy," Gert said gently. "You saw her again. Remember? You saw her in the scrying pool."

I knew exactly what Gert was talking about, but I didn't want to acknowledge it. So maybe I'd had a vision of my mom in a new apartment somewhere, pathetically cuddled up to my favorite sweater. And maybe in the vision she'd been clean. But if that was true, it was just as pathetic. She'd had to lose me, her house, and her entire life in order to get her act together? If she'd been a real mom she'd have managed it while I was still around. Normal people didn't need tragedy to tell them not to blow the rest of their lives chasing their painkillers with booze.

"How do I even know if that was real?" I asked. "She could

be passed out in a ditch somewhere for all I know. Or dead by now."

"She isn't dead," Mombi said, looking a little exasperated. "We found her in a broadsheet!" she added proudly.

"A what?"

"A sheet with news and announcements," Gert said slowly, as if talking to an idiot. "In the Other Place they have pictures"—she turned to Glamora—"can you believe that? Pictures! I think that's a splendid idea."

"You mean a *newspaper*?" All three witches looked at me, and in spite of myself, I stifled a giggle. "Okay, right. So she was in the newspaper."

"The broadsheet described the movements of the tornado survivors," Mombi explained importantly. "*I* used that information and compared it to a map of the surrounding countryside." She brandished a tattered old highway map that looked like she'd found it in a culvert.

"You could have just Googled her," I said, laughing.

"I don't know that spell," Mombi said gruffly.

Mombi had saved the newspaper with the details of the post-tornado emergency cleanup effort. My mom had been moved to temporary emergency housing along with everyone else from this area who lost their homes in the tornado and didn't have anywhere else to go—which, as far as I could tell, was our entire trailer park.

"Great," I muttered. "It'll be a Dusty Acres reunion. I can't wait."

We talked for a while about what my plan should be, but the truth was that none of us really knew what we were doing. All we had to go on was a Wickedly half-baked theory that Dorothy's maybe-mythical magical shoes were somewhere in my old high school, and if they were I would be able to find them. It didn't even make sense. None of this made sense. Plus, if the shoes had worked to bring Dorothy back *from* Oz, who knew whether they'd succeed in taking all of us *to* Oz even if I could find them? None of us could use our full magic. We were totally making up this whole thing as we were going along.

But the prospect of action left me weirdly cheerful. Anything was better than sitting around waiting for the end—even visiting a mom I'd been only too happy to leave behind. It was a crazy, stupid, and probably impossible mission, but it wasn't exactly my first crazy, stupid, and probably impossible mission. Once I decided to do it, I felt almost relieved.

Nox hadn't come back inside, and I pretended I didn't care. "You might as well get a little rest," Glamora suggested. "It's not even dawn yet—you can go see your mother later in the morning." I wasn't going to argue with that logic. As I settled into a corner of the tent, wrapping myself up in a soft cashmere blanket the color of Nox's eyes (oh *please*, I told myself, *knock it off*), I was almost surprised to realize how tired I was. It made sense, of course. I'd been through a lot, and it wasn't like we'd been taking naps in between battles. But I was tired all the way through to my bones. I felt like I could sleep for a thousand years without waking up, and the thought was tempting. I wasn't just physically tired—I was tired of everything. Of fighting, of running, of losing. I wanted someone else to take up the burden of saving Oz for a while.

Get some rest, Amy, I heard Gert say in my head.

A warm tingle started in my toes and spread through my body, relaxing my muscles one by one as if I was sinking into a giant bubble bath. It felt just like the healing pool in the cave where I'd first been taken to the Order. Before I knew it, I was actually *there*. The purple walls of the cavern, studded with glittering amethyst stalactites, met in a high arch overhead. The massive tree, whose roots seemed to reach deep into the very heart of the earth, stretched toward the ceiling with gnarled branches covered in tiny white blossoms that drifted down around me like sweetly scented snow. I was floating in the deep, foamy pool, its water as warm as a bath. My clothes dissolved around me as the water drew out my aches and pains and exhaustion. I knew somewhere inside that I couldn't possibly be back in Oz, that the vision was Gert's doing, but I didn't fight it. I drifted off into a deep, dreamless sleep.

The witches let me sleep in. The tent was empty and I could see through its delicate silk walls that the sun was high in the sky by the time I sat up, yawning and stretching. I didn't feel all the way rested, exactly, but I did feel a lot better. I wondered how long it had been noon for, and then I remembered we weren't in Oz anymore. The sun here moved because the earth was spinning on its axis, not because some crazy power-hungry bitch decided it should be sunny for as long as she felt like it. I wasn't thrilled about being back in Kansas, but that part at least was a nice change.

"Oh good, you're awake," Glamora said, sticking her head through the tent flap. "Mombi ate all the bacon, but I'm sure we can whip up some more. She says it's important to sample the local delicacies as long as we're here." I laughed out loud at the idea of anyone calling bacon a "local delicacy," but my stomach growled loudly, and even Glamora giggled.

I couldn't use magic to fix myself up, so I dragged my fingers through my dirty hair and straightened my clothes as best I could. Gert's magical cleansing vision had been all in my head. I was pretty distinctly in need of a real bath, but I decided not to worry about that either. If my mom wanted a pretty princess, she could brush my hair herself. I'd had about enough of other people's expectations.

Nox was wrapping himself up in his Quadrant cloak, obviously preparing to go somewhere. He refused to meet my eyes. The distance between us that had sprung up last night felt even stronger now. I wanted to say something to him, reach out. But I didn't know how to cross the gulf I'd somehow created. I'd been the one to push him away, but I was already regretting it.

"Where are you going?" I asked in a low voice, and he practically flinched.

"Gert and Glamora want me to protect—" he began, but Glamora cut him off with a breezy wave of her hand. Gert and Glamora exchanged glances.

"We're sending him out to do reconnaissance. Make sure the area is safe."

Safe? That was a joke. The scariest thing about Dusty Acres was how empty it was. There was obviously something they weren't telling me. Nox mumbled something incoherent that could have been "good-bye," "I love you," or "go to hell," and stalked off toward the road into town.

I caught Gert studying me with a soulful expression that seemed almost sympathetic. They were trying to keep us apart, I realized. If Nox and I couldn't be together, the witches were going to make sure we weren't around to distract each other. I felt a brief surge of fury. Shouldn't that be up to us? Did I not get a say in my own life? What game were they playing anyway? I'd already decided to keep my distance from Nox. But that was *my* decision, not theirs.

After a picnic-style breakfast of bacon and eggs, Glamora waved the dishes and picnic blanket away, and I stood up. "I want to get this over with," I said tiredly. "Where's my mom?"

Apparently, Gert had been using her extended involuntary Kansas vacation for recon as well as recovery. "I used what we already knew from the vision of your mother you saw in my cave," she explained. "Her hut is right near the high school."

"At least I won't have to take the bus to school," I said. "And it's called an apartment."

Mombi snorted. "Keep your attitude in check, missy."

The apartment where my mom was living wasn't far from Dusty Acres, either, and we all agreed it would be better if I just walked there. Glamora was more tired than she should have been from whipping up our tent and breakfast, and Gert and Mombi admitted Kansas was having an effect on their magic, too. At least it wasn't just me who was suffering, although it wasn't much comfort knowing the witches would have a hard time helping me if anything went wrong. Quadrant or no Quadrant, I was on my own.

It seemed like a bad idea to use their power to transport me a distance I was perfectly capable of walking. The witches offered to escort me, but I only laughed.

"Yeah, right," I said. "No offense, but this is the twenty-first century. I'm going to have a hard enough time explaining how *I* got here, let alone three old bats who look like extras from a senior citizens' Dungeons and Dragons role-playing party."

Mombi smoothed her blue cloak huffily. "We don't have dragons in Oz," she said.

"Never mind," I said, shaking my head. "I'm fine on my own."

Gert stepped forward and hugged me, and for a second I let myself get lost in her familiar, comforting embrace. No matter how much the witches had kept from me, and no matter how much I felt like they were using me half the time for some secret, complicated plan of their own, Gert's hugs were still the best. Somehow, she always managed to make me feel like everything was going to be okay. Even when it pretty clearly wasn't.

"We won't be with you here, Amy," she said. "Mombi will take us all into the Darklands to wait. We'll be safe there, and we can conserve our power."

"Great," I said. "So I can't use my magic, I'm completely on my own, I have barely any time to accomplish the basically impossible task you've given me, and on top of all that, I have to move back in with my mom."

Glamora nodded earnestly, her blue eyes wide. "Yes," she said. "That's really all you have to do."

I sighed. Sarcasm was wasted on pretty much everyone in Oz except Lulu. *And Nox,* a little voice piped up in the back of my head. I told it to shut up.

"We'll be with you in spirit," Gert said, squeezing my hands. "And when you need us—when you're ready to use the shoes to open the portal back to Oz—send us a sign, and we'll rejoin you."

"What, like the bat signal?" I said, rolling my eyes.

"What do bats have to do with anything?" Mombi asked.

"Never mind," I said.

The three of them hugged me in turn—even Mombi—and then joined hands. Mombi closed her eyes and muttered something under her breath. Weakened as she was, she was still far more powerful than I was—I'd only ever managed to get myself into the Darklands for a brief period when I was fighting Dorothy, and she was taking two other people for an indefinite stay without even batting an eyelash. Not that Mombi really had much in the way of eyelashes. Slowly, the witches began to turn gray and then fade, like watching a color movie degrade into black-and-white. The brightness seeped from their bodies and their images flattened and grew transparent. Gert opened her eyes and blew me a kiss, and then they faded away altogether.

This was it. Yet again, I was on my own, and the future of everything was in my hands. I sighed and started walking.

My mom's new apartment was right downtown in Flat Hill—if *downtown* was the right word for a town that didn't have an up. The downtown of my hometown consisted of four blocks of struggling businesses: an always-empty Chinese restaurant, a coffee shop that also sold dusty stuffed animals and sad-looking helium balloons with cheery slogans for holidays long since passed, three bars (luckily for my mom, since she'd been 86'd for life from two of them), a drugstore, a feed store, and a hardware store that still rented VHS tapes out of a curtained room in the back you had to be eighteen with ID to enter. I'd always known my hometown was a dump, but seeing it again after the magic and beauty of Oz was like being punched in the gut. How could anyone stand to live here? How had I managed to do it for sixteen years? I'd known there were other places—I'd just never been to any of them.

And then it hit me—of course. Dorothy must have felt the

same way. And in Dorothy's Kansas, they didn't even have indoor plumbing. No wonder she'd wanted to go back to Oz, and no wonder she'd fought so desperately to stay. Everyone kept alluding to how the magic of Oz ended up transforming people from the Other Place—people like me and Dorothy. If she and I were alike in one way, did that mean I was destined to . . . *No*, I told myself fiercely. I wasn't anything like Dorothy. I would never do the kinds of things she did.

You already have. I buried that thought so far down that I'd never be able to dig it up again. I had enough to deal with already.

Looking at Flat Hill made me strangely grateful for the tornado that had given me a free ride out of this hellhole. Sure, things had been tough in Oz, but at least a lot of the time they'd been beautiful, too. Most of the people I went to high school with wouldn't ever see the next state over, let alone a flying monkey or a waterfall made out of rainbows.

Suddenly, I remembered one of the last things my mom had ever said to me. *One second, you have everything, your whole life ahead of you. And then, boom. They just suck it all out of you like little vampires till there's nothing left of you*. She'd been talking about me.

Unexpectedly, I felt tears well up in my eyes, and I scrubbed them away angrily with the heel of my hand. I didn't need this shit. Not now, not ever. I almost turned around right there. Gert and Mombi and Glamora could go to hell. I'd figure something else out. I always had.

But what? I couldn't get back to Oz without Dorothy's stupid shoes, and it's not like I was going to set up a trailer of my very own in Flat Hill. So maybe my only option right now was my mom. That didn't mean I had to like it. Or forgive her. I blinked away the last of my tears and kept walking.

The tornado had wiped out Dusty Acres, but it had missed most of the main part of town. Here and there I saw scattered piles of debris, and one house at the edge of town had had its roof lifted clean off, though the rest of the building was untouched. Someone had tacked blue tarps over the gaping hole where the roof had been. One of them was coming loose and flapped idly in the humid breeze.

Otherwise, Flat Hill was exactly as I preferred not to remember it. Balding, patchy lawns surrounded by picket fences whose white paint had peeled away years ago. Bedraggled flower beds overgrown with weeds. Televisions flickering behind closed windows, even though it was the middle of the day. The late-morning sun already baking down into the carless streets while a dirty-faced girl on a tricycle wheeled around in bored circles. Flat Hill was a place people took their dreams to die, if they'd had any in the first place. I'd never loved Flat Hill, but after Oz it looked even uglier, dirtier, and poorer.

My mom's new apartment building hadn't been fixed up much despite the fact that it was now housing people again, and it had seen better days. It was just four stories, and didn't look like it had more than a dozen apartments. The siding was a shabby, sad gray that was falling off in places. Some of the windows were boarded up. From the looks of things, they had been that way since long before the tornado. The awning was torn and flapping in the wind, and the glass in the building's front door was cracked. I ran one finger down the list of names next to the intercom until I found *Gumm* in grimy pencil next to apartment 3B. Maybe she at least had a prairie view. I took a deep breath and pressed the buzzer.

After a minute, the intercom crackled. "Hello?" The voice was cautious, but it was definitely hers. I cleared my throat.

"Hi, Mom," I said finally. "It's me. Amy."

There was silence for a second—a long second—and then the intercom blasted me with a shriek so loud I covered my ears. "*Amy?* Oh my god, honey—don't move, don't do a thing, I'll be right down—" The intercom crackled again and my mom was gone. A minute later, she was flinging open the front door of the building and sweeping me up in her arms. Instinctively, I stiffened, and she let me go awkwardly.

She looked just like she'd always looked on one of her supposedly good days—too-short skirt, too-low top cut to reveal way too much of her overtanned cleavage, too much cheap makeup hiding the fact that if you took away the tacky clothes and terrible eye shadow she was actually still pretty. But there was something different about her, too. Something sharper, brighter. More alert. She held me at arm's length and looked at me hard, her eyes welling up with tears, and I realized what it was. They were red, but red from crying, not from pills. She didn't smell like booze. Was it actually possible my mom was sober? I'd believe it when monkeys flew. Oh, right. Well, I wasn't ready to believe it yet.

"Amy, it's really you," she said, still crying. "Where have you *been*?"

Oh, crap. Where *had* I been? I couldn't believe it hadn't occurred to any of us to think up a story to explain my month-long absence. It's not like I was going to tell my mom I'd been spending my time hanging out with a band of witches learning to cast spells, beheading the Cowardly Lion, and fighting a glitter-spackled chick no one in Kansas believed existed. "Uh," I said, "I was—I was in the hospital. In Topeka. The tornado picked me up with the trailer and I, um, I got—hurt. So, that's where I've been."

My mom stared at me for a minute. "But I searched all the hospitals. When you disappeared—wait, what am I thinking?" she said suddenly, shaking her head. "Come upstairs. I still can't believe this is happening. I missed you so much." She gave me another fierce hug I couldn't dodge and then beckoned me into the building.

Inside wasn't much better than the outside, and I couldn't help but notice a faint but unmistakable whiff of eau de cat pee in the hallway. I followed my mom up three flights of stairs to a short corridor lined with doors painted an industrial gray green. My mom opened the door to 3B and I followed her into the living room.

It was sort of depressing that this crappy apartment was way nicer than our trailer had ever been. It was twice as big, for one thing, and a picture window at the far end of the living room let in the afternoon sun. It was sparsely furnished with just a couch and a little card table with two chairs, but she had tacked a couple of cheerful prints on the walls and there was a bright rainbow-patterned rug on the floor. None of the furniture was the same as our old stuff, obviously—the government must have given her some kind of stash of emergency funds, because it's not like we'd had money for new stuff before. But it wasn't just that the apartment was nicer—it was clean.

Reflexively, I checked the couch for my mom's usual nest of Newport cartons and takeout containers and blankets, but it was bare. The apartment didn't even smell of cigarette smoke. Three doors lined one wall, suggesting that this apartment actually had bedrooms. Maybe even more than one. My mom was coming up in the world.

"It's not much," my mom said from behind me. "Just until I can save up enough to get something nicer. I lost everything in the storm." She looked away for a second. "Including you," she added quietly. I must have looked uncomfortable because her tone shifted and she brightened.

"Here," she said, patting the couch. "Let me make you some tea. Sit. We have a lot to talk about." I perched gingerly on the edge of the couch as she bustled around the tiny kitchenette, boiling water and putting tea bags into two mugs. I wasn't sure my pre-Oz mom even knew tea existed. When we both had steaming mugs of tea, she settled into the opposite end of the couch as if she was afraid I'd run away if she got too close. Like I was a wild animal.

"I'm sorry you were so worried." Looking at the emotion in my mom's eyes, I *was* sorry. "I couldn't leave the hospital," I explained. "Because, um, I had amnesia," I added in a fit of inspiration. "I lost my wallet and everything in the tornado, and I got hit on the head really bad. So I was in a coma for a while. When I woke up, I didn't know who I was. The hospital kept me while they tried to find my parents. And then, um, I just woke up the other day and remembered who I was, and they—um, they must have contacted the emergency housing place, because they told me where you were, and here I am." I took a sip of my tea.

It was an insane story with about a million holes—who had paid for the hospital visit? How on earth had I even survived being carried that far by a freaking tornado? Why hadn't the doctors contacted my mom themselves? How had I gotten from Topeka to Flat Hill? I found myself holding my breath as Mom's eyes drifted back and forth while she thought it all through.

"That must be why I never found you," she said. "If you didn't know your own name, you couldn't have told the doctors." She frowned. "But why didn't they realize I might be your mother, if you were the only patient with amnesia? I made flyers and passed them out, I went to every hospital—"

It took everything I had not to scream at her to just shut up. How many times had my mother lied to me in my life? *I'll take you to Disney World next year. I don't know where the cash in your underwear drawer went. Of course I haven't been drinking.* If I tried to make a list of every lie, it would take me a year. The least she could do for me now was just let it go.

Mom looked at me carefully. "Your hair's different," she said.

Right. Back in the caves, at the Order's headquarters, Glamora had magically changed my hair from pink to blond. That definitely didn't fit too well into my "I spent the last month in a hospital" story either. I opened my mouth to say something, and my mom shook her head.

It was like she knew exactly what I was thinking. It was like she could hear all my complaints. She might not have known everything that had happened, but she *understood*. If that wasn't a first, it was close. She really had come a long way, I guess.

"All that matters is that you're home now," she said firmly, and I relaxed a little. She paused. "But . . . I should call your dad."

I had not seen my father since I was a single digit. And I never wanted to see him again. I had thought that was one thing that Mom and I agreed on no matter what her blood alcohol level read.

Seeing the shock on my face, my mom scrambled to explain. "I had to tell him, Amy. I thought maybe he could help."

I laughed. It felt—and sounded—bitter. "I'm sure he was out there combing Dusty Acres looking for me."

"He sent a check," my mom said simply. "Amy," she went on, "I really owe you an apology. A big one. Not just for leaving you when the tornado came. I don't know if I'll ever forgive myself for that. But for everything before that, too."

She was crying again, and this time she wouldn't meet my eyes. "I've been a terrible parent," she said. "For a long time. I don't expect you to forgive me, but I want you to know I know, and I'm sorry."

I raised my eyebrows. This, I had not expected. "What happened to the pills?" I asked bluntly, and she flinched.

"When I"—her voice broke—"lost you, I realized what had happened to me. What I'd let myself become. I quit cold turkey, Amy. I knew I had to be there for you when you came back. I looked for you everywhere after the storm, but it was like you'd just vanished into thin air. Somehow I always knew that you'd come back to me, though, and I wanted to deserve it when you did." She smiled through her tears. "I'm even working," she said. "I got a job at the hardware store as a cashier."

"You quit cold turkey?" I asked, surprised. "That must have been tough."

"It was the hardest thing I've ever done," she said, looking down at her lap. "It was awful." Her tears spilled over, running down her cheeks. "But it was nothing compared to what it felt like when I thought I'd lost you."

Some part of me wanted to reach across the distance between us and hug her, but I'd fallen for her promises one too many times before. If she'd quit using when the tornado hit, that meant she'd only been sober a month. And a month was nowhere near enough time to trust anything had really changed. But if she'd made flyers and searched frantically from hospital to hospital, that was the biggest effort she'd made for me—for anything other than a bottle of pills—in a really long time. Either way, it didn't matter, I told myself. I'd already made up my mind that I was going back to Oz. There was nothing for me here. I'd learned to live without my mom. I could do it again. We were both silent for a minute.

"Mom?" I said finally. "I'm really sorry, but Star—um, she didn't make it."

My mom gave me a sad, are-you-kidding-me smile. "Honey," she said, "Star's a rat. If I have to choose between a rat and my daughter, I'll take the kid every time." She cleared her throat. "Well," she said, with a note of false cheer in her voice, "do you want to see your room?"

"My room?"

"I had to fight for a two bedroom. They wanted to give me a studio. But I knew you'd be back." She got up and opened one of the doors off the living room. I looked over her shoulder and my eyes widened in surprise. Like the rest of the apartment, the room had barely any furniture—just a narrow twin bed and a little bedside table and lamp. But my mom had painted the walls a pretty, pale pink, and hung bright white curtains over the window. She'd bought a bottle of my favorite perfume, too, and left it next to the lamp.

"This is nice," I said cautiously. "Thanks."

"It's nothing," she said. "I'm going to get us something better really soon. Even though I just started at the hardware store, I'm already saving. You must be tired—do you want to rest?"

"No," I said. "I'm okay." I realized with surprise that I was telling the truth for once. Sleeping in had done me good, and I was feeling weirdly energized to be home. My mom clapped her hands together.

"Then today calls for a special treat. Why don't you get cleaned up, and I'll take you out to buy some new clothes. Tonight we can order pizza and watch old movies."

Back in the pre-accident days, my mom and I had loved watching corny old black-and-white movies together. Our favorites were always the funny ones, where Audrey Hepburn or some other super-glamorous actress goofed around while rich, handsome guys fell all over her. Sometimes it seemed like things might not work out for her for a minute, but the handsome guy always came to the rescue at the end.

Part of me felt way too old for that now. No, not even too old. Too *tired*. Too experienced. I'd fought in a war. I'd seen too much of the world to believe in any of that crap, even for an hour.

But at the same time, being back home, and seeing my mom like this, was doing something funny to me. It was like everything that had happened in Oz was drifting away. It was like I was waking up and looking around and realizing, slowly, that it all had just been a weird, terrible dream.

It hadn't been a dream. But I *did* need new clothes. If I was going to try being a high school student again, I needed something to wear. And it had been so long since I'd seen a movie.

"I don't need anything new," I said. "We can just go to the thrift store." *Salvation Amy strikes again,* I thought bitterly. My mom might have changed, but nothing else in Kansas had. I tried not to think about the clothes I'd worn in Oz. My fighting gear, the way I'd been able to magic myself into a glittering, unrecognizable version of that sad, poor, trailer-trash girl I used to be.

"No," my mom said firmly. "I want things to be different, Amy. I mean it."

"Sure," I said. "That sounds good."

SIX

I took a long, hot shower in my mom's new bathroom. She'd even bought a bottle of the strawberry body wash I liked, although now the glitter suspended in the thick pink liquid, so reminiscent of Glinda, made me want to puke. I'd had enough of glitter for the next few lifetimes. I shampooed my hair twice. Maybe the real thing was more effective than magic. I wondered how witches and princesses dealt with scalp buildup in Oz, and collapsed into near-hysterical giggles on the bathtub floor while the hot water turned slowly cold. Okay, maybe I wasn't handling this return-to-Kansas thing with as much badass attitude as I'd thought. I'd have to look for a post-travel-to-a-fictional-kingdom PTSD support group. But the fact that I might be this close to falling apart was just one of the many things I couldn't tell my mom about what I'd been up to in the month of Kansas time I'd been gone. *Mom, I really need therapy—between literally turning into a monster and killing a bunch of people in a magical world you only think is made up, I'm not feeling too great?* Yeah, right.

Come on, Amy, I told myself, picking myself up off the floor of the tub. *Get it together.* If I lost it in front of my mom, there was no telling what she might do or where she might send me. I couldn't talk about anything that had happened to me and I couldn't let what I'd been through show. I had to keep being a warrior. This was what I'd practiced for. This was what I'd trained for. And this was no time to forget that.

As I brushed out my long hair—no invisible magic stylists in Kansas, sadly—I saw myself as my mom must have seen me, standing on her threshold. There were dark circles under my eyes that no amount of sleep was going to erase anytime soon. I looked about ten years older than I had before that tornado had plucked me out of Dusty Acres. Mostly, I just looked sad. Without magic to hide behind, I was going to have to do my best with concealer.

I spent a long time doing my makeup. I'd never cared about it before, but my mom loved girly stuff, and I knew she'd know I was doing it for her. I remembered suddenly the way Nox had looked at me what felt like a million years ago, when Glamora had taught me how to glam out with magic, and felt a quick, sharp pang. I tugged the brush through my hair with one last savage yank, pulled on the dirty clothes I'd been wearing, and opened the bathroom door. My mom's smile was so bright and so genuine that I was glad I'd gone to the trouble of borrowing her mascara and lipstick.

Of course there was no mall in Flat Hill. There wasn't even

a place to buy clothes, unless you counted the overalls they sold at the feed store. There was a bus, though, that ran once an hour to the biggest nearby town, where you could stock up on slightly outdated ensembles at one of those giant box stores that also sold kitchenware, hunting rifles, and kids' toys.

The bus ride passed quickly enough, and soon we were walking in the front door. I let my mom pick out the clothes she wanted to buy me; I didn't care what I wore. As she flipped through a rack of pastel sweatshirts with rhinestone slogans like CUTE and FLIRT, I said casually, "I guess I should start back to school tomorrow."

She stopped short. "School?" she asked.

I shrugged. "I mean, it's not like I can get out of going forever."

"Honey," my mom said, "you just got home. I think you can take a week or two to settle in." She paused. "I don't know if you remember," she said delicately, "but before you disappeared—I mean, before the tornado picked you up—you got suspended. We'll probably have to deal with that, too."

Suspended? I had no idea for a moment what she was talking about, and then it all came rushing back. Madison. The fight she'd picked with me the day the tornado hit—how she'd pretended it was my fault and told the assistant principal, Mr. Strachan, that I'd assaulted her. After battling Dorothy, Madison Pendleton seemed like a pretty pathetic enemy. It was hard to believe I'd once lived in terror of her. Poor little Salvation Amy had gone to ninja camp. Now that I thought about it, I was kind of looking forward to seeing Madison again.

"Right," I said. "I forgot about that."

"I can go talk to Mr. Strachan tomorrow before I go to work," my mom offered. "I'm sure we can figure something out if you're sure you're well enough to go back. I know you missed a lot of school, but I'll ask if you can make up the work you were absent for and still graduate on time." Graduate? Right. That, too, was something from a life that seemed so far away I could barely even think about it. In every way that really mattered, I had already graduated.

"Sure, thanks," I said. My mom gave me a thoughtful look, but she turned back to the rack of clothes.

She ended up buying me a couple of T-shirts and sweatshirts, and one pair of jeans. She didn't say it out loud, but I knew that was all she could afford—and she couldn't really afford even that. She didn't say anything about money later that night either, when we ordered an extra-large pizza with extra pepperoni from the chain store a couple of blocks over—what constituted fine dining in Flat Hill. My mom flipped through channels on the beat-up old TV she told me she'd gotten from the Salvation Army.

So maybe it was true. Maybe I always was going to be Salvation Amy.

So what? I didn't care. I didn't care about anything here anymore, except finding those stupid shoes and going back to Oz. Somehow, without really thinking about it, I'd decided already: I didn't belong in Kansas anymore, no matter how happy my mom was to see me. I couldn't just go back to being the same person I'd been before. Not after everything I'd seen and done. I couldn't go back to a place where no one would believe anything that had happened to me was real. I'd watched people I cared about die. I'd risked my life. I'd used magic. I'd fallen—okay, fine, I'd fallen in love. And there was no one in Kansas I could share any of that with. It was as if Oz had made the decision for me. Or maybe I just didn't have much of a choice.

"Oh, look!" my mom said happily. "*The Wizard of Oz* is on. Remember how we used to love that movie?"

I almost dropped my slice of pizza on the sad shag rug. There she was, in all her glory—Judy Garland singing her heart out as the Lion, the Tin Man, and the Scarecrow skipped along behind her. Everyone looked so happy, and not scary at all. Dorothy was a young, innocent girl with a cute little dog. The Tin Man was an actor in silver makeup, with a silly funnel on top of his head. The Scarecrow was a dopey guy in burlap, and the Lion was just a man in a plush suit with a bow in his fake mane. I remembered the real Lion, swallowing Star in one gulp, and shuddered. "It's all wrong," I muttered under my breath.

"You're telling me," my mom said. "You know Judy Garland was already on pills when they were shooting this? The things they did to that poor girl. If you think I was a bad mother, you should have seen hers."

That was a point I wasn't about to argue. "I'm kind of sick of this movie. Do you mind if we watch something else?"

"Fine by me," my mom said. "It's not quite the same when you know the truth, is it?"

I wished I could explain myself to her. My mom was finally being honest with me, for the first time ever, and it sort of sucked that the shoe was on the other foot now. But if I told my mom the Cowardly Lion was real—and I knew because I'd killed him myself, after he ate her beloved pet rat—she'd do a lot more than go talk to Assistant Principal Strachan tomorrow. She'd go straight to a psychiatrist instead, and I'd be going to the mental hospital, not back to high school.

When it was time for bed, I hugged my mom good night. She smelled like she'd smelled when I was a kid, before the accident and the pills and the Newports: sweet and flowery, like springtime. She hugged me back. I looked over her shoulder into her room, taking it in without really thinking, and then something clicked. "Where's your bed?" I asked, releasing her.

"Oh." She laughed, giving a little shrug. "I couldn't really afford two, so I'll just sleep on the couch. A couple more paychecks and I should be able to get myself a bed, too."

"Mom, come on. I can sleep on the couch. You take my bed."

"I've been selfish for way too much of your life," she said, looking me straight in the eye. "I can handle a few weeks on the couch." Guilt welled up in my heart like blood from a paper cut. My mom had transformed her life in the hopes I was coming back, and all I could think about was how I was going to leave her again. What would it do to her when I disappeared again?

You can't think about that and you can't get used to this, I told myself. *You're only here to get the shoes*. It was easier for everyone if my mom and I didn't get too close. If I closed myself off, the way I'd learned to do in Oz. Caring too much only meant you were that much easier to hurt. And if I was going to leave Kansas for good, I couldn't let my armor crack for a second.

"Suit yourself," I said, making my voice hard and cold, and I closed my bedroom door to the look of hurt on her face. But all I could think about as I tossed and turned in the unfamiliar, narrow bed was the tears welling up in her eyes as I'd shut her out. Nox, my mom . . . who was going to be next on the list of people I had to hurt in order to survive?

SEVEN

My mom left the house early the next morning, and I got busy. I dragged out her battered old laptop—you could practically hear the gears turning when I logged online. Before I looked up the history of Flat Hill, I couldn't resist. I had to Google it. A video called "Tornado Girl Tragedy" popped up instantly. On one side was Nancy Grace, the CNN reporter who always covered big trials and missing person cases. And on the other, my mother's best friend, Tawny. Nancy had a habit of lambasting bad mothers who happened to be nowhere to be found while their kids were going missing.

"So where was your friend, Tornado Girl's mom, when the tornado hit?"

"She was with me—we were at a tornado party," Tawny said dramatically, and then burst into guilty tears.

"Tornado party," Nancy repeated, her southern drawl wrapping around the words, making it sound even more awful.

At the word *party*, I clicked on the X to close the screen. I had seen enough. I turned to my real mission.

For hours, I looked through websites about prairie history, old farmers' journals, and black-and-white pictures of the people who had come to Kansas back in Dorothy's era to make a better life for themselves. I wasn't sure what I was looking for; I just knew I'd know it when I saw it. And after reading about a million articles on devastating blizzards, crop failures, droughts, disease, and poverty, I couldn't help but feel sorry for Dorothy. Whatever she'd turned into in Oz, her life in Kansas had been harder than anything I could imagine. *The Wonderful Wizard of Oz* might have portrayed her life with Uncle Henry and Aunt Em as idyllic, but it didn't take much reading for me to realize that life on a Kansas farm as a dirt-poor orphan probably hadn't been a walk in the park.

And then I found it—on a historical website dedicated to printing techniques in old newspapers. I sat up straight on my mom's couch with a gasp. "Area reporter interviews Kansas tornado survivor." It was a scan of a yellowing, torn newspaper article from the *Daily Kansan*, dated 1897. The paper was so faded I could barely make out the words, and most of the article was missing. But I saw enough to know what I was looking at. "Miss D. Gale, of Flat Hill, Kansas, population twenty-five, describes her experiences in the tornado as 'truly wondrous,' but the most wonderful aspect of her story is that she survived the devastating tornado that destroyed her home. Miss Gale reports extraordinary visions experienced during the storm, including wonderful creatures and an enchanted ci—" The page was torn off there, so neatly that it almost looked as though someone had done it on purpose. And then I saw the author's byline: Mr. L. F. Baum.

"Holy *shit*," I said out loud into my mom's empty apartment. Dorothy *had* been real. She *had* lived here in the very town where I'd grown up. And L. Frank Baum had *interviewed* her. How did no one *know* about this? I didn't know much about the history of Baum's books, but I was pretty sure that I would have heard about it if people realized Dorothy was based on a real person. She'd told him the whole thing, everything that happened to her, and he'd taken her entire story and turned it into a book. She'd come back to Kansas, just like I had, dumped back into her ordinary, crappy life. No one could possibly have believed her—not even Baum himself.

But if Baum had put Dorothy's shoes in *The Wonderful Wizard of Oz*, that meant she'd told him about them. And the rest of the article might be a clue to where they were now. Dorothy might not have looked for the shoes the first time she returned to Kansas, but she hadn't hesitated to take up the offer of a second trip to Oz. If she hadn't looked for them then, they had to still be here. And if I could find the rest of the paper, I'd be that much closer to figuring out where they were.

Extraordinary visions, all right. How had no one else found what I'd just stumbled across? How was it possible that no one else had realized Dorothy was real? There was something else going on here. Something big. I had to find the rest of that article. But how?

I heard a key turning in the lock, and I scrambled to delete my search history. I'd barely managed to return the computer to where I'd found it—under a pile of papers and magazines on the table by the couch—when my mom walked in. She looked startled to see me there, standing in the middle of her apartment like an idiot. "Uh, hi," I said. "I just, uh, woke up." I shot a glance at the wall clock in the kitchen. It was four in the afternoon. Oh well, let her think I was lazy. It was better than trying to explain myself.

"Hi, honey," she said. Her voice was cautious, and I remembered what I'd done to her the night before. I felt another flash of guilt and shoved it aside.

"Good news," she said. "I talked to Assistant Principal Strachan. He says since the circumstances are so unusual, you can consider your suspension over."

"Great," I said. "So I can go to school tomorrow?"

She shot me a strange look. "Are you sure you want to, honey? You've been through a lot. I thought you might want to take a few days to rest up before you went back. We could even see if there's a way for you to finish out the quarter at home."

"I have to get out of here," I said without thinking. She flinched visibly. "I mean, I really just want to—to get back to normal," I added quickly. "You know, jump back into things. I think it's the best way."

My mom sighed. "Whatever you want, Amy. I just . . ." She trailed off and then shrugged helplessly. I knew I'd hurt her again, but there was no way around it. "Assistant Principal

Strachan wasn't happy about it," my mom warned. "You're going to have to be on your best behavior. And Amy—Madison will still be there. I know she picks on you, but you have to get better at dealing with it." She looked down at the ground. "I can help you, if you need me."

I almost laughed. At this point, there wasn't much Madison Pendleton could say to me that would bother me at all. But I realized immediately I'd hurt my mom's feelings—again. Of course. She'd been offering to help, and now she thought I was laughing at her, instead of Madison. I felt awful, and then I felt awful for feeling awful. It would be better for both of us if I kept my distance. But she was trying so hard—and I was starting to believe the change was real and not just an act. I'd miss my new, improved mom. But my mom wasn't enough to keep me in Flat Hill. Right? I couldn't afford to let myself think any other way. I'd made up my mind to go back to Oz. Which meant I *had* to find those shoes—and I had an idea of how to do it.

EIGHT

The next morning, dressed in my new jeans and one of the shirts my mom had picked out for me, I was once again a senior at Dwight D. Eisenhower Senior High. The halls were the same dull linoleum, smelling of mop bucket and ancient cafeteria tater tots. The lockers were the same dull gray metal that even a fresh coat of paint couldn't make look new. The lights overhead flickered like mood lighting in a prison camp. But this time, everything was different. Before, I'd been nobody. Salvation Amy, trailer-trash nobody. If people bothered to look at me, it was only with scorn in their eyes. This time around, I was a celebrity. And I definitely didn't like it.

Everywhere I walked, whispers followed me, and people turned to stare as I passed. More than a few of them said hi in sickly sweet tones that made me want to roll my eyes. They'd never talked to me before in their lives; they just wanted to be close to the drama. My disappearance and miraculous return was the most interesting thing that had happened at Dwight D. Eisenhower Senior High since Dustin knocked up Madison Pendleton. I wasn't dumb enough to fall for the fake warmth. I knew who my real friends were in Flat Hill: nobody.

Go ahead and look, I thought. They *should* look. Because whatever they thought happened to me while I had been gone, the truth was so much crazier. And anyway, I wasn't here to run for prom queen. I was here to save the Whole. Damn. World. The only annoying thing was that these people would never even know it.

It took me a minute to find my own locker—because I didn't recognize it. It had practically been turned into a shrine. Ribbons looped around the bare metal. Dried flowers were stuck through the vents. Cards and notes were taped to every inch of its surface—"Missing You," "Come Home Soon," a heart cut out of construction paper with MISS U AMIE written on it in loopy cursive that looked like a kindergartener's. Someone had even taped a picture of me with sequins glued in the shape of a heart around my face. Where the photo had come from, I had no idea. Pre-Oz Amy glared balefully out at me in her dirty thrift-store jeans, ready for a fight.

The whole thing made me sick. I wanted to pull the cards and flowers off my locker and throw them to the ground, trample them into scraps. None of these people had given a shit about me until they thought I was dead. Until I'd given them an excuse to feel sad, important, useful. Until I'd finally done something interesting by getting myself killed. My stomach turned over and I flipped my lock through its old combination, the numbers coming to me effortlessly. *The more things change, the more they stay the same,* I thought bitterly.

"Do you like it? I'm the one who organized the decorating committee."

No matter how much time I spent in Oz, I'd never forget that voice. I turned slowly. "Hi, Madison," I said. I mean, what else was I supposed to say?

My mouth dropped open when I saw her. Pregnant Madison was now new-mom Madison, and she beamed with pride at me over the wrinkly faced infant strapped to her chest in one of those weird baby slings that always look like they're designed to suffocate the kid. Baby or no baby, she was still Madison. She was wearing a hot-pink sequin-covered crop top that bared a surprisingly toned postbaby belly, pink velour track pants with a huge, glittery pink heart over her ass, and pink platform sneakers. She also smelled intensely of strawberry body spray and her lips were slicked with a thick coat of pink gloss.

"If it isn't Amy Gumm, back from the dead," she said. "We all thought you were a goner, you know." She giggled. "Of course, once you weren't around for a while—you know, I almost missed you. *Almost*. This is Dustin Jr., by the way." She patted the baby, who made a burbling noise. Madison's baby was downright ugly. Then again, I guess most new babies are. He looked like a little old man who couldn't find his dentures. His cheeks were too fat and his face was squashed-looking, as if someone had stepped on his head. Plus, he was bald as an egg. But I felt bad for him. It wasn't his fault that his mom was the biggest bitch in Kansas—well, second biggest, now that I was back.

Anyway, I'd long since learned I could tackle bitches way bigger than Madison Pendleton of Flat Hill. Although come to think of it, Madison was as fond of sparkly pink crap as Glinda. Maybe when you signed up for Super Evil Archenemy status somebody sent you a gallon of glitter body spray. Or maybe everybody evil just had the same tacky taste. Either way, I was apparently going to be cursed with a glittery pink nemesis everywhere I went.

"He's, uh, really cute," I said. This lying thing was getting easier and easier, wasn't it? I'd slayed monsters in Oz—she'd just given birth to one.

She smiled, and weirdly, it wasn't her usual cat-about-to-chomp-down-on-the-canary grin. It was a real smile—almost tender. She looked down at Dustin Jr. and stroked the top of his bald head gently with one finger. "I know," she said blissfully. "It's kind of crazy how much stuff can change in a month."

"Tell me about it," I muttered. I looked back at my locker. "Thanks for, uh, all this," I said. For some reason, Madison was not moving.

She shrugged. "I mean, it was the least I could do, you know? I know we didn't always get along, but I didn't want for you to, like, *die*. Honestly . . ." She trailed off, chewing at one pink-manicured nail. I raised an eyebrow. "Honestly, I guess I *was* kind of a bitch to you sometimes," she said in a rush. "I mean, you made it easy, you know? You were pretty shitty to me, too. And you kept going after my boyfriend."

"I did not!" I protested.

She rolled her eyes. *"Please,"* she said. Her voice took on a high-pitched note. "'Oh, Dustin, of course I'll do your algebra. Oh, Dustin, let me *tutor* you.' You weren't even *trying* to be subtle."

"He kept asking," I said.

"Dustin's not very smart," Madison said. "But he knows a sucker when he sees one."

I stared at her, not sure whether to laugh or hit her. Was Madison—in her own weird, mean, Madison way—trying to be *friends* with me? By making fun of her jock boyfriend? I'd always had a soft spot for Dustin—she was right about that. But she was also right that he wasn't exactly the brightest bulb in the chandelier.

"Look," she said, shrugging again. "When you disappeared like that I realized that you're, like, one of the only interesting people around here. It was boring without you, Sal—Amy." She popped her finger back in her mouth again, chewing away at her nail and grinning at me. "Gonna be late for homeroom. See you around," she said, and sauntered away as Dustin Jr. trailed spit down her shoulder.

So that was pretty weird. But it was nowhere close to the weirdest thing that would happen to me that day.

NINE

Mr. Strachan had given my mom my old schedule, and in each classroom, the story was the same. A loud buzz of chatter would die down immediately as soon as I walked in the door. Everyone—and I mean *everyone*—would turn to look at me as I slunk toward my seat, doing my best to pretend I was invisible. A few seconds later, the talk would start again—this time, low whispers I wasn't meant to hear, although I couldn't help catching some of it. *"Went crazy and . . ." "Totally ran away with some guy, just like her mom . . ." "Was blackout drunk for, like, the entire* month *and then lied about being in a hospital . . ."* Okay, so nobody bought the hospital story. Too damn bad. I sat with my back straight and my eyes fixed on the front of the room, I wrote down my homework assignments, and I spoke when I was spoken to—which was never, conveniently leaving me plenty of time to think about how I was going to start my search for the shoes. Even my teachers wouldn't meet my eyes. *Whatever,*

I thought. *It's not like I had friends before either.* At least this time no one was throwing food at me, or yelling "Get those shoes at Kmart, Salvation Amy?" as I tried to slink by. Being a total pariah had its definite advantages.

At lunch, I made my way through a cloud of silence that followed me across the room and exploded into hissing whispers the moment I passed. I kept my head high and my back straight, pretending I was walking across Dorothy's banquet hall. I found an empty table by the window at the far corner of the cafeteria and pulled my sandwich out of the paper lunch bag my mom had packed for me. A scrap of paper fluttered to the floor, and I recognized my mom's loopy cursive when I bent down to pick it up. *I love you, Amy. I'm so glad you're home.*

Notes in my bag lunch? She was working her way up to Oscar material for her new role as Concerned and Caring Mom. But even as I tried to shrug off her effort, some part of me was seriously touched. I remembered the mom who'd baked a cake for my ninth birthday party and poured me a bucketful of Sprite to drown my sorrows when no one showed up. But I couldn't think like that, I reminded myself. I couldn't. I tucked the note in my jeans pocket.

And then, to my total surprise, two figures sank down into chairs on either side of me. "Hi, Amy," Dustin said shyly. "Hi, again," Madison said. "Lrrbbble," added Dustin Jr.

"Okay," I said, putting down my sandwich. "Quit screwing with me, Madison. Maybe you're having some kind of postpartum thing, only instead of getting really depressed you got all friendly. But I am not interested. What do you want?"

"I want to eat lunch with you," she said calmly. Her own lunch—a roast beef sandwich on thick, expensive white bread—the kind you bought by the loaf at the grocery store and sliced yourself—was packed neatly into a Tupperware container that had room for carrot sticks and apple slices, too. She offered Dustin Jr. a carrot stick but he let loose with a lusty wail.

"Isn't he too little for solid food?" I asked cautiously. Madison shrugged.

"I'm trying to get him to advance," she said. "Breastfeeding totally sucks." And then, without further ado, she pulled up her shirt as if daring me to say something. Dustin Jr. latched on to his lunch with gusto.

Dustin Sr. had opted for cafeteria pizza. The smell was something else. If there was anything that would seal my decision to bail on Kansas forever, it was cafeteria pizza. "Mmmmm," he said unconvincingly.

"D, that stuff is major no way," Madison said, rolling her eyes.

"No, seriously, rewind," I said. "Why are you guys here? What is this about?" I waited for the other shoe to drop. For Madison to play whatever mean joke she had up her sleeve, or to say something horrible about my hair or my clothes, or drag the whole cafeteria over to laugh at me.

Dustin looked between us nervously. "It's not like that, Sal—um, Amy," he said. "I mean, not anymore. I know Madison was kind of uncool to you—"

"Kind of *uncool?*" For all the things I'd endured in Oz, I couldn't keep the hurt out of my voice. Madison had made my life in Kansas a living hell. She was the one who'd made sure I didn't have any friends. She was the one who made sure I got mocked every day for my secondhand clothes. She was the one who'd spread rumors about all the times my mom had come home too drunk to even walk straight, or with strange guys who didn't even stay the night. I don't even think she knew how close to the truth they were.

"All right, look," Madison said. "Real talk, okay? I know I was a bitch. I know I *am* a bitch. At least I *own* it. But see where I'm coming from. I thought I was on top of the world—" Her voice dripped scorn as she waved a hand around the cafeteria. "Queen of this entire shithole—what a high-class job, am I right? And then I got knocked up, and it was too late to do anything about it by the time I realized I was pregnant—I mean, we're in the middle of Kansas, it's not like I could find somebody to drive me to New York to take care of it. Football-star's-fiancée-prom-queen-preggo Madison Pendleton was everybody's idea of a great mascot—but slutty-single-mom Madison Pendleton dragging her *bastard* kid all over Dwight D. Eisenhower Senior High after she ruined the football star's life? Not so much. I was supposed to drop out when I popped the kid out so no one had to look at us, or adopt him out, or act sorry, and I didn't do any of that stuff. I had to stand in Strachan's office for twenty minutes, screaming, before he finally agreed to let me bring the kid to school so I can actually graduate on time. And so now, if you want to know the truth, Amy Gumm, *I* don't have any friends either. It's you and me, babe. Now we can be boss bitches together. Assuming you've got it in you."

"Hey, don't forget *me*," Dustin said, half wounded. Madison smiled at him, that same warm smile she'd given his kid, but her eyes were sad. "She didn't ruin my life," he added. "I blew out my knee in a game right before Dustin Jr. was born anyway."

I stared at Madison, totally speechless. I'd never heard her talk so much at one time without letting an insult fly, let alone admit anything like vulnerability. I thought suddenly of all the times I'd pretended to be something I wasn't in Oz—to protect myself, to get by. And I thought about what it must have been like for Madison, pregnant and barely seventeen, knowing she was probably going to be stuck in this dump for the rest of her life. I didn't forgive her, exactly, but I thought I might understand her.

"What about . . ." I made a vague gesture, trying to remember the names of Madison's Clone Wars besties.

"Amber?" Madison snorted and looked across the cafeteria. Amber—dressed in an outfit uncannily identical to the glitter-heavy blinged-out gear Madison was sporting—was holding court at the head of the popular table, surrounded by admiring jocks, acolytes in matching ensembles, and a couple of hangers-on. As if she could sense the force of Madison's gaze, she glanced over at us and sneered. Madison raised a single, slow middle finger. Amber blanched and looked away. Queen bee or no queen bee, Madison was still pretty scary. "I got demoted," she said almost cheerfully. "Whatever. Saves me a lot of time."

"But you and Dustin could get married," I said. "You could get a babysitter for the kid so you can finish school."

"My parents threw me out of the house," she said matter-of-factly. "So no free child care. And Dustin and I broke up." She looked at him and raised an eyebrow.

Even though Madison seemed genuine, and had gotten a taste of her own medicine, I was definitely not ready to trust her. She had made a sport out of hurting me, like it was an extracurricular activity.

But there was an intimacy in the bully/bullied relationship. I knew Madison better than most other people. I'd needed to, to be able to avoid her, or to anticipate when the next insult was coming and get myself ready. And I'd never seen this side of Madison. She actually *almost* seemed contrite. But maybe motherhood had just given her a better poker face.

I realized Dustin had continued talking while I'd been trying to figure out Madison. "I mean, of course I help with the baby. My parents are pretty cool, they're letting Madison stay with us until we figure out something better." He sighed and put his head in his hands. "We just knew we weren't right for each other, even though we still care about each other. It's a lot," he said. "But we'll figure it out." Madison put her head on his shoulder, and he gave her a squeeze. The thing was, they *did* love each other. It was obvious in the little glances they shot each other when they thought I wasn't looking. Madison and Dustin had formed some kind of post-breakup peace. It was kind of weird. But there are lots of different kinds of love, I guess. And it was totally obvious, too, that they both loved Dustin Jr. As if she could read my thoughts, Madison handed the baby over to Dustin, who rocked him gently with an expression of total bliss while Madison looked at both of them with affection.

If I couldn't have Nox in my life the way I wanted, could I have him in my life like this?

Madison cleared her throat. "Okay, Amy, spill," she said. "Where the hell have you *been*? Obviously not in a hospital. You couldn't even fool Strachan with that line of crap, although that's the story he fed the school. Count your blessings, I guess."

There was no way I could tell them. Absolutely none. But in spite of myself, I was starting to like this weird, new Team Madison. And I was weirdly touched by how nice they were being to me. Could I trust them? Did it matter? What the hell, it wasn't like I had anyone else.

"I have a better idea," I said. "Why don't you guys help me out with something."

Dustin Jr. let out an excited burble and vomited. Madison, not missing a beat as she swabbed him off with a handful of napkins, raised a perfectly plucked eyebrow. "What kind of something?"

"Something secret," I said.

Madison's eyes lit up. "I *love* secrets," she said as her baby giggled. "I *knew* there was a reason I missed you."

"Remember your book report on Dorothy?" She nodded. "You're going to help me find that bitch's shoes."

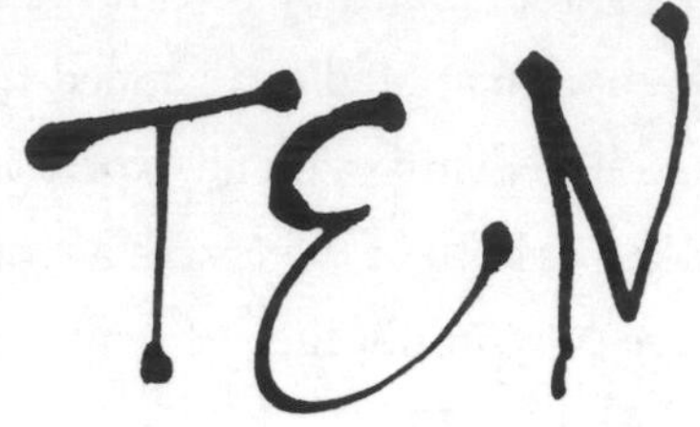

"Dorothy's *shoes?*" Madison's eyes were wide in disbelief. "You really *did* get hit on the head, right? News flash, babe. Dorothy isn't a real person."

"Well . . . ," I said, hesitating. "I can explain—" But I was cut off by the bell for fifth period. Dustin and Madison were staring at me. Dustin Jr. burped and closed his eyes. "Meet me after school," I said in a rush. "On the front steps. It will make sense. Sort of. I promise." But they were gathering up their books and bags.

"Gotta hose this little dude off," Madison said, not meeting my eyes. Okay, fine. Madison had been the worst thing in my life before I left for Oz, and Dustin had just been a dopey dreamer who I thought I had something in common with. Who was I kidding? We weren't friends. And it didn't matter, because I didn't need them. I'd done everything else on my own. I could do this, too. Dustin gave me a little wave as they walked away from me.

I waved back. At least he'd always been nice. Even if it was only because he wanted something from me.

I needed a plan, but I didn't even know where to start. Gert, Mombi, and Glamora hadn't given me much to go on. In between pre-calc and PE I ducked into the girls' bathroom, locked myself in a stall, and did my best to send out a couple of tendrils of magic just to see if I suddenly could. But it was no use. I was going to have to do this the hard way, and I didn't have a clue where to start.

To make my day even worse, I had a hot date with Assistant Principal Strachan. He'd told my mom I'd have to come in and meet with him on my first day back. The last thing I wanted was to make waves, so I made sure I was at his office ten minutes early. The receptionist, Mrs. Perkins, had probably been working at the high school when my grandmother was in diapers. She was a sweet older lady who always wore matching twinsets, no matter the weather, and kept a stash of lollipops in her desk drawer. Which I knew, because I'd spent a lot of time in Assistant Principal Strachan's office. But Mrs. Perkins never judged me no matter how many times I got in trouble. I think secretly she was on my side.

"Amy!" she exclaimed as I walked into the school office. "It's been a while since you visited!" She winked at me and dug a lollipop out of her drawer before I even asked. "The principal will be with you in just a moment. Have a seat."

"Cherry! You remembered," I said, sitting in one of the uncomfortable plastic chairs. I didn't really care that much about

Mrs. Perkins's lollipops, but she always seemed so happy when I took one that I pretended to be excited. A few minutes later, I could hear Assistant Principal Strachan yelling for me from behind his door. Mrs. Perkins winked at me again as I took a deep breath and walked into his office.

If I'd changed in the last month, Assistant Principal Strachan definitely hadn't. His wire-rimmed glasses were slipping down his big, bulbous nose. His pitch-black toupee was slightly askew, revealing a thin tuft of graying hair underneath. His suit was the same one he wore every single day—and probably had been wearing every single day since around 1995. His beady brown eyes peered at me through his glasses. And, as usual, he didn't look happy to see me.

"Miss Gumm," he growled, pointing to a chair in the corner like I was a kid. I guess I did still have that lollipop. "Very nice of you to rejoin us after your little sojourn."

"I was in the hospital," I said.

"Your mother has already shared her concerns with me," he said, ignoring me. "She felt we should accommodate you given your circumstances, but I'm not so sure I agree. You've started fights repeatedly—"

"I've never started them!" I protested, and he scowled.

He clucked his tongue. "Already arguing with me. I see you haven't changed much. Look here, young lady. Your mother told me your story about being in the hospital. I think all three of us know that's a lie. I don't know where you've been the last month, Miss Gumm, but one whiff of trouble from you and you'll be expelled. Permanently. Am I making myself clear?"

I opened my mouth to protest again and then shut it. If I got kicked out of school, I'd have no possible way to search for the shoes, which meant no way to get back to Oz—for me or for anyone else. "Yes sir," I said meekly, swallowing my pride. "I'm sorry."

"You should be suspended," he grumbled, but my apology seemed to mollify him. "Get back to class. Don't let me see you in my office again." I nodded obediently. As I left, Mrs. Perkins snuck me another lollipop.

On my way back to class, I stopped in front of the tired old glass-cased diorama by the school's front doors. It was a display dedicated to Kansas's most famous export, *The Wizard of Oz*: a dollhouse-sized farm with a backdrop of a painted tornado and, in the distance, a faint, glittering image of Oz. There were even little cows grazing in the fake grass that surrounded the farm, and a plastic Dorothy in a tiny checked dress shading her eyes as she looked toward the descending tornado. A tiny plastic Toto capered at her feet. When it was new, the diorama must have been nice, but that had been a long time ago. Over the years, dust had crept in and thickly furred the figurines, hiding their features under a layer of gray. The grass was patchy and balding, and several of the cows had fallen over.

I'd never thought much about the diorama before, but it had a whole new significance now—especially since I'd found the scrap of article. Even though I *knew* Dorothy was real—she'd almost killed me enough times—it was still sinking in that

Dorothy was *real*. She'd been a farm girl on this very patch of land. Her enchanted shoes were probably—hopefully—still here. But if the witches were right, how was it that no one knew? I'd found the article without much trouble by doing a basic internet search. Everyone knew about Dorothy's story. So how was it possible that in a hundred years no one had figured out it was true? Had someone tried to cover it up? It was the only explanation I could come up with, but I couldn't imagine who—or why.

There was no point in worrying about that now; I had way bigger problems. If the shoes were really here, I'd have to figure out a way to search for them without getting caught, stay out of trouble, keep Assistant Principal Strachan happy, and convince my mom that everything was okay. And I couldn't help but think about what he'd said in his office about all three of us knowing that I'd lied about being in the hospital. Was that why my mom had accepted my totally implausible story—because she'd known all along I was making it up? Did she think I had just run away? Had she pretended to believe me because she thought the truth might hurt too much for her to hear? I filed that under "things to figure out later" and ran back to chemistry. I had a lot of work to make up, and I needed everyone to believe I was happy to be home until I had another chance to escape.

ELEVEN

After they'd ditched me in the cafeteria, I wasn't expecting to see Madison and Dustin waiting for me on the front steps after school, just like I'd asked them to. I did a comical double take, and Madison grinned. "I don't know what your deal is," she said, "but you're the most interesting thing that's happened in Flat Hill since some dumbass thought a hill could be flat."

The feeling of relief that overwhelmed me took me by surprise. I wasn't *totally* alone—at least, not for the moment. If you'd told the old Amy Gumm that she'd be hanging out after school with Madison, Dustin, and their drooling newborn, I'd have said you were completely nuts. But then again, a lot had happened to that Amy Gumm. I could take this in stride, too.

"It's kind of a long story," I said, thinking fast. I had to come up with *something* to convince them Dorothy was real, but I couldn't tell them anything close to the whole truth.

"So let's go get ice cream downtown and talk it over," Madison said. She laughed at the expression on my face. Madison? Eating food with calories? It really was a whole new world. "What? So maybe I never got over my pregnancy cravings. That thing about pickles is totally true, too."

"She eats, like, a pint of rocky road a *day*," Dustin said.

"Shut up," Madison said, hitting him.

"Lead the way," I said.

Flat Hill's downtown drugstore was like something straight out of the 1950s. It probably *was* straight out of the 1950s—and no one had bothered to clean since then either. The long old-fashioned lunch counter was always sticky, the bar-stool upholstery was cracked and peeling, revealing the gross yellow foam padding underneath, and they only served three flavors of ice cream—vanilla, chocolate, and strawberry. But there was nowhere else to go. Kids from school were already piling into the booths by the window, giving me and Madison dirty looks, but Madison held her head high and ignored them, settling regally onto a bar stool with Dustin Jr. in his baby wrap and Dustin Sr. on her other side.

"Okay, so," I began, once Madison had ordered a triple-decker chocolate sundae—"With extra syrup!" she barked—and was busy spooning ice cream into her mouth. "You know how in *The Wonderful Wizard of Oz* Dorothy is from Kansas?"

"Yes, Amy, we know that," Madison said drily.

"I found part of this newspaper article from 1897," I explained. "It was *by* L. Frank Baum, the guy who wrote the original books, and it was an interview with a girl named Dorothy who survived a tornado that struck Flat Hill that year. She talked about having crazy visions of a wonderful place."

Madison and Dustin looked at me expectantly. "And?" Dustin asked.

"Well, that proves Dorothy was real, right? So her shoes must be real," I said. Okay, so maybe I hadn't quite worked out the most convincing argument.

Dustin's forehead creased and Madison smiled. "That's his thinking face," she said affectionately. He gave her a dirty look.

"Amy," he said slowly, "even if this thing you found proves that *Dorothy* was real, *Oz* isn't real. She was just a girl who hit her head during a tornado and hallucinated. So her shoes can't be real, because in the story she got the shoes in Oz, and Oz doesn't exist."

"Right," I said. "It's, uh, I want to like—*metaphorically* look for her shoes. I mean . . ." I thought fast. "I mean, we can prove she was real if we find the rest of that article. And then we'll, uh, be famous!" I added brightly. "Totally famous. We'll go viral. It's our ticket out of Flat Hill."

Madison stared at me, her eyes narrowed. "So what's the part you're not telling us?"

"Which part?"

"Amy, this story is insane. Your house gets wiped out by a tornado. You disappear for a *month*. You come back and tell everyone you were in the hospital, which is clearly not true, and now you're obsessed with proving that a character in a cheesy old movie was a real person?"

"I . . . Well, yeah," I said. "I mean, I'll do it by myself. I understand if you don't want to help me."

"Help you do *what*, exactly?" Madison asked patiently, like I had the brain development of Dustin Jr.

"Find Dorothy's sho—find, uh, more evidence that Dorothy existed," I said lamely. "You know, like . . . I couldn't even find the rest of the article. But I know there has to be some kind of . . . I don't know, newspaper collection or something. Her farm was where the high school is now. I mean, there has to be more about her."

"How do you know Dorothy's supposedly real farm was in the same place as the high school?" Madison asked.

"I, uh . . . ," I faltered. "I just, um, guessed." They were both looking at me like I had grown an extra head. "Come on, you guys, if we can prove Dorothy existed, we'll be completely famous. On TV. Interviews and stuff. You name it." Madison was starting to look intrigued instead of suspicious. "Anyway, I thought maybe I could start by trying to find the whole Baum article and, uh, starting from there."

"Why don't you just go to the library?" Dustin asked.

"The library?"

"Flat Hill's historical archive is in the library at the high school," he pointed out. "I had detention one time and they made me dust back there."

"Oh my god, Dustin, you're a genius," I breathed. Of course. It was so obvious. Here I was, worrying about magic, when all I needed was to find an old newspaper.

"He's okay," Madison said, patting him on the shoulder.

"The only thing is, they keep the really old stuff locked up, and you have to have special permission to get back there," Dustin added. "I think you have to be writing a paper about it or something." My heart sank. Great, just what I needed. Everything I needed was locked up in some dusty old room no one really cared about, and I couldn't even break in using magic.

"Maybe I could sneak into school at night," I said.

"Wow, you are *really* serious about this," Madison said. "Why don't you just get detention?"

"What?"

"If that's how Dustin got back there, it'll probably work for you, too," Madison said reasonably. "We can get detention, too, if you want company," she added, holding Dustin Jr. aloft with a wicked gleam in her eye. "Pissing off Strachan is like my new full-time job. Dustin can pee on his desk or something."

"No way," Dustin said.

"I meant the baby."

"I *know* you meant the baby. I mean no way can you piss off Strachan, Mad. He's itching for an excuse to throw you out of school. But if you want help looking, Amy, I can go with you. I just have to show up late for class a couple of times."

Madison stuck out her glossy lower lip in a fake pout. "You're so boring," she sighed.

"Strachan would love to throw me out, too," I mused. "I have to figure out a way to get in trouble without actually getting in trouble."

"Don't you have detention already? Like, technically?"

Madison asked, batting her eyelashes. "I seem to remember a certain hallway fight with a defenseless pregnant chick."

"Of course," I said, practically slapping my forehead with the heel of my hand. "I'll just tell him I feel bad getting out of my suspension. You're totally brilliant, Madison."

"I know," she said airily, polishing off her sundae and eyeballing the dish like she was ready to order another. How was she so fit? "Breastfeeding," she said, answering my unasked question. "Plus, carrying this little sucker around all day is a total workout. I'm in the best shape of my life."

"If I watch you eat any more ice cream, I'm going to puke," Dustin said firmly, pushing the plate away. Dustin Jr. woke up and wailed aloud as if in protest. Heads turned as Madison tried unsuccessfully to shush him. "We better get home," Dustin said to me. "But I'll see you tomorrow in the clink." He grinned, and I wanted to hug them both. For the first time since I'd gotten back to Kansas, I had a plan.

"See you tomorrow," I said.

TWELVE

I let myself into my mom's apartment building. The hallway was dim and quiet. Someone's cat slunk past me—probably the source of the cat-pee smell in the hallway. My mom was home, and the apartment was full of delicious cooking smells. A guy I didn't recognize was sitting on the couch.

"Hi," he said, jumping to his feet eagerly as I walked in. "You must be Amy. I've heard so much about you. I'm Jake." He held out one hand and I stared at him for a second before realizing he meant for me to shake it.

"Uh, hi," I said. He was pretty handsome, in a farmer kind of way—he hadn't shaved in a couple of days, but his stubble gave him a rugged, manly look instead of a scruffy one. He was wearing a T-shirt that revealed tan, muscled arms, and jeans that were clean but far from new. He took off his John Deere baseball cap as he shook my hand.

"Amy?" My mom came into the room from the kitchen. She

was wearing her favorite (and shortest) skirt and a low-cut top that showed off her cleavage. Her hair was piled in a messy, flattering bun on top of her head, and her cheeks were bright with pink blush. But she had an apron on over her bar-hopping ensemble, and she was holding a long-handled wooden spoon in one hand. She gave me a one-armed hug. "How was school? You met Jake?"

"School was fine," I said. "And yeah, we just met."

"Jake lives down the hall," my mom said, but from the look she gave him, I had the feeling he was a lot more than just her new neighbor. "He lost his place in the tornado, too."

"You're from Dusty Acres?" I asked, surprised. I was pretty sure I'd have remembered this guy if I'd seen him before.

"No, from Montrose," he said, naming a town even smaller than ours a couple of miles away. "We were basically flattened in the tornado, but the nearest emergency housing was here. I lost everything—my farm, my whole house. Your mom's been really kind to me since I moved in here. I don't know what I'd do without her."

I bet, I thought sourly. They were looking at each other in a way that made me want to barf at the same time it made me think of Nox. I cleared my throat, and my mom jumped.

"Sorry, honey!" she chirped. "I should have told you Jake might be coming over for dinner. I'm making spaghetti!"

You should have told me Jake existed, I thought. But my mom looked so happy I didn't want to say it out loud. Still, I was a little hurt. She hadn't been too sad about my absence to start up a juicy romance with the hot neighbor. I walked past them into the kitchen and helped myself to a Coke. That, at least, was one good thing Kansas had that Oz didn't.

Dinner was so normal it was kind of weird. I told my mom and Jake about my day at school while my mom passed around a big plate of spaghetti and a basket of rolls. Anyone watching us would have thought we were any old family sitting down for a meal together. Obviously, I left out the part about plotting a secret search with Madison and Dustin—and I also didn't bring up my meeting with Assistant Principal Strachan. But after Jake went back to his place—giving my mom a big kiss on the lips that I totally ignored—I followed her into the living room and sat down next to her on the couch.

"You didn't have to send him away," I said. "I kind of liked him."

My mom beamed at me. "Isn't he great? He's nothing like the other guys I've dated." *Like my dad?* I wondered. "I don't think I was ready for someone decent before, you know? I mean, I didn't really have my act together." She got quiet all of a sudden. "As you know," she said softly.

"Listen, Mom," I said, ignoring her overshare. I didn't want to get into another conversation about our feelings where I'd just end up hurting hers. "I met with Assistant Principal Strachan today and he said you didn't believe me about the hospital. Is that true?"

She looked down at her hands and sighed. "I wish he hadn't told you that," she said.

"So it is true."

"Amy—" She turned to me, and I saw to my surprise that her eyes were welling up with tears. "Look, Amy, like I said, I know I've been a pretty crappy parent for the last few years."

I couldn't help it. The mom I'd left behind in Dusty Acres had done a lot of damage. "More than a few," I said before I could stop myself.

She nodded. "Okay, more than a few. When the tornado hit—well, let's just say I don't blame you for using it as an excuse to leave. I'm just so grateful you gave me another chance and came back." She paused. "Are you—were you—*okay* while you were gone? Were you safe?"

Not even close, I thought, but I knew what she was asking. She was thinking of real-world girls-on-milk-cartons stuff: scary strangers, dark vans, *SVU* episodes. She'd probably spent every minute since I'd gotten back wondering just what trauma I was repressing.

"Yeah," I said. "I met some nice people and they, um, took care of me. It was nothing like—I mean, what you're thinking." Her face sagged in relief. I knew she wanted me to tell her more. But I'd already tried to come up with too many stories for one day. "I'm sorry, I just—I'm really tired. Being back, school and everything. I'll tell you later, I promise." As long as *later* never came, it was a promise I wouldn't have to actually break.

"Of course, honey. But if you want to talk about what happened while you were gone, I'll always listen. Okay?"

I wished I *could* tell my mom what had happened in Oz. I

wanted to talk to someone human—and at least relatively sane. But I knew that even if I trusted her—which I didn't—there was no way I could ever begin to explain everything that had happened to me, and no way she'd believe me if I tried. For the first time, I wished I'd never gone to Oz at all. My life in Kansas had sucked, but I hadn't had to watch anyone I cared about die. I hadn't turned into a monster, and I hadn't had to kill. As bad as Kansas was, Oz might have been even worse. I'd been a hero in Oz, sure, but no one had really treated me like one. No one had looked at me the way my mom was looking at me now—as if I was the only person in the world, whose safety mattered more than anything else.

"Ready for bed? You have a big day at school tomorrow."

"Yeah, right," I said, laughing. "Chemistry is no match for me."

She smiled and hugged me. "That's my girl."

As I pulled away, I saw her. It was Mombi. She was standing in the corner, behind my mom, and she looked pissed.

"Get it together, Amy!" the witch whispered. "We're not here for you to win daughter of the year."

With that, she disappeared.

THIRTEEN

The next morning, I practically ran to Assistant Principal Strachan's office. Bonding with my mom was nice and all, but I had work to do: like save an entire enchanted kingdom before a magic-crazed nightmare razed it to the ground. Assistant Principal Strachan was about to meet the new, improved Amy Gumm. And I was going to find out the truth about Dorothy.

I had to wait to see him, but luckily I'd gotten to school early. Mrs. Perkins gave me another lollipop and I crunched it while I waited. I couldn't help thinking about Gert, Mombi, and Glamora, lurking in their weird limbo state, waiting for me to accomplish something. Anything. And Nox. Where was he? Was he thinking about me, too? Was he wondering if I was safe? Did he care? Was it possible to drive yourself completely insane in fifteen minutes in a plastic chair in a hallway or did it just feel that way? Finally, Assistant Principal Strachan called me into his office, looking none too pleased to see me.

"What is it now, Miss Gumm?"

"Sir, I've been thinking about what you said yesterday. I'm just so grateful you've lifted my suspension, but it really doesn't seem fair."

He raised an eyebrow, but said nothing as I continued. "I understand I was so much trouble before, and I want to convince you I've changed." I tried to remember the speech my mom had used on me. "I know I don't deserve forgiveness," I added, "but I'm going to work for it all the same."

"I beg your pardon?"

"I want to serve detention, sir. After school, for the same amount of time as I should have been suspended."

Assistant Principal Strachan stared at me. "You *want* detention?"

"It's the only way to show you I mean what I say," I explained. This didn't really make sense, even to me, but he seemed to buy it. Or at least he couldn't figure out a sinister motive behind my sudden desire to scrub the hallways and dust the library.

"Very well," he said, his eyes narrowed. "You will serve out your suspension as a detention for the next two weeks. I don't know what you're up to, Miss Gumm, but if I find out you're doing anything shady—"

"You won't, sir!" I said quickly, grabbing my bag and resisting the urge to give him a big kiss on the cheek. He was still staring after me in confusion as I ran out the door.

I was so ready to start searching that I didn't pay attention to much of anything that day. I ate lunch with Dustin and Madison again; true to his word, Dustin had shown up so late for first period that he, too, was sentenced to after-school purgatory. "Aren't you worried they'll kick you out of school, too?" I asked him.

"Are you kidding? I was on the football team," he said. Madison snorted in disgust and muttered something that sounded a lot like "bullshit double standards."

I was practically bouncing in my seat on the long hard cafeteria bench. Dustin Jr. was in a cheerful mood, waving his arms around and drooling on his terry-cloth onesie. Watching Madison taking care of her baby, I was struck by how much she had changed. She was still tough, but now it seemed protective. You could tell she didn't really know what she was doing. Sometimes she seemed almost terrified of the baby, as if she might drop him or do something totally wrong. Dustin obviously had no clue how to deal with an infant either. But they both looked at the little guy with so much love. It was strange to see the person who'd made my life miserable for so long this caring and vulnerable. Madison had been good at everything without even trying. But I guess even Madison was no match for ten pounds of screaming, spit-covered, easily damaged newborn.

I wondered if my own mom had been anything like that when I was a baby. If she and my dad had looked at me with that same expression of dopey, helpless, animal love. If anyone would ever love me like that again. *Nox*. I shoved that thought into a closet at the back of my brain and slammed the door. Nox had made his choice and I didn't blame him. I knew Oz would always come first in his heart. If I felt that strongly about a place, I'd put it before people, too. Maybe I just wasn't meant to have a home. But the least I could do was help Nox save his.

"What are you thinking, Amy?" Madison, having secured Dustin Jr. in his baby wrap again, was looking at me. "You look like you went to another planet. A really, like, sad planet."

"Nothing," I said, a little too sharply. But she didn't seem to mind.

"Yeah," she said. "I know all about that." For a second I wanted to snap at her. What did Madison know about real sadness? And then I thought of what her life must be like now, how her so-called friends had bailed on her the second she'd turned into a teen-mom warning story, and I realized that Madison probably knew a lot more about suffering than I gave her credit for.

After-school detention was a motley collection of the school's biggest losers (whose number I probably would've counted among even if I *hadn't* offered to serve out my sentence): a couple of potheads, a guy I recognized from one of my classes junior year who was always getting in fights in the halls, and a girl with a bleach-blond ratty perm and stonewashed jeans straight out of 1997 who rolled her eyes at me as I eagerly accepted my vacuum cleaner and dust rag. The shop teacher, Mr. Stone, handed out supplies to my fellow detainees, and then mumbled instructions so low that he might as well have been speaking another language. Just then, the door swung open and Dustin walked in.

"Hi, Amy," he said. "We should—"

"No socializing!" Mr. Stone said, coming to life a little. Dustin apologized and accepted his bottle of glass cleaner. "Help Gumm with the science classrooms," Mr. Stone added.

"Actually, sir, I thought we could clean the library," Dustin said innocently. "That was my job last time. I'm a real expert."

Mr. Stone stared at Dustin as if he was up to something—which, of course, he was. Sort of. But Dustin just looked back with a vacant, innocent expression. I had to look away or else I'd start cracking up.

"Fine," Mr. Stone growled. "But I'll be checking up on you. Any hanky-panky . . ." He stopped short and then flushed red. One of the potheads snickered and sneezed the name of a venereal disease.

"That's enough!" Mr. Stone barked. "For that, you're on bathroom duty, Carson." Mr. Stone tossed Dustin a set of keys, and I hid another smile as I followed him to the library.

I'd never spent any time in the high school library. From what I could tell, nobody else had either. Dustin unlocked the door to what was more or less a glorified janitor's closet: a tiny, windowless room full of rusting metal shelves crammed with books that hadn't been new when my mom was going to school here. It looked like the shelves hadn't been dusted since the last time Dustin served detention. The sad little book display arranged on a tiny table near the door was springtime-themed—despite the fact that it was October. There wasn't even a librarian; if you wanted to check out books, you were supposed to borrow a teacher's keys and use the honor system. Literature theft wasn't exactly a high-concern crime in our neck of the prairie. The school probably would've been excited just to learn that someone could actually read.

The "archive" turned out to be a closet at the back of the library. Dustin flipped through the keys Mr. Stone had given him, but none of them fit the lock. "Shoot," he said. I looked at the flimsy wooden door, and then at Dustin. He grinned. "Really?"

"Come on," I said. "I did your homework for you for a year. You owe me."

He nodded solemnly. "You do have a point there." Bracing one foot against the doorframe, he grabbed the doorknob and pulled. Muscles bulged under the soft fabric of his cornflower-blue T-shirt, and I remembered with a pang that I'd once had a major crush on the guy. Dustin might be a little dumb, but he was hot. The door creaked alarmingly, and with one final tug it came away from the frame with a splintering crack.

"Wow," I said. "I didn't think that would actually work. You're really strong."

Dustin blushed modestly. "It's just, like, laminate," he mumbled.

"We're going to be in so much trouble," I said, looking at the ruined lock.

"Nah," he said. "Nobody comes in here. They won't notice for years."

Eagerly, I looked over his shoulder at the contents of the closet: a teetering stack of dusty cardboard boxes, piles of faded fabric, and, weirdly enough, a rusty old hoe. That was it. The entire historical archive of Flat Hill, Kansas.

"I guess this place was always a dump," I said. Dustin pulled the top box off the stack, grunting with surprise at how heavy it was. I lifted the lid, revealing a stack of ancient yearbooks. The top one was dated 1967.

"Far out," Dustin said, leafing through it. "Check out this dude's hair." He pointed to a blissed-out-looking hippie guy with shampoo-commercial-worthy blond waves past his shoulders.

"Totally not fair," I said. I shoved the box aside and went for the next one while Dustin looked at old yearbooks. More yearbooks, a box of old newspapers—none of them dating back to the time of Baum's article—a leather-bound book whose title, *Tales of the Prairie*, was embossed on the front in frilly letters. Nothing. My heart sank. The piles of fabric were old-fashioned aprons and a frayed blue banner with CONGRATULATIONS CLASS OF 1934 sewn on in bright red letters.

"I guess that's it," Dustin said in disappointment.

"There's one more box," I said. "Way at the back."

"I don't see it."

I reached for the box and then yanked my hands back with a yelp. It had *stung* me. I popped a finger into my mouth, tasting blood. "There's something sharp back there," I said.

"I don't even see what you're trying to grab."

I reached in again, more cautiously this time, and then I felt it, like a halo around the battered old box: the unmistakable buzz of magic. A thrill ran through me. I'd been *right*. There was something here—and someone had tried to hide it. Someone powerful enough to use magic in Kansas. Someone who'd been able to keep the truth about Dorothy a secret for over a century. Someone who *had* to be from Oz.

"Give me those dust cloths," I said. Just as Dustin handed them to me, the library door swung open, and we both froze.

"I don't see much cleaning happening in here," Mr. Stone growled. Dustin's eyes were huge.

"Oh, shit," he mouthed.

FOURTEEN

"What's going on in here?" Mr. Stone asked peevishly, stepping into the library. We were hidden by the shelves, but if he came any farther into the room he'd see us, and there was no way we could explain what we were doing going through a stack of old boxes next to a busted closet door. Dustin jumped up and headed for the door. Instinctively, I threw the old graduation banner over myself and the pile of boxes. My arm brushed up against the last box I'd found. It didn't sting me this time; it *burned*. Like the feeling of metal cold enough to freeze to your skin and peel away the outer layer. And then the awful burning faded and a strange sensation crawled across my skin, like the chill you feel when you've been out in the snow too long.

Everything around me dimmed until the edges of the room were lost in dense, thickening shadow. Tendrils of darkness crept across the floor toward me. A slender, silvery form stepped out of the shadows and looked down at me. It was mostly hidden by the darkness, but I could make out swirling black robes and a pale, bald skull topped with a twisted iron crown.

So, it hissed. I heard its voice inside my head rather than out loud and clapped my hands over my ears in a futile attempt to shut it out. *You have found what I have hidden, little witch. My congratulations.*

I struggled to say something, but the creature's magic had glued my mouth shut. *Who are you?* I thought desperately.

I could *feel* its smile cutting into my thoughts.

You'll find out soon enough, little witch. You are strong and clever to have uncovered so easily what I had concealed so carefully. Your witches could not see what I had put away here so many years ago. Even your Dorothy could not find what once had been hers. But you found it without magic, as if it was calling to you. You are very strong indeed—perhaps even stronger than my other little friend.

What other little friend? Did it mean Dorothy?

We will see each other again, my dear. I am beginning to think you shall be quite useful to me. But now is not the time for explanations. Give my regards to your . . . friends.

A knife-sharp flash of pain stabbed into my skull and I cried out in agony. I could *see* Mombi, Gert, and Glamora, darkness swirling around them, looking up in fear and alarm. Nox, out on the prairie somewhere, staring upward as if he knew I was looking down at him, opening his mouth to say something. The creature laughed and flicked its fingers, and a roiling cloud of darkness descended on the four of them, erasing their faces from my mind.

Until next time, little witch. Watch your back. Not all your friends are trustworthy. And then it stepped back into the shadows and disappeared. I felt its magic loosen its grip on me and I slumped to the floor, tears of pain leaking from my eyes.

". . . Amy? She's in the bathroom," Dustin was saying. "Everything's cool here, Mr. Stone."

The shop teacher grumbled something I didn't catch and the library door swung closed again. "Phew," Dustin sighed, his footsteps coming toward me. "That was, like, really clo—Amy? Where are you?"

"I'm right here," I said thickly. My mouth tasted like ashes and dirt. With effort, I pushed away the graduation banner and sat up. Dustin was staring at me with his mouth open.

"How did you do that?" he breathed.

"Do what?"

"You just . . . you weren't there," he said. "Amy, you weren't *there*. And then you were. You just, like, appeared. Are you okay?"

"I'm fine," I said, faking a sneeze. "I didn't go anywhere, I hid under this dumb banner." I was still stunned from the effects of the creature's magic, but I had to convince Dustin he hadn't seen anything out of the ordinary. "It's so dark back here, you just missed me. I totally thought I could *hide* under this thing, can you believe that?" I babbled. "Like a little kid playing hide-and-seek, ha-ha. So silly. Um, anyway, there's another box in there."

Dustin was still looking at me like—well, like I'd vanished

and then reappeared out of thin air. But the fact that it wasn't physically *possible* to vanish and reappear out of thin air was working in my favor. Whatever explanation he was coming up with for what he'd just seen, it definitely wasn't "some kind of really scary mind-stabbing supernatural entity just walked out of the walls, made Amy briefly invisible in order to drop a bunch of vague sinister hints, and then disappeared."

"What's in it?" he asked, his curiosity getting the better of him. Wrapping my hands in the dust cloths, I gingerly lifted the box from the back of the closet. But whatever magic had been protecting it had disappeared with the mysterious visitor, and it felt like an ordinary box this time when I touched it. It was light and small, but something thumped inside it. I lifted the flaps, and breathlessly, we looked in.

There was nothing in the box but an old notebook. I took it out and flipped through the pages. Every one of them was blank. My heart sank as I stared at the book, turning the pages over and over again as if looking at them again would make words appear. A secret, a spell—heck, even a map to Dorothy's shoes. Nothing. I wanted to cry. All this, and for what? I'd never find the stupid shoes, even if they existed. The witches and I were stuck in Kansas forever. Dorothy was going to destroy Oz, and we had no way to stop her.

"Amy, what's wrong?"

"I was just hoping for an answer," I said.. Whoever the mysterious visitor had been, it had been wasting its time protecting a blank book.

"We can keep looking, Amy," Dustin said, anxious to cheer me up. "We can—I don't know, Topeka probably has a library. I can drive you over there if you want as long as Mad doesn't mind watching the baby. It's no big—"

The library door swung open again and we both nearly jumped out of our skins. "Time's up!" Mr. Stone bellowed. "Go home, you little miscreants." Thankfully, he stomped off without bothering to check our work. I shoved the boxes back in the closet and covered them with the banner. At the last minute I shoved the notebook into my bag. Maybe I was trying to remind myself that my mission was more hopeless than finding a needle in a haystack. We locked the library door behind us and returned the keys and our vacuum to a sullen Mr. Stone.

"I can give you a ride home," Dustin offered.

"Thanks," I said.

I was silent in the car, leaning my head against the glass and looking out, trying to see some beauty in the dull gray sky and flat, dusty earth. *I might as well get used to it,* I thought. *This time, I'm here for good.*

FIFTEEN

My mom and Jake were sitting side by side on the couch when I got back to her apartment, holding hands and watching the news. When I walked in they jumped apart, blushing, like I'd just caught them doing something actually scandalous. I stifled a giggle.

"Honey!" my mom exclaimed. "I wasn't expecting you to be so late. Where have you been?"

I was definitely not in the mood for conversation, but I'd already been enough of a jerk to my mom. I explained about detention, and she beamed at me. "What a mature decision to make, Amy. I'm so proud of you." Even Jake was nodding. At least I'd done something right, even if it was for the wrong reasons.

That night, Jake cooked. He was so nice to my mom it was hard not to like him, against my better judgment. My mom had had a few boyfriends here and there—if "boyfriend" was the right word for the losers who hung around the trailer for a month or two, eating all our food and burping in front of the TV with a six-pack before disappearing again—and she had an unerring instinct for jerks, deadbeats, and creeps.

There was the guy who liked to follow me around when she wasn't home, eyeing me in a way that made me start carrying pepper spray everywhere I went. Thankfully, he didn't last long. There was the guy who "borrowed" a bunch of money from her and then vanished without paying her back. Amazingly, she was surprised. There was the guy I never saw sober. But Jake actually seemed nice. Maybe he even *was* nice, not just putting on a show until he got whatever it was he wanted. My mom turned off the TV, and we sat around her little card table and ate the casserole he'd made like we were an actual family. I kept waiting for him to say something mean to my mom, or stare at my boobs, or spout off something really sexist or racist or just gross, but he was actually . . . normal. I'd only been gone a month of my mom's time, but it was like I had come home to a different planet.

"How was school today, Amy? It must be hard to adjust to being back after your—" He paused, as if he wasn't quite sure what to say. "Accident," he finished. I wondered how much my mom had told him about her theories about my disappearance. "It was fine," I said politely. "I'm not as far behind as I thought I would be, actually. Dwight D. Eisenhower Senior High isn't exactly Harvard." He laughed at my dumb joke as if I'd said something incredibly funny. My mom smiled as he asked me more questions about myself. What books did I like to read?

What were my favorite movies? How about favorite foods? If he was trying this hard to impress me, he must be really into my mom. I was surprised by how happy I was for her. I needed him to be this good for after. For when I was gone again.

Jake even did the dishes after dinner—I offered, but he insisted. I told Jake and my mom that I was tired, although mostly I just wanted to give them some privacy—and be alone to think. No sooner had I shut my door than the air in front of me began to shimmer, and Mombi materialized. "Again?" I hissed. "I can't exactly explain away a random old lady standing in my room if my mom comes in!"

"'Old lady' isn't very polite, missy," Mombi growled. "That's 'old witch' to you. Anyway, I'm not really here. Gert, Glamora, and I are still hiding out in the Darklands. I'm just projecting to check in. You and I need to talk."

"I thought your magic was too weak to just zip around like you're on vacation," I said. "Or are all bets off when it comes to spying on me?"

"I only spy because I care," Mombi hissed. "Unlike some people who seem to have forgotten what they're here for."

"I haven't forgotten a thing," I snapped. "Now what's going on?"

"We seem to be adjusting to being outside of Oz. Still a long way from shipshape, but at least we're getting strong enough for a little astral projection."

"I'm not sure that's going to help," I said dully. I sank down onto my bed and told her everything. About the newspaper article, breaking into the library closet, finding the mysterious box. When I got to the creature who'd dropped in on my and Dustin's party, Mombi stopped me.

"Tell me this part again," she said, her voice low and urgent. "What did you see?"

"Something tall and skinny. Black clothes. Bald. I think it had a crown."

"And what did it say to you?"

I struggled to remember, but it was like trying to look through fog. "I can't remember exactly. Something about how I'd found what it had hidden. I think it has to be the person who covered up the truth about Dorothy—that she was real, I mean." I shuddered. "Dustin couldn't see it."

"He wouldn't be able to," Mombi said grimly. She stared off into space for a moment, rubbing her chin with one thumb. "It can't be him," she muttered. "Ozma thwarted him. Has he really been here all this time?"

"Who?" I asked. Mombi kept talking to herself. "Mombi, *who*?"

She sighed and shook her head. "The Nome King," she said. "I think what you saw was the Nome King. But if it was . . . we are in a mess of trouble indeed."

"What's a Nome King? It sounds like a kind of mushroom."

Mombi snorted. "Who, not what," she said. "*Who*. The Nome King is a king of the Nomes," she said. "That's nome with an *n* not a *g*, mind you. Don't screw it up. He gets very prissy about the spelling. He pulled one of his diggers limb from limb while he was still alive just because he pronounced it with a *g*."

I swallowed. That fit pretty well with the creepy dude who'd magically dropped in on me in the library. My interest in meeting up with him again was at—well, let's say an all-time low. "Diggers? He digs stuff? What is he, like some kind of a troll? Don't they live in mountains?"

Mombi gave an exasperated sigh. "All that time Glamora spent teaching you the difference between a scone and a crumpet, and no one ever bothered to teach you about the Nome King. Typical."

"Well, don't blame me," I said.

Mombi spoke through gritted teeth like it hurt her to have to explain something so elementary. "A troll is a big, stupid monster. You bop it hard enough over the head—no more troll. A troll is easy-peasy. A Nome is more like a cross between a fairy and a demon. Nasty things. They live in the underworld of Ev, across the Deadly Desert."

"Never heard of it," I said.

"Frankly, it's not much to write home about," Mombi said. "The point is, the Nome King tried to invade Oz, ages ago, but Ozma stopped him. Made him swear an oath to leave Oz in peace as long as she ruled . . ." Mombi trailed off and looked at me as she let it sink in.

"Ozma isn't in power anymore," I said. "Congratulations, teacher's pet." I ignored her witchy sneer. "But if he's trying to invade Oz, what's he doing here?"

"I don't know yet. But at least part of it makes sense. If he's the one who erased any proof that Dorothy was a real person, he *must* know about the shoes. It's possible he's using them to travel back and forth—or he has some other power of his own. Magic in Ev isn't like magic in Oz. It doesn't follow the same rules. Ev is as different from Oz as the Other Place is. What exactly he's up to is impossible to guess, but there's no way it's good news for us."

"He said something about how I was stronger than the 'other one.' I think he meant Dorothy. And he told me not to trust anyone," I said, remembering.

"Oh dear," Mombi said quietly. Her leathery face went white. That's when I knew we were in serious trouble. "He knew who you *were*? That's not good at all."

"You're not being very reassuring."

"It just means we have to find the shoes before he does anything else. Do that, and we may be back in business. Maybe." She frowned. "But I don't like the sound of that, little missy. You be on your toes. If he's using Dorothy somehow and decides you'll make a more valuable pet . . ." She didn't have to finish. I didn't want to think about the rest of that sentence. Not here, in the one place I'd almost felt safe for the first time in months: the frilly little pink bedroom my mom had created as she held out for my return. I knew the safety was an illusion. I'd learned in Oz that safety always was. But I couldn't help it. Some part of me wanted to pretend it was enough to protect me. That I could just stay here and go back to being ordinary. That I could check out of this neverending mission and let someone else take over for a while.

But I couldn't tell the old witch any of that—even though, from the way she was looking at me, I was pretty sure she could guess at least some of it. I turned my thoughts back to the mission. Which was, after all, in pretty serious trouble on its own.

"Mombi, I don't know how to find the shoes. I thought I could find something in the library, but that turned out to be a dead end."

"Why would the Nome King descend on you in a pool of darkness if you were looking at a dead end, Amy?" She had a point there.

"But I didn't find anything. Just this old blank notebook."

"Let me see it," she ordered. I dug through my bag and pulled out the notebook, handing it to her, but it passed through her hands. "Goddamn projecting," she muttered. "I always forget. Turn the pages for me." Yet again, I flipped through the book as Mombi's keen eyes watched the blank pages turn.

"I can feel the power in that book. Can't you?" I closed my eyes, concentrating on the weight of the book in my palms. And once I paid attention, I understood what Mombi meant. It was barely there, but unmistakable—like the charge on a television screen after you turn it off. "You're right," I said. "There's something there."

"I'm going to funnel my magic through you," Mombi said. "It should work—you won't need any power of your own, you'll just need to be a conduit. But it may be too much for me to unlock whatever that book is hiding and keep projecting myself here. If I disappear—you're going to be on your own again. And if there's no clue about how to find the shoes . . ."

She didn't have to finish. If I didn't find the shoes, we were screwed.

"Let's do it," I said with more confidence than I felt. The idea of Mombi using me as a funnel was weird and kind of scary, but at least we were doing something. If Mombi wasn't ready to give up, neither was I. "No one would go to this much trouble to hide a book if it didn't hold something important."

Mombi eyed me appraisingly, and I saw something like respect flicker in her eyes. It was kind of nice. We hadn't always seen eye to eye, and I still had no idea if she even had my best interests at heart. (Let's face it: probably not.) But it still meant something to me to have the old witch's respect. She closed her eyes and began to mouth the words to a spell. Suddenly, I remembered what I'd seen when the Nome King had paralyzed me. The witches, looking out in fear. And Nox, all alone out on the prairie somewhere. Was what I'd seen real? What was he doing out there?

"Wait!" I said. She opened her eyes again, this time looking slightly irritated. Too bad. "How's Nox? Where is he?" Mombi gave me a look so withering that if she had actually been in the room I probably would have flinched.

"He's *fine*, and you don't need to know anything else," she said disgustedly. "Are you ready now?"

I wanted to ask more, but I knew better than to push my luck. Wherever Nox was, he either couldn't or wouldn't contact me—and neither option was all that appealing. If the witches had sent him on some secret mission, Mombi obviously wasn't going to tell me. Mombi had already closed her eyes and was going back to her spell. The book in my hands began to radiate heat.

I could feel Mombi's magic moving through me, but it was strange and alien, not the familiar feeling of sharing power that I'd tapped into before. Like I was just a piece of pipe that her power was pouring through, as unimportant as a lifeless hunk of plastic. I struggled to let go of the feeling of wrongness, to let Mombi work through me.

"Don't fight me," she hissed between gritted teeth. The strain of the spell was evident on her face. She was pale, and the deep wrinkles on her seamed old cheeks stood out in harsh relief. The book flapped open in my hands of its own volition, its pages riffling frantically in an invisible breeze. I gasped out loud and nearly dropped it as a tiny black cloud of swirling ink formed over the pages, dripping downward and shaping itself into tiny lines that became letters. The pages whipped faster and faster, filling with words. The book blazed with heat in my hands, its cover smoking. I couldn't take it anymore; I dropped it on the ground with a yelp and heard its spine crack as it slammed to the floor.

"Amy!" Mombi gasped. "You have to—" But her outline was already fading, and whatever else she had to say was lost as her image flickered and vanished.

"Everything okay in there, honey?" my mom called, rapping lightly on the door.

"Great!" I yelped, kicking the still-smoking book under my bed.

"Were you asking me something?"

"Just talking to myself!" I reassured her. She said good night again and I heard her settle back on the couch with a sigh. I waited long minutes until I heard her soft snores through the door, and then I got out the book. It had cooled enough to touch, but I still handled it gingerly, half expecting it to bite me.

It was still just an ordinary old journal, the leather cover blackened in places where Mombi's spell had singed it, but now the pages were filled with a cramped, old-fashioned cursive script. I opened it to a random page and, squinting, tried to make out the tiny, elegant letters.

. . . Millie is growing so beautifuly. Every day she lays at least 1 egg. Em says she will be a Prize Layer & maybe I can even entre her in the Fair next summer! I wood be so proud if she won a meddle!

Toto is so cute today. I am teching him to fetch but he only wants to play!

"Holy *shit*," I breathed. This was it. It had to be. There was only one kid in Kansas who'd had an aunt named Em and a dog named Toto: Dorothy Gale, the little girl who'd gone to Oz. I turned the pages, skimming Dorothy's diary entries. More about her chickens, her dog, her farm chores. And then: two blank pages, and after that, in a bolder, more jagged handwriting:

NO ONE BELEVES ME. BUT I WENT. THEY'LL BE SORRY ONE DAY EVERY ONE THAT SAID I LYED.

That was it. The journal ended there. The rest of the pages were blank. Nothing about her shoes, her return to Kansas, or anything that had happened in Oz. If there was any more writing hidden there, Mombi's spell hadn't revealed it. I sighed and closed the diary. All I'd discovered was that Dorothy was real—which I really, definitely already knew—and that someone had wanted to hide that fact. Someone with a lot of power. Someone who I was pretty sure wasn't on my side. I hid Dorothy's journal under my mattress and closed my eyes. I'd figure something else out in the morning. But for now, I was exhausted.

I tossed and turned for a while on my narrow bed, and when I finally fell asleep, I dreamed terrible dreams, reliving some of the worst moments I'd had in Oz. The spell I'd used to permanently separate Pete and Ozma while Ozma screamed in pain. Beheading the Lion, the fountain of his blood spurting all over me. Polychrome's broken body. And in the background, Dorothy cackled away, mocking my inability to defeat her, her red shoes pulsing with that awful light.

Everything else faded away, and then I faced her alone on an open, dusty plain that looked strangely familiar. Gray-green lightning struck the barren earth around us, and thunder boomed in the distance. Dorothy's eyes were crazy, and a hot wind whipped her checked dress and blew dust in my eyes until I could barely see. I reached deep within myself to find the magic to fight her, but there was nothing there. She laughed as she watched me struggle, and then snapped her fingers. Helpless, I watched swirling darkness gather itself over her open palm. She raised one hand to fling it toward me, and I threw up my arms as if that would somehow protect me. I could hear someone shouting my name, but faintly, as if he was far away. Someone familiar. Someone who could protect me. Dorothy advanced toward me, shrieking with laughter, and I knew she was about to kill me.

"But you're just a girl," I said, and her face creased in confusion. "You're just a girl from Kansas. Just like me."

"No!" she screamed, raising her hand. "I'm not like you! I'll never be that little girl again!"

"Amy!" shouted the faraway voice. "Amy, no!" Suddenly, I knew who he was.

"Nox!" I screamed his name into my dark room, sitting bolt upright with my heart pounding. Seconds later, my mom flung open the door to my room and came running in.

"Amy? Amy, are you okay? What on earth is happening?"

It took me a long time to remember where I was. "I had a bad dream," I whispered. My mom made a sympathetic noise, and put her arms around me, humming a snatch of a song she used to sing me to sleep with when I wasn't much more than a baby.

"It's okay," she said gently. "I'm right here. I'm not going anywhere." If I *was* going back to Oz, I couldn't let myself get weak. Nobody sings you lullabies in the middle of a war.

"I'm fine," I said gruffly. "Just go back to sleep."

"Okay, honey," she said softly, and turned to go, closing the door behind her. It took all the willpower I had not to call her back. I just wanted someone to hold me and tell me everything was going to be okay. But that would have been a lie. Nothing was going to be okay again as long as Dorothy was alive.

As I fell asleep, I thought one last time about Nox. The dream had felt so real—I could have sworn I'd really heard him, as if he really was trying to help me. But I had no idea where he was, or if he wanted to help me even if he could. Mombi was gone and I had no way of contacting her. I had no idea how to get back to Oz, and no clue what to do next. This time, I was completely on my own. I felt tears dampening my pillow as I slid back into a dark and mercifully dreamless sleep.

SIXTEEN

Jake was gone the next morning, but my mom was up before I was and had made me scrambled eggs and toast. Really, really burned toast. I took a couple of triangles to be polite, and she sighed. "I'm still getting the hang of this domestic thing," she admitted. "You don't have to eat them."

"The blackened part is good for you," I reassured her, but when her back was turned I tossed my toast into the garbage.

She pressed another bag lunch into my hand as I headed for the door. "See you tonight!" she called. "I won't be home late from work." She paused for just a second as I opened the door. "Love you, Amy," she said softly. I hesitated, and the door swung closed on her anxious face.

"You too," I murmured as I walked away.

Dustin and Madison were waiting for me when I got to school. There was some part of me that almost longed for this halfway normal new life with a mom who cared about taking care of me and actual friends who weren't Munchkins or talking monkeys. I hadn't realized how much I had wanted this kind of normal life until I had it (sort of). But then I remembered that Dustin and Madison were only being nice to me and my mom had only gotten her act together because I'd vanished for a month. If I'd stayed in Kansas, my normal life would have kept on the same as ever: one long, crappy day after another. It was too strange to think about, and so I decided not to.

"Ready for day two of detention?" Dustin asked me as we walked toward first period. I'd left Dorothy's journal at home, figuring it was safe under my mattress. "Maybe we'll find something else in the library." I was about to tell him I didn't think that was likely when it hit me. If Baum had interviewed the real Dorothy, maybe the secret to her shoes was somewhere in his books. At the very least, I could look up the Nome King. Baum had used the real Dorothy's memories to write his stories, even though he'd probably thought she was making everything up. If he'd described the Nome King, I might find out something that could help.

We were just passing the dusty old Dorothy diorama when Dustin stopped short. "Here comes trouble," he said under his breath. "Mad, maybe you should get out of here." Assistant Principal Strachan was heading straight for us, and he looked *really* pissed.

"I'm not going to abandon you guys," Madison protested. Dustin Jr. started to cry.

"Miss Gumm, Mr. Cheever," Assistant Principal Strachan

said icily as he descended on us. "I have a few questions for you about the cleaning job you did yesterday afternoon." He stressed the word *cleaning* with unmistakable sarcasm. "Miss Pendleton, you may go to class."

"But—" Madison protested as the first bell rang.

"Is there a *problem*, Miss Pendleton?"

Madison stared him down, and for a second I thought she was actually going to fight him. When Madison's scariness was on my side, it was pretty awesome. Even Assistant Principal Strachan looked a little intimidated. But after a tense pause, she shrugged. "Not today, *sir*," she drawled, bouncing the still-crying Dustin Jr. in his baby wrap. "See you guys around," she added, giving Dustin Sr. an ostentatious kiss on the mouth with a satisfied smack before she turned around and sauntered away, her pink-velour-clad butt swishing saucily. I had to hand it to the girl. She had attitude.

The hallway had cleared, and it was just me, Dustin, and Assistant Principal Strachan standing in front of the dusty old glass case. I cleared my throat. "Did you need something from us, sir?"

Assistant Principal Strachan's eyes narrowed. "I have questions for you, Amy," he hissed. "Perhaps they are better answered in my office." There was a strange, silvery glint in his eyes. Next to me, Dustin stiffened. I could sense it, too. Something wasn't right. Assistant Principal Strachan had never called me by my first name. And there was something weird about his voice. It almost seemed to echo inside my head. Like the Nome King in the library. As soon as the thought crossed my mind, Assistant Principal Strachan smiled.

"Very like indeed, Amy Gumm," he snarled. I hadn't said anything out loud.

"Amy?" Dustin asked, a note of fear creeping into his voice.

"Dustin, get out of here," I said in a low voice. *"Now."* But it was too late. Assistant Principal Strachan's face was stretching in front of me, his features melting away and dripping down his chest to reveal the twisted, cruel face of the creature that had confronted me in the library. His shapeless old suit peeled away from his body. Bones snapped and popped as he grew taller. And this time, Dustin could definitely see it.

"Amy, what's happening?" he asked as the husk that had been Assistant Principal Strachan crumpled to the ground and the Nome King took a step toward us.

"Be silent, little boy," the Nome King hissed, flicking his fingers. I felt his magic as it moved through the air like a shock wave—straight toward Dustin.

"Get down!" I yelled, throwing myself at him and bringing us both to the ground. The Nome King's magic zap missed us by inches and slammed into the wall behind us with a huge, echoing boom. The building shuddered and ceiling tiles crashed down around us.

"Little Dorothy's grip on Oz is weakening," the Nome King said, his voice eerily calm. "Soon the magic of Oz will have sapped her strength entirely and she will be no good to me whatsoever. But you, my dear Miss Gumm, are made of stronger stuff. I think you might be very useful indeed."

Absurdly, I thought of those old episodes of *Scooby-Doo* where a character that everyone thought was friendly is revealed to be the villain in disguise. "I could have gotten away with it, too, if it wasn't for you meddling kids!" he snaps as he's taken away. It's always hard to tell if it's supposed to be scary or funny.

But this situation wasn't at all funny. Without my magic, I had no way to defend myself—and I was on my own. I had to get us out of here before the Nome King killed Dustin and grabbed me, and I had no idea how I was going to do it.

"What do you mean, useful? What did you do with the real Assistant Principal Strachan?" If I couldn't fight him, maybe I could distract him long enough for Dustin to get away. His eyes flicked involuntarily toward the Dorothy diorama, and for the first time I noticed an extra figurine—the spitting image of Assistant Principal Strachan, down to the frumpy suit and scuffed shoes. I shivered. I'd never liked the guy, but I wouldn't have wished *that* for him. And then I noticed something else. Miniature Dorothy was wearing a miniature pair of shoes that glinted under a layer of dust. Silver shoes.

Once you learn how to recognize it, magic is unmistakable. You just need to know what to look for. It's like this talent my mom has for spotting the one shirt on the rack with a tiny hole in it, so she can get a discount. And the silver shoes in the diorama were magic as hell. They were so magic that just standing this close to them was giving me a tingly feeling in my stomach.

I'd found them. I had no idea how they'd gotten there, but the shoes had been right in front of me the whole time.

The Nome King smiled. "Indeed," he said. "Hidden in plain sight all this time. I thought they might come in useful someday. I have no trouble moving between worlds, dear Miss Gumm, but not everyone is so lucky. If you are to be the next ruler of Oz, you will need a way to get back. Might I offer you a new pair of footwear?"

The next ruler of Oz? What was he talking about? If the Nome King wanted control of Oz himself, what possible use could I be? Had he been the one behind Dorothy's return to Oz—and if so, why?

"Maybe we can reach an agreement," I said carefully, giving Dustin a shove. As confused as he was, he got the message. While I slowly got to my feet, staring down the Nome King, Dustin scooted away on his hands and knees.

The Nome King laughed. "An agreement? I don't think you're in a position to bargain, Amy Gumm."

"She's not," said a familiar voice behind me. "But I might be."

The Nome King's smile widened, his toothy grin even scarier than his regular expression. "How thrilling," he said. "Welcome to the party, little wizard."

SEVENTEEN

"Nox," I hissed. "What are you doing here?"

"You can't use magic, Amy. There's no way you can fight the Nome King by yourself."

"Did Mombi send you?" He didn't answer, his eyes on the Nome King, which made me think he had come here on his own. I had no idea what the consequences were for a witch who disobeyed Quadrant orders, but I was guessing Gert, Glamora, and Mombi wouldn't be too happy with Nox's solo mission.

The Nome King was obviously enjoying the moment. "Do you really think you can protect her against *me*, little boy? *Your* magic barely works here. You're weak and far from home. I urge you to let the matter rest. I have no wish to do harm to your *friend*." The way he stressed the word clearly indicated that he guessed Nox and I had feelings for each other—and that he found it funny.

"This isn't a game," Nox said in a low voice. I knew what Nox was doing. After all, he'd trained me. He was testing the Nome King's defenses, looking for a weakness. But the Nome King had already said his magic didn't work like ours.

"Amy, who are those people? What—what happened to Assistant Principal Strachan?" Shit. I'd forgotten about Dustin. He was still in the hallway.

"Dustin, I mean it! Get out of here!" I hissed.

"I'm not going to just leave you!"

"I can take care of myself!" He didn't budge. "Go call the police!" I yelled. There was nothing a Kansas cop could do to stop a creature like the Nome King, but at least that would get Dustin out of harm's way.

"I'm not leaving you!" he repeated.

"Just *do* it!"

The Nome King lunged forward, reaching out his long thin fingers for me.

"Amy!" Nox shouted.

"I see!" I ducked under the Nome King's arms, my own training kicking in as I somersaulted across the hallway and landed in a crouch next to the display case. But the Nome King hadn't been coming for me at all: he'd been going for Nox, who threw up a quick shield that the Nome King batted away as if it was made of cobwebs.

"This matter does not concern you, child," he said evenly. "If you wish to leave, you will leave us now."

"I'm not a child," Nox said grimly. He raised glowing hands, tendrils of fire licking along his fingers and condensing into a ball of flame in his palms. The Nome King laughed—that same awful, sinister laughter that slid into my skull like a knife blade. I howled with pain, clapping my hands to my ears. Nox was doubled over, too, tongues of fire dripping harmlessly off his fingers. I had to get us out of here. We couldn't possibly fight off the Nome King if I didn't have magic. I had no doubt he'd kill Nox if he got in the way of whatever the king wanted with me.

Could be worse, I thought. *At least he's not into glitter.*

The silver shoes were the only chance I had for Nox and me to escape. But the Nome King wanted me to take them. What was I getting myself into if I was accidentally obeying him while I tried to save Nox's life? The Nome King advanced toward Nox, grinning, the long spidery fingers of each hand lengthening and turning silver like the Tin Woodman's knife-fingered minions. If I didn't act now, Nox was toast. I pulled off my sweatshirt, wrapped it twice around my arm, and brought my elbow down on the glass diorama case with all my strength. Pain blazed up my arm, and for a second I thought I'd been dumb enough to break my arm instead of the glass. But a long, satisfying crack had appeared on the glass case. One more blow, and the case shattered. Behind me, Nox and the Nome King were circling each other, the Nome King moving easily and Nox's movements tight with anxiety. The Nome King was toying with him like a cat batting a mouse around before she kills it. But at least his sick little game was keeping Nox alive for the moment.

"Amy!" Nox gasped. "What are you doing?"

"Trying to save your life I'm sure," said the Nome King,

sounding bored. "I can't imagine why she'd bother."

"You don't really seem like a guy who knows much about friends," I snarled, grabbing the Dorothy figurine out of the shards of broken glass. As soon as I touched the shoes, I could feel the magic running through them like an electric current. They began to glow with a gentle, warm light that filled the hallway. Dustin, Nox, and the Nome King froze. The shoes grew in my hands like one of those little sponge animals you soak in water until they looked exactly the right size for my feet. I kicked off my sneakers and slipped the shoes over my feet.

"Very good, Amy," the Nome King purred at the exact moment Dustin yelled, "Amy, no! It has to be a trap!"

I wasn't an idiot. The possibility had already occurred to me. But I didn't know what other choice we had. I had to get Nox and Dustin to safety before the Nome King killed them both.

But something incredible was happening. As soon as I put the shoes on, they began to change. The soles thickened and the thin silk fabric, covered with dozens of hand-sewn sequins, crept up my ankles. Silver laces threaded themselves through polished silver grommets.

Dorothy's magic shoes had turned into a pair of diamond-studded leather combat boots—and they fit me better than any shoe I'd ever owned. I couldn't describe the feeling of wearing them. It was like being hugged by an old, dear friend. *Everything's going to be just fine,* the shoes seemed to sigh. Their gentle presence filled me from my toes to the top of my head. I held my hands up and saw that they glowed with the same beautiful silver light that had come from the shoes. I could feel magic flowing through my body as though I was a hollow log in a clear stream. I was calm, calmer than I'd ever been. Nothing mattered anymore. I felt a thousand miles away from the chaos in the hallway. I knew if I asked them the shoes would take me anywhere I wanted. And I knew where I wanted to go: back to Oz. I closed my eyes and prepared to summon the power to go home.

"Amy!" Nox cried, and my eyes flew open again. How had I forgotten him? What was I doing? I stared down at my glowing feet. If the shoes were part of the Nome King's plan, how could I possibly trust their magic?

I didn't have time to worry about that. The Nome King clapped his hands in delight when he saw the shoes on my feet. Nox lunged forward, trying to knock the Nome King off his feet, just as Dustin leapt into the fray. His eyes were huge with fear but his face was set in determination. He would get himself killed fighting for me—even though he had no idea what he was up against.

"Dustin, stop!" I yelled, but it was too late. The Nome King whipped a fireball at him so fast I didn't even see his hands move.

"No!" I yelled, reaching for it with my free hand. My boots blazed with light and power and, at last, I could feel the answering pull of my own magic as a web of dull, flickering strands of light spun out of my fingertips. It wasn't enough to deflect the Nome King's fireball, but my net sucked some of the force of his weapon away before it smacked Dustin squarely in the chest. His mouth dropped open into a round O of surprise as he stared down at the blackened crater spreading across his chest, and then he let out a low moan and toppled slowly backward. "Dustin!" I screamed. I heard pounding and shouts in the hallway and a siren in the distance.

A handful of teachers rounded the corner at a run. The Nome King raised his hands, and another shock wave sent them flying backward. Nox, abandoning magic, barreled into the Nome King's stomach, but the Nome King kicked him away easily. The Nome King reached upward and pulled a mass of long, thin strands of darkness out of the air that began to swirl and expand, whirling faster and faster.

"My dear Miss Gumm," he said lightly, his slithering voice sending chills down my spine. "I'm afraid it's time to bid adieu to your little beau. I'm taking you back to Oz now, where you belong." The swirling mass of darkness ballooned upward, tearing tiles off the floor and sending them spinning through the shattered windows. Suddenly, I knew what he was doing. He'd summoned a tornado. I had Dorothy's shoes and I knew the Nome King wanted to send me back to Oz. And I knew he wasn't just going to leave Nox behind—he couldn't risk leaving one of the Quadrant. He was going to kill him.

We didn't have much time. In fact, we didn't have any. I wanted to help Dustin. I wanted to tell Madison how much I hoped she got out of Flat Hill someday. I wanted to say good-bye to my mom for the last time. But I didn't have a choice. It was either return to Oz, or watch Nox die in this hallway.

"Nox!" I screamed. "Come on!" He took in my shoes with a

single glance and darted away from the Nome King, wrapping his arms around me. "Take us home!" I yelled above the furious howl of the tornado. The shoes shot out rays of white light, and we floated up—*into* the eye of the storm.

Standing in the middle of the ruined hallway, surrounded by shattered glass, blood, and rubble, the Nome King watched us go. A huge, terrifying smile spread slowly across his face. *I'll see you very soon, Miss Gumm,* his awful voice sliced into my head. And then the tornado had us, and everything went dark.

EIGHTEEN

The first thing I heard was birdsong. Panic seized me. If I didn't get my butt in gear, I was going to be late for school. My eyelids seemed to be stuck shut. I lifted one hand to rub them, and winced as pain coursed through my body. Everything hurt, from my head to my toes. Moving only made it worse. Something heavy was pinning down my other arm. And the birdsong I was hearing was nothing anyone in Kansas would recognize. For one thing, it was all the wrong notes. For another, it was coming from the ground.

"Amy? Are you okay?" The voice was familiar. Rough and low. A boy's voice. "Hold still," it said again. "I think you might be hurt." The weight on my unmoving arm shifted, and gentle fingers touched my cheek. "We need to get you help."

Finally, I opened my eyes. Inches from my face, someone was looking down at me in concern. Someone I recognized. I struggled to remember his name.

"Nox," I croaked. "What happened? Where are we?"

"You did it, Amy," he said. "We're back in Oz. Outside the Tin Woodman's old palace. I think we landed in the vegetable garden."

In spite of myself, I started to laugh. It hurt like hell, but I didn't care. "I think I might be pissed at you," I said.

"I know," he said, and then he kissed me.

I couldn't move without pain surging through my body, and I figured Nox was in about the same shape—he just happened to be lying on top of me. He tasted like Oz: like a field of singing, sweet-smelling flowers, or a handful of Lulu's sunfruit—wild and clean. His lips were so soft. Everything still hurt, but suddenly I didn't care. I closed my eyes again and lost myself in the sensation of the kiss. He shifted his weight and grunted with pain, and I started to laugh again. After a second, he laughed, too. His mouth moved to my neck, and then my ear. "Amy," he said softly, his voice rough with emotion. "I am so not supposed to be doing this, but—"

I knew kisses didn't solve what was wrong with us. But I wanted his lips on mine. I wanted him this close for as long as it lasted. The kiss tasted stolen.

Someone coughed loudly, and he jerked his head up. I yelped as his movement set off a new chain of aches in my body, and then opened my eyes reluctantly. Mombi loomed over us, a frown of disapproval across her face.

"How did you get here?" Nox said, bewildered.

"How do you think? We're all bound together through the magic of the Quadrant."

"As one of the Quadrant witches, Nox, you are connected to us now," Gert explained. "We can see what you see and feel what you feel." Wait—did that mean I'd just made out with *all* of them? That thought was too disgusting for words. Gert raised an eyebrow at me before continuing. "We realized what was happening as soon as you found Dorothy's original shoes and we were able to piggyback on the magic that pulled you both back to Oz."

"This was the first safe place we could think of, so we teleported you here," Glamora added. "The palace is abandoned; the Winkies are gone, the Woodman's dead, and it's not a likely place for anyone to look for us. But it won't be long before Dorothy and Glinda figure out where we are. We can't hide forever from their magic."

I waited for them to tell me what a good job I'd done in finding the shoes, but Mombi wasn't done tearing Nox a new one.

"You *know* better," she snapped at Nox. "This isn't a game. You disobeyed us in the Other Place and you're disobeying us now."

"I thought we were equals now as members of the Quadrant," Nox said matter-of-factly. Had Nox ignored their orders in Kansas in order to watch over me? That would explain why he'd shown up out of nowhere at the school. I darted a glance at him but he wouldn't meet my eyes.

"You have a responsibility to Oz now that is far greater than anything else," Mombi yelled. "Is that somehow unclear?"

Mombi was the most pissed I'd ever seen her, and that was saying something. Nox looked like a little kid who'd gotten busted stealing cookies as he jumped to his feet, apologizing in a babble.

"I know, Mombi," he said. "I'm so sorry. You're right."

She was still looking at him like he was a piece of something rotten she'd gotten on her shoe. "Do you take the Quadrant seriously or not, Nox? There are others who could take your place."

There were? I glanced at him. He looked startled. If there were other witches who could take Nox's place, maybe that wasn't a bad thing. Maybe he could just . . . retire. Maybe we had a chance at being together.

Stop it, I told myself. I was behaving like I was back in high school. This was way more important than my feelings—or Nox's.

"I will do my duty," he said quickly, not looking at me. I couldn't help a flash of hurt at how easy it was for him to give me up, but I told myself to quit being such a baby.

"We believe you, Nox," Gert said, much more gently than Mombi. "I know this is difficult for you." She looked at me. "We must all sacrifice for the greater good," she said, and I felt certain her words were directed at me. "Amy, you're badly hurt," she added. "You need the healing pool, but I'm afraid we don't have that luxury here. Hold still, please."

I could feel the warmth of her magic spreading from her palms and flowing through me. I could sense it probing outward into my arms and legs. At first it felt good, like getting a really great massage.

But you know how there's always that moment during a

massage when you're like *okay, that's enough?* Gert crossed that line, and then some.

I yelped in agony as her spell wrenched my bones and muscles, shoving them into place and knitting them back together. It felt like my entire body was being squeezed through a tiny keyhole.

Just when I thought I couldn't endure the pain a second longer, it stopped. I wiggled my fingers cautiously, and then moved my arms and legs. Gert had done it again. I was still bruised, worn out, a little angry, and a little sad. But I was here, and I was alive.

The source of the birdsong chirped again, and I looked down to see a little yellow frog regarding me with bright eyes and trilling merrily. "Singing frogs?" I said. "How did I miss those?"

"The singing frogs of Oz are indigenous to Winkie country," Glamora said.

"We've got more important things to talk about than frogs," Mombi growled. Nox glanced at my feet, and I followed his gaze to where the silver boots gleamed softly on my feet. The events of the past few days came flooding back. Madison. Dustin. The Nome King. Dorothy. My mom.

"Why are we at the Woodman's palace?" I asked. "And where's Dorothy?"

"Come on," Mombi said, beckoning. "Let's have this conversation inside."

NINETEEN

The Winkies' palace was actually pretty gross. What did I expect, I guess, considering that its previous tenants had been the Tin Woodman, and before him, the Wicked Witch of the West.

It basically looked like the palace had been sacked. Dusty tapestries hung crazily from the walls, and most of the doors were splintered as though they'd been kicked open. Here and there, the floors or walls were stained with something that looked suspiciously like blood. All of the furniture was overturned or broken. Mombi waved a hand as we entered the palace's banquet hall, and an invisible hand righted a few chairs and arranged them around a table.

I flexed my fingers, feeling my own power tingle to life in response. Whatever had happened to my magic in Kansas, it was back now. And it felt different in a way I couldn't explain. *The shoes,* I thought. The shoes were doing something to me, that much I was sure. But was that a good thing or a bad one?

And could I even use magic anymore without it turning me into Dorothy?

"First things first," Mombi said. "We don't know where Dorothy is. We're assuming she went back to the Emerald City as soon as she returned to Oz, but we have no way of knowing yet. And we have to move fast before she figures out we found a way back ourselves." She turned to Glamora. "It's time to summon the rest of the Wicked," she said, and Glamora nodded in agreement. "The Nome King is moving against Oz, and now we have three enemies to deal with. All our old plans are off the table. This is a whole new ball game."

The final confrontation with the Nome King came flooding back. "The Nome King *wanted* me to come back to Oz," I blurted. "He said that Dorothy wasn't useful to him anymore but that I might be."

Mombi and Gert exchanged glances. "I don't like the sound of that at all," Mombi growled.

"Is it possible . . ." Glamora trailed off and the witches stared at each other.

"Glinda brought Dorothy back to Oz," Gert said. "We've assumed all along that she's been orchestrating Dorothy's return to power in order to put herself behind the throne. But if she's been working with the Nome King . . ."

"Or under his control," Mombi said quietly. "We have no real idea how powerful he is. He can move back and forth between Ev, Oz, and the Other Place. He's wanted to take power in Oz for centuries."

"Centuries?" I asked.

"He's very, very old," Glamora said. "Some say he's even older than Ozma's ancestor Lurline, the first fairy who came to Oz."

Magic's dangerous for outlanders. You're not built for it. Nox had warned me what felt like a lifetime ago, when I'd begun my training in the secret underground caverns of the Wicked. "Dorothy's not useful to him anymore because Oz's magic has corrupted her," I said. If Dorothy's magic was so destructive it had transformed her from the sweet, innocent girl who'd written about her chickens and her dog into the bloodthirsty, insane tyrant she was now, what was it going to do to me? Because as soon as I started thinking of her as a real person, it was easy to see how much like me she had once been. The Nome King had told me I was stronger than Dorothy, but Oz's magic had already turned me into a monster.

Gert nodded, reading my mind. "That settles it," she said. "You can't use magic any longer, Amy. It's too dangerous."

"But how can I fight without magic?" I protested. "You're the ones who trained me. You made me into what I am. You want me to just pretend none of that ever happened?"

Nox had been quiet as we talked, but now he spoke up. "It's not worth it, Amy," he said. I remembered the conversation we'd had what felt like months ago but had just been a few days. If Oz's magic turned me into another Dorothy, the Quadrant would have to kill me. And I knew Nox would do it, too. He'd see it as an act of mercy—and it would be. I thought of what

Dorothy had done, and shivered. I'd rather die than end up like that. But how could I protect myself in Oz if I couldn't use my powers? I had Dorothy's shoes, but what if using them again was just playing further into the Nome King's plans?

Suddenly, I thought of my mom. Magic for me was as destructive as pills had been for her. The same addiction—and the same results. I'd fallen in love with power the way she'd fallen in love with oblivion. I'd hated her for what her addiction had done to her—to us—but was I really any different?

Where was she now? What did she think had happened to me? What time was it in Kansas? How much of the school had been destroyed by the tornado? Someone must have told her I was gone again by now. Another tornado sweeping me away—what were the odds of that one? This time, Dustin had watched me get swallowed up by the storm. And Dustin—had he survived the battle with the Nome King? Eventually, the police would have to declare me dead. How did that stuff even work? How long would it take before my mom was forced to give up hope for good? And what then? Would she start using again with no reason to stop, no one to stay sober for? If she thought I was never coming back, there was no telling what she might do. I felt tears welling up in my eyes. I was stuck in Oz with no ability to protect myself, dependent on a boy who couldn't love me, unable to save my mom from the thing that was going to destroy her. It was too much to think about.

"I need some air," I said, shoving my chair back from the table.

"Amy, you have to be careful," Gert said. "Dorothy could be anywhere."

I heard Mombi behind me, murmuring, "It's all right, let her go. We can protect her if anything happens."

I didn't know where to go, so I took the first staircase up I saw, and then the next. After a few minutes of stumbling through the palace, I came to a big room that looked like it had once been a bedchamber. The air smelled faintly of machine oil. There wasn't a bed, only a tall wooden cupboard at the far end of the room that was blackened as though someone had tried to set it on fire. I remembered the Tin Woodman's chambers at the Emerald Palace, and I felt a creepy shiver up my spine as I realized what I'd found. He slept standing up. I was in his old bedroom.

Directly across from where I assumed he stood was a portrait of Dorothy. I had taken the heart right out of his chest, but standing here now in his room I realized—if he had never met Dorothy, he would never have become so evil. I wonder what I would be if I had never met Nox.

I almost turned to leave but then I saw a set of double doors that led outside and I pushed through them, gulping in the fresh air as I stepped onto a balcony with a panoramic view of the kingdom.

It was some view. First, the gardens surrounding the palace, which were overgrown and trampled in places. But beyond them, I could see all the way to the mountains in one direction and the Queendom of the Wingless Ones in the other. Underneath bright blue, wide-open sky—with all of Oz laid out before me—I still felt invisible walls closing in on me. I had traveled so far, had learned so much, and fought so many battles, and I didn't feel like it had made any difference at all. If anything, Oz seemed worse off than it had been before I came along.

"Amy?" Nox's voice was tentative behind me. I didn't turn around.

"I want to be alone, Nox."

But I heard footsteps, and a moment later he was standing next to me. We were both silent for a long time.

"I used to think it was so beautiful," I said, still not looking at him. "Even when things got really bad, it was still beautiful, you know? It was still, like, *amazing*. Now, though, it's like it doesn't matter how beautiful it is. It's just more stuff for someone to ruin."

"You're right," he said.

Now I looked at him. He seemed much older than he had when I'd first met him, even though it really hadn't been so long ago.

"I don't want to be right," I said.

"What do you want me to say?" He brushed a strand of hair from his face. "You're right. Everything got so messed up. And you know what I wonder sometimes?"

"Do I *want* to know?"

"Sometimes I wonder if it's even Dorothy's fault, or if this place was just rotten from the start, underneath everything. If maybe that's the price you pay for magic."

"My world doesn't have any magic, and it's pretty messed up, too."

"Is it? It seemed okay to me. Better, at least."

"You didn't see much of it."

"Yeah, I know," he replied. "But you know what I liked about it?"

"What?"

"It reminded me of you. Everywhere I looked, I couldn't stop thinking, *This is where Amy's from. This is the dirt that she walked on. This is the sky that she grew up under.* It's the place that made you who you are. And that's what made me like it."

"It's made Dorothy, too."

"Oh, screw her," Nox said. And we both laughed. But just a little bit, because it really wasn't that funny at all.

"I wish I could see where *you* came from," I said.

"You're looking at it, aren't you?"

"No, I mean, like, where you *really* came from. Your village. The house you grew up in. All that stupid little stuff."

He winced. "It's gone," he said bitterly. The pain in his voice shot through me like it was my pain, too. At this point, maybe it was. "You know that. Burned to the damn ground."

"I know," I said. "I wish I could see it anyway."

"The rivers were full of sprites who sing to you while you go swimming. In the summer, you could walk through the Singing Forest and watch the mountains rearrange themselves . . ." He trailed off, with a sad, faraway look in his eyes.

"Maybe . . . ," I started. Maybe *what*? Maybe everything will be okay? Maybe things aren't really so bad? There was no way to finish the sentence without sounding faker than the knockoff

Prada purse that my dad sent me for my thirteenth birthday, with the label misspelled to read *Praba*.

I didn't need to finish, though, because Nox did it for me. "Maybe it's not worth fighting for," he said. "Maybe we should just give up."

"No!" I said. "That's not what I meant."

"I know. It's what *I* meant. I don't think I've ever said it aloud, but it's what I really think sometimes. Like, maybe it would be better to just let them all kill each other off. Mombi, Glinda, Dorothy—everyone. Let them keep fighting until they've destroyed every single thing. And then maybe it would all grow back. I bet it would. Eventually, I mean."

"No," I said. "I mean, maybe you're right; I don't know. But we can't give up. Not after all of this."

A minute ago, I had been ready to give up myself. But hearing Nox say it made me realize how wrong I had been to even think about doing something like that.

"Look," I said. "Things aren't all they're cracked up to be in my world either. You think wandering around Kansas camping on the prairie for a couple of days was good? Yeah, so it's beautiful out there, but our planet is freaking out. The oceans are rising, people are fighting more and more wars every day, plants and animals are dying out, every other week some kid takes one of his parents' guns to school and starts shooting. . . ." I stopped short at the look on Nox's face. "The world I grew up in is gone, too," I said quietly. "But that doesn't mean I'm going to give up on it. Because if you give up—then what is there left to live for?"

We were both silent for a long time, looking deep into each other's eyes. He was so close to me. I could smell his faint rich sandalwood smell. I could have reached up to brush the hair out of his eyes. I could have leaned in the barest amount and our mouths would have met. And I wanted it so badly my heart was thundering in my chest.

"How about this?" Nox asked, not looking away from me. The purple-pink light from the setting sun reflected in his gray eyes, making them look practically neon. "How about you and I just leave. Let them have their war. We'll just find a place to hide, just the two of us, and then, when it's all over, we'll climb out from the wreckage, and start the whole thing all over again. We'll rebuild it all. Together."

He reached forward and took my hand, and my heart nearly skipped a beat. It sounded so beautiful. Just him and me. On our own. No more war, no more suffering. No more running. It was like a beautiful dream—except that it was impossible, no matter how much some part of me wished it could come true. I couldn't sacrifice the people I loved just to be with the boy I wanted. And I knew Nox well enough by now to know he'd never be able to do it either. It would tear him apart. And then we'd just be two bitter, brokenhearted people in a dead and ruined world. I knew it. And so did he.

"You don't believe that," I said.

"What if I do?"

"You don't. That's the most selfish thing I've ever heard you say. It's not you."

"Maybe I'm an asshole."

"You might be an asshole, but you're not a selfish asshole."

"How do you know that, Amy?"

"Because I couldn't possibly love a selfish person," I said.

His eyes widened in shock. "Amy," he said hoarsely, "I . . ." But he didn't finish. He was staring over my shoulder, at the view below the Tin Woodman's balcony.

"You what?" I said softly, not sure if I had said too much.

That was when I realized it wasn't what I had said that had surprised him. It wasn't even me he was looking at anymore. He was staring over my shoulder out onto the horizon.

"I think we're in trouble," he said. I whirled around.

In the plain below the palace, an army was waiting for us. But not just any army. They were clones. A sea of creepy clones with cornflower-blue eyes and clear, ageless skin. Tendrils of golden hair spilled from their helmets. They were all virtually identical, and behind those flat blue eyes there was a terrifying blankness. And there was no mistaking the glittering pink figure who floated at its head.

Or the girl and the boy in chains at her side.

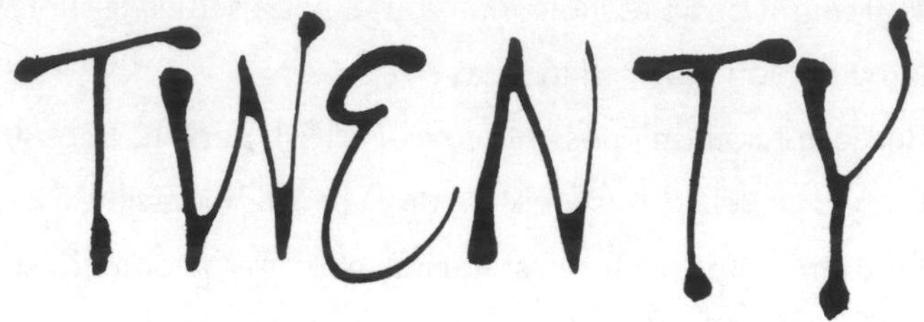

“Go get the Wicked,” Nox hissed, tugging me down so that Glinda couldn’t see us over the railing of the balcony. *“Now.”* He didn’t have to tell me twice. I pelted down the stairs until I crashed directly into—

“Melindra!” I gasped. She looked the same as she had when I’d last seen her, tall, fierce, and ready for battle. The blond hair on the human half of her head was shorn close to the skull, and the tin half of her body was dented and battered. Behind her stood Annabel, the red-haired unicorn girl with the purple scar on her forehead who’d trained with me, too. There were more people in the room I didn’t recognize, all of them with the same tough, wary warrior’s stance. Glamora was rubbing Gert’s back, and Gert looked exhausted. She must have used her power to summon the Wicked one at a time.

“Amy, what is it?” Gert asked when I crashed into the room.

“It’s happening!” I gasped. “Upstairs, now!” I turned around and ran back to Nox, not waiting to see if they were following me.

Glinda had come prepared for battle: instead of her usual ruffled dresses, she was dressed in a tight pink catsuit that looked like leather studded with little scales. Her golden hair was drawn back in a severe bun, and she carried a huge pink staff in one slender hand.

"Oh dear," Gert said as she gazed down at Glinda and her legions. They wore matching silver armor, polished to a blinding glow that made me think uncomfortably of the Tin Woodman, and their silver-tipped spears glittered like diamonds.

"When did she get an army?" I asked.

"She's always had an army," Mombi said. "She just doesn't use it very often."

"What do you mean, very *often*?"

"General Jinjur invaded the Emerald City and deposed the Scarecrow before Dorothy returned to Oz," Melindra said. "Didn't they teach you this?"

"I skipped the history lesson on the way to the battle."

Melindra rolled her eyes. Whatever problem she had with me, she hadn't gotten over it. Great.

"Glinda summoned her army then and drove Jinjur out of the palace," Mombi filled in. "Together, Glinda and the Scarecrow put Ozma on the throne."

"Wait, I thought Ozma was the one who banished Glinda," I said, confused.

Gert nodded. "She was. Glinda thought she'd be able to control Ozma—to rule Oz through her. But Ozma has—had—a will of her own. Glinda tried to oust her. Ozma banished her. It wasn't until Dorothy returned to Oz that Glinda was freed."

"Dorothy's not with her," Gert said, looking down at the battlefield, where Glinda's troops were moving into formation.

"If she's moving against us without Dorothy, that's a big deal," Melindra said. "She's never openly gone against Dorothy's wishes before. She couldn't be more clear about trying to take power for herself now if she posted it on a banner."

"If she is working with the Nome King somehow, he could have forced her hand," Mombi said. "Either way, I don't like it. Facing a united Dorothy and Glinda is bad enough—but with both of them acting on their own . . ."

"Don't make the mistake of thinking those pretty little girls won't tear you to pieces," Melindra said. "Trains 'em herself, Glinda does, and you can imagine the kinds of exercises she thinks up." We all shuddered collectively. "They'll gut you soon as look at you. Some of the best fighters in Oz."

"They used to be some of the only fighters in Oz," Gert said.

"Well, those days are long gone," Mombi said shortly, "and they'll shoot us off the balcony if we stand here like fools for much longer. Nothing to do but go inside and prepare for battle. Luckily the walls are three feet thick. The palace will be easy enough to defend, as long as we stay inside."

"We haven't prepared for this," Melindra said, and the tough girl sounded almost plaintive.

"You've trained for battle," Nox said curtly. "That means

you've trained for this." Melindra flashed him a hurt look and I tried not to gloat.

Glinda's army had finished moving into tight formations and the Sorceress hovered above them at the center of it all. Flanking her, Pete and Ozma sagged in their chains. The enchanted princess was staring around her with that all-too-familiar vacant air. Pete looked miserable and sullen. *You deserve it*, I thought in disgust, remembering the way he'd betrayed me and Nox to Glinda in Polychrome's palace. Pete had escaped with Glinda—if escape was the right word for what she'd done to him.

I didn't care if he was suffering now. I remembered Polychrome's crumpled body, Rainbow Falls burning. Polychrome's unicorn-cat Heathcliff lying broken and bloody. Pete could go to hell for all I cared. But Ozma was different.

Ozma was an innocent in all of this. But it was more than that, too. She was also the rightful ruler of Oz. There was every chance that she was the only one with the power to change anything. If only we could unlock it.

"We have to rescue her," Nox said, echoing my thoughts.

"There's got to be a way," I agreed, and was gratified to see the flash of approval in his eyes. Maybe I was faking it until I made it, but Nox was right. Acting confident did give me a renewed sense of strength. How could what we faced possibly be worse than what we'd already been through?

Below us, a trumpet sounded, and Glinda rose even higher in the air to hover over her army.

"Good afternoon, dear Wicked," she said, and even though she was speaking quietly and still hundreds of feet away, she sounded as if she was close enough to reach out and touch.

She and all her soldiers had smeared their faces with PermaSmile, and their white teeth glinted out of terrifying grins as they looked up at us. "Welcome back to Oz. We're *so* glad you've returned to see the *new* era that's coming."

"Meet the new witch, same as the old bitch," Mombi muttered.

"Where is Dorothy, sister dear?" Glamora cooed.

"Is it you, darling?" Glinda squealed. "I haven't seen you in ages! Not since I gave you that *tremendously* satisfying facelift."

"I haven't forgotten," Glamora replied icily.

The way they were talking to each other was eerie—it was as if they were having an intimate—if tense—conversation over tea and pastries.

Mombi didn't have any patience for their banter. "What do you want, Glinda?" she bellowed.

"I thought we could be friends," Glinda purred. "Your little Quadrant party hasn't gone unnoticed, you know. I was so hoping you might invite me." Her voice was pouty, but the PermaSmile wouldn't let her frown.

"We must have forgotten," Mombi growled.

"No, I don't think you did," Glinda hissed. "Did you think you could join forces without me, my witchly sisters?"

"Funny, going behind *our* backs didn't seem to bother you when you wiped out the memories of Oz's queen and brought a tyrant to power," Gert snapped.

Next to me, Nox tugged my shoulder. "We need to get back downstairs. If there's an opportunity to rescue Ozma while they're going back and forth, we have to take it." I nodded, and Nox signaled to Melindra, Annabel, and a couple of other warriors. We began to creep stealthily toward the staircase. Mombi shook her head at us.

"Enough with this nonsense," she said abruptly. "We join forces as a Quadrant and go down there to take her out. We hadn't planned on it happening this soon, but we knew it was inevitable. East, West, North, South. We work as four. Nox, we need you."

"No," Glamora said. We all looked at her in surprise. Her blue eyes, eerie twins of Glinda's, burned with a fierce, lightning-hot energy. "She's my sister, and this is my fight."

"My dear," Gert said, "you can't possibly mean to go up against her alone. She has an entire army at her disposal—and she nearly killed you the last time you fought." Reflexively, Glamora touched her face where, long ago, she'd lifted the veil of glamour to show me the gruesome scar Glinda had carved into her cheek.

I'd fought next to Glamora. But I'd never seen her look the way she looked now. Powerful and fierce, yeah, but something else, too.

Elated. Hungry. Out for blood. I remembered back in the cave where I'd first met the Wicked, when Glamora had taught me the art of glamour. I'd wondered then if she was scarier than

Glinda. Watching her now, I didn't have any doubts at all.

"I have been waiting for this moment since the first time I faced her all those years ago," Glamora said calmly. "I've been waiting to end her life, the way she would have ended mine if she'd had the chance. This is my chance to rid Oz of her evil, and this is my battle alone." Calmly, she ran her hand along her face, wiping away all of the glamours she wore like makeup and revealing the gaping, half-moon scar that ran from her ear, down her cheekbone, and across her chin. It still looked as fresh as if she'd gotten it this morning.

I could tell Gert and Mombi wanted to protest, but they knew as well as I did that Glamora wouldn't have hesitated to strike all of us down on the way to destroy her sister. The gleam in her eyes was almost unhinged, and the air around her shimmered like she was a pot of water about to boil.

"I do not see the wisdom of this course of action," Mombi muttered, but Glamora ignored her.

"Wait here for me," she said, and rose up into the air.

"She's right," Gert said. "This is her battle. Let her fight it, Mombi."

"This is a terrible idea," Mombi growled, shaking off Gert's restraining hand. But like the rest of us, she hurried anxiously to the edge of the balcony, peering over it.

Even from the balcony I could see the tension in the line of Glinda's shoulders. Despite her army, despite all her magic, it was clear that some part of her was afraid. Glamora had waited so long for this moment, carrying this hatred and desire for vengeance for years. I'd be afraid even if I had an army at my back, too.

No, I *was* afraid.

"There's no use trying to stop her," Gert said in a low voice. "But we need to come up with a backup plan—*now*. Dorothy will likely be on her way any minute. If Glinda found us here, she can't be far behind."

While Gert spoke, Glamora was floating regally toward her sister, and as she moved through the air her gown fell away, leaving her naked. It barely registered, because then she was shedding her skin, too, like a snake sheds its scales. Underneath it, her body was purple and glittering in the sun.

Instead of giving herself armor, Glamora had *become* the armor. Her hair, her skin, her limbs. All of her was now bright and faceted. She was now a living jewel. Everyone was speechless at the sight of it.

The only one who didn't look shocked at the transformation was Glinda, who simply nodded in acknowledgment.

The two witches now circled each other in the air, Glamora a bright shadow of her sister's form. Glinda's usually sweet face was set in a mask of naked hatred made even more terrifying by the sickly sweet PermaSmile.

The air turned dark and thick, forming itself into a cloud that slowly took the shape of a huge serpent with its head rearing back to strike. Glinda flicked an arm upward and a spear of pink light struck Glamora's serpent in the chest, dissolving it momentarily. Glamora brought her arm down, and the serpent re-formed, undulating around her in black coils. She snapped her wrist, and a bolt of pure power shot toward Glinda, who ducked at the last minute. Instinctively, I reached for my knife—and it materialized in my hand.

"Amy, what are you doing?" Nox hissed.

"If Glinda is distracted, we can rescue Ozma—and Pete, too," I said, heading for the door.

"You can't use magic!" Mombi barked.

"The knife doesn't count," I said. "It was a present." Nox opened his mouth to protest and then shut it again, shaking his head.

Mombi sighed. "I'll stay here with Gert to see if there's a way we can help Glamora. Nox, you, Melindra, and Amy look for a way to rescue the princess and her traitorous other half. Annabel, we'll need fighters here, too." The girls nodded.

But I wasn't the only one who'd had the brilliant idea of taking action while the sisters battled it out. Suddenly, the castle shuddered around us. We hurried back to the edge of the balcony and looked down. Glinda's girl army had moved a battering ram up to the castle doors—but this wasn't an ordinary battering ram. It was huge, glittery, pink, and shaped like—

"Is that a *Munchkin*?" Nox gasped in horror. Glinda's twisted magic had transformed an ordinary Ozian into a giant, fossilized pink weapon. The Munchkin's face was twisted in horror, his eyes squeezed shut as though he was still in terrible pain. Pink flames burned in his open mouth, dripping onto the ground where they sizzled and smoked like molten pink lava. Even as we watched, Glinda's soldiers drew back and lunged forward, slamming into the door with terrific force.

"We can't help him now, and that door won't hold forever," Gert said grimly. "We'd better prepare ourselves."

TWENTY-ONE

None of us needed a second prompting. We raced downstairs to the palace's main entryway, where the big wooden doors were already splintering. Gert, Mombi, and Nox joined hands, power flickering around them as they prepared to face Glinda's army. I tightened my grip on my knife. With a huge cracking noise, the doors burst open, sending chunks of wood flying through the air. Mombi flicked her fingers, and the pieces froze in midair and then clattered harmlessly to the ground. The first girls were already clambering through the hole in the doors, spears at the ready. Nox hurled a ball of magic at the invaders, and one girl shrieked in agony as it struck her full in the torso. She fell to the ground, her armor smoking, but more girls were already climbing over her inert body.

I ran forward, my knife raised. Up close, Glinda's soldiers were terrifying. They'd filed their gleaming white teeth into sharp points bared by their eerie PermaSmile grins. Their armor crawled with tiny pink bugs that jumped at their opponents, buzzing and stinging. I knocked a soldier's spear out of her hand with one blow and cut her throat on the reverse swing, kicking her body out of the way as another girl came for me in her place. "Are they clones?" I screamed across the hall to Nox, who was battling two more of Glinda's soldiers. The girls didn't even register my question, and Nox was too busy to answer it. "What are you?" I asked the girl I fought now. "Why are you fighting for Glinda?" She bared her sharp teeth and lunged toward my throat. "Fine," I said, and stabbed her through the heart.

"Behind you!" Nox yelled, and I turned just in time to dodge another blow. Nox sliced his way toward me. Right as he reached me, another soldier raised her sword, readying herself to stab him through the back. I hurled him to the ground and deflected her blow. A second later he leapt to his feet, kicking her legs out from under her with unearthly speed and grace.

Nox and I were fighting back-to-back—the way we always had. I couldn't help it. It just felt right. On either side of us Annabel, Melindra, and the other members of the Order slashed and stabbed. Gert and Mombi darted around the room, casting spells as they saw an opening. More girls pulled down the remnants of the palace doors, and soon the battle spilled out into the courtyard. Glinda and Glamora, in her jeweled form, hovered overhead, swooping and diving through the air like human comets as they hurled fireballs and sizzling, lightning-shaped bolts of pink magic at one another.

"Over there!" Gert called. I dispatched my newest opponent

with a hard punch and looked up. Pete and Ozma were huddled up against a rock, wide-eyed and clinging to each other, still in chains. Pink chains, I saw with disgust. *After all of this is over, I'm never wearing the color pink again*, I thought.

"Now's your chance, Amy!" Gert shouted, clearing the way to the prisoners with a huge ball of fire. I raced through the gap in the melee to Ozma's side. "Ozma! Are you all right?"

"The corn harvest will be ready soon," she said politely.

"She's fine," Pete gasped. His face was bruised and bloodied, as if someone had beaten him up recently. I had a pretty good guess as to who that might be. And I wasn't too sorry about it either. "You have to get us out of here," he pleaded.

"So you can sell us out to Glinda again?" I snarled. "Worked out pretty well for you last time, huh?"

"I was desperate!" he cried. "Polychrome was going to kill me. You know that!"

"Well, she can't kill you now, because she's dead," I said.

Pete's eyes widened. "Behind you!"

Right. I was in the middle of a battle. I whipped around, knife at the ready, but Nox had already made short work of the girl soldier who'd been about to run me through like a shish kebab. "If it isn't the little prince," he said with disgust, breathing hard as he stared at Pete.

"We can't just leave him here to die," I said reluctantly. "We have to get them both out of here."

"Are you sure?" Nox growled. His hands burned with magical fire as he pulled at Pete's chains, but as soon as he touched them, the flame dissipated into smoke and the pink metal glowed white-hot. Pete yelped in pain, but the chains didn't budge. "Hurts!" Pete gasped. "Please, stop!" Nox's spell had no effect on Ozma's bindings either, although she watched him work with detached interest.

"We'll have tea in the west garden, don't you think?" she offered.

Nox shook his head. "Glinda's magic is too powerful. We have to get them back into the palace and hide them until we have more time to undo the spell." Pete grabbed a rock off the ground and held it up, as if he was going to bludgeon the next girl soldier to death.

"Let me help!" I yelled.

"No!" Nox yelled back. "Amy, you *can't* use magic!"

"I won't be using any magic at all if I'm dead!" I retorted. He shook his head, but he knew I was right. And I had Dorothy's shoes. I sent a tendril of power snaking down to my feet and felt an answering pulse from the shoes. *Help me*, I thought. *Whatever you are. Please, just help me.*

The boots twinkled as if in response. Suddenly, I was surrounded by a dazzling cloud of tiny fireflies winking and glittering like diamonds—because they *were* made of diamonds, I realized. All around me, the battlefield went silent as though I'd stepped into a sparkling silver bubble. I could still see it dimly, as if I was looking through a screen, but another image was superimposed over the carnage.

I was standing in an old farmhouse. Everything was worn

and shabby but scrupulously clean. Once-bright yellow curtains, patched neatly in a dozen places, were pulled open to reveal windows that looked out on endless, undulating prairie. An old man and woman were sitting at a rough kitchen table that had been worn smooth by the years, and a rosy-cheeked young girl was serving them pie as they looked at her with obvious pride. Her face was sweet and pretty; her blue eyes sparkled, and her glossy auburn hair was pulled into two neat braids. "I know my crust will *never* be as good as Aunt Em's," she was saying, "but I tried *so* hard on this one to make it perfect!"

"I'm sure it's delicious, Dorothy," said the woman. A shock ran through me. This was Dorothy? But this girl bore no resemblance to the tarted-up villain I'd been trying to kill for what felt like forever. This person was just a child.

This was the Dorothy whose journal I'd found. Dorothy looked up, straight at me—and straight through me. She couldn't see me. But then her eyes narrowed, and her face began to change. Her blue gaze took on that tint of menace that was so familiar, and her smiling mouth twisted into a sneer. "Amy Gumm," she said. And then her gaze dropped to my feet and her eyes widened. "My *shoes*," she whispered. "Where did you find them?" Her voice was tinged with wonder, and for a second she was that sweet little girl again.

"Dorothy? Who are you talking to?" Aunt Em asked, and Dorothy's expression wavered. But then she flicked her fingers dismissively, and Aunt Em, Uncle Henry, and the farmhouse disappeared. We were standing on an open plain underneath a violent gray-green sea of clouds, like the sky just before a tornado. As I watched, Dorothy grew taller and her features sharpened, losing the gentle baby fat of the little girl in the farmhouse. Her dress wrapped around her, the shabby, mended gingham transforming to a sleek, tight, plated bodysuit like Glinda's. "Don't think you can use our connection to take me on a trip down memory lane," she said coldly. "I'm coming for you, Amy Gumm, and I'm coming for my shoes. I'm going to find a way to make you die."

"Amy! *Amy!*" Someone was calling my name. I blinked, and snapped out of the empty field back into the heat of battle. Nox was shaking me and calling my name. "Amy!" he cried frantically. "What happened? Where did you go?"

"I tried to use the shoes," I gasped. "But they're still connected to Dorothy. She knows where we are now. She's on her way."

"We have to warn the Quadrant," Nox said urgently. I looked up. Glinda and Glamora were still going at it. Glinda's hair had come loose from its bun and surrounded her head in a wild halo. Her armor was rent in a dozen places, and her face and hands were smeared with blood. But Glamora wasn't looking much better. Her amethyst form was chipped and cracked, and though both of them were still flying at each other, she held one arm close to her chest as though she couldn't move it. I could see flashes of power as Mombi and Gert fought on the ground, but like Nox and me, they were surrounded. The ground was littered with the broken and bloody bodies of Glinda's soldiers and the air smelled like blood and the electric haze of spent magic. I couldn't see Melindra or Annabel or any of the other Wicked. None of us could hold out for much longer. If we didn't do something soon, all of us were going to go down fighting for Oz right here.

Suddenly, a terrifying howl split the air. Pete's face went white. I turned to see what he was looking at. "Oh no," I said. Beside me, Nox drew his breath in sharply.

Dorothy had found us.

She wasn't alone.

TWENTY-TWO

Dorothy looked even worse than she had when I'd seen her in Kansas, as though she couldn't suck magic out of the ground fast enough to keep herself going. Her dress was still in tatters, and she'd painted on her maniacal smile with a garish red lipstick that looked like a bloody slash across her face. Her shoes blazed with red light. But she wasn't the scariest thing we faced anymore—not by a long shot. That honor fell to her steed: a three-headed monster the size of a truck. It was covered in sharp-edged, reptilian scales. Behind it swung a long tail crowned in a bristle of spikes. Its legs ended in paws with huge, serrated claws. The teeth in each of its three mouths were as long as my forearm. It threw back first one head, then another, and then a third, and roared. And then I spotted a red velveteen ribbon around each of its thick, muscular necks.

"Oh my god," I gasped. "That's *Toto*." That is, something that had once been Toto. But this Toto was like the 'roid-rage version of Dorothy's little dog, twisted and terrifying.

At Dorothy's back was yet another army—this one made up of the Tin Man's gruesome hybrid creations. Creatures lurched and hopped, brandishing arms and legs that ended in spikes and saws and pincers. Some rolled along on bicycle wheels. Others bounded on all fours, but their bodies were replaced by metal torsos. Most of them looked like they'd been pieced together in a hurry. Bloody wounds seeped fluid where jagged metal edges met living flesh, and some of them limped or dragged themselves along, their blank faces showing no sign that they were in pain but the trail of blood they left behind them suggesting otherwise.

Dorothy, seated astride Toto's broad back, laughed out loud. "Did you miss me?" she called. "It's so good to see you again, Amy. All my old friends in one place." Her eyes flicked upward to Glinda and Glamora, who'd paused their battle and hung there watching her.

"Dorothy," Glinda called. I thought I heard a hint of panic in her voice. She hadn't expected Dorothy to find us so quickly. *She was hoping she could take us out first,* I realized. Glinda wasn't strong enough to face the Wicked *and* Dorothy at the same time.

"I'm *so* disappointed to see your army here," Dorothy said. "It's like you're going behind my back, Glinda, and you know I just hate secrets, unless they belong to me."

"Dorothy, you misunderstand—" Glinda began, but before the words were out of her mouth Dorothy pointed her fingers and shot a fireball directly at the hovering witch. Glinda spun and dodged, her wand at the ready.

"No, I don't think I do," Dorothy said coldly. "*I'm* the Queen of Oz, Glinda, have you forgotten? Any army that acts without *my* command is acting against me. And you know what I do to traitors."

Toto snarled, rearing on his scale-plated hind legs as his huge claws dug into the earth. "Forward!" Dorothy screamed, and her army surged ahead to meet Glinda's. Dorothy's awful zombie-like soldiers cut and hacked mechanically at the mass of identical girls. They might look bedraggled, but they were terrifying. Dead-eyed and robotic, they kept swinging even as Glinda's soldiers cut them into pieces. I watched in horror as a girl beheaded one of Dorothy's minions. The creature's body advanced relentlessly, chopping away with paws that ended in a bristle of jagged, rusty knives. I turned my head away, not wanting to see the rest.

For the moment, the four of us were sheltered by the rock that had hidden Pete and Ozma, but it was only a matter of seconds before both armies tore us apart. There were too many of them for Nox and me to possibly be able to fight off.

Toto reared against his leash and landed with a thump that shook the ground. Dorothy was almost on top of us. Without thinking, I grabbed Nox's hand, and his fingers tightened around mine. "Amy," he said, low and urgent. "I just want you to know—I mean, I want you to understand that I . . ." His voice caught and my eyes filled with tears.

"I'm sorry I couldn't save Oz."

He drew me to him so tightly it knocked the wind out of me.

"I'm sorry, too," he said, and then he kissed me in a way that made my knees buckle until I kissed him back even harder. A kiss about the end of the world. A kiss that said good-bye, and I'm sorry, and I wish things could have been different. A kiss full of longing for the life we'd never have together, the things we'd never know about each other. But it wasn't long enough; it couldn't be. We were about to die.

Nox broke away and I raised my knife as Glinda's soldiers surged around us.

"Loooooo!" Ozma trilled next to my ear, tugging at my sleeve, and I jumped back. "Looo looo looo!" she said eagerly.

I didn't have time to figure out what Ozma wanted. The girl soldier nearest me raised her spear and I brought up my knife to deflect it. And then her piercing howl of triumph ended in a scream as a mass of something sticky, flaming, and unbelievably foul-smelling hit her squarely in the face.

"What the—" Pete began.

"LOOO!" Ozma shouted, pointing upward. We all looked, not understanding what we were seeing, until Nox whooped aloud as comprehension dawned.

"The monkeys!" he cried. "It's the monkeys!"

"LULU!" Ozma shouted in joy as the monkeys descended.

TWENTY-THREE

"That's right, little miss!" Lulu bellowed, lobbing another ball of the mystery flaming goop at a soldier with a tiny catapult and flapping down to land next to us. "Never send a human to do a monkey's job. It's what I've been saying for years, but does anyone listen to me? Of course not." She was dressed in a dapper military uniform, complete with an admiral's stars pinned to the breast, and a little leather flight cap. Her wings were made out of an elaborate combination of wire, leather, and string. Monkeys—both winged and Wingless Ones wearing homemade wings like Lulu's—were landing all around us, fighting to clear a space. Toto's three heads whipped around as he snapped at the monkeys in midair. Glamora was clutching a bright pink crossbow, firing bolts that trailed pink flames at her sister as Glinda struggled to get out of the way and simultaneously fight off a flock of the beastly attackers.

I was so glad to see the monkeys that I almost grabbed Lulu

and hugged her, but there wasn't time for rejoicing. "Can you get Pete and Ozma back to the castle?" I asked. With a nod, Lulu barked an order, and several monkeys detached from their formation and hoisted Pete and Ozma into the air like baggage. Ozma kicked her feet delightedly as the monkeys carried them over Dorothy's and Glinda's troops. Lulu covered them from the ground, catapulting wads of the monkeys' fiery weapon at Glinda's soldiers. "What *is* that stuff?" I yelled over the noise of the battle.

"Sunfruit napalm!" Lulu said proudly, adjusting her leather cap and taking out another of Glinda's soldiers. "Family recipe. Sunfruit, rotten bananas, and you-know-what." She jerked a thumb toward her backside. That explained the smell.

"Dorothy's got bats in her belfry," Lulu said, shaking her head as she lobbed more sunfruit napalm into the fray. "She's been unhinged since the beginning, but this is a whole new level of nuts. Assuming we get out of here alive"—she crossed herself briskly—"which, at this point, does seem a lot to ask, I'm definitely having a word with the Wizard."

Of course. She had no idea how much had happened since we'd split up at the Emerald City.

"The Wizard's dead," I said. "He used me and Dorothy to open a portal to the Other Place, and then Dorothy killed him." One of Dorothy's mechanical soldiers lunged at Lulu, and Nox ran it through before she could react. It struggled violently at the end of his blade. Shuddering in disgust, I chopped it into pieces. As if he could hear me, Toto roared. From across the battlefield,

Mombi and Gert were throwing long chains of magic, trying to restrain Toto as he charged into the fray. But his tough, scaly hide was magic-repellent, and Dorothy only cackled as their magic bounced harmlessly away. His spiked tail swept in both directions behind him, knocking out Glinda's soldiers—and plenty of Dorothy's—like dominoes. His six red eyes glowed with hatred as he snatched monkeys out of the air and devoured them in one or two bites. Nox and I might be able to hold off Dorothy's and Glinda's soldiers, but nothing could stand in the way of Toto.

"We have to take out that damn dog," Lulu said grimly as she fought.

"I don't know how we'll get close enough," I panted, lopping the metal head off one of Dorothy's soldiers with my knife. It flew through the air and landed at my feet, gears whirring. A single eye stared up at me, blood running from its socket like tears. Disgusted, I kicked the head away. The Tin Woodman and the Scarecrow might be dead, but Dorothy had simply picked up where they left off.

"I do," Lulu said. I looked at the brave little monkey and realized what she meant.

"Lulu, you can't. He'll eat you out of the air."

She shrugged. "Die in a blaze of glory, right? You want to get close to the pooch from hell, I'll take you. Just don't say I never did anything for you."

"Amy," Nox began, but another of Dorothy's soldiers interrupted us.

"No time!" Lulu yelled, hoisting me into the air as Nox parried the soldier's blow. My stomach lurched as Lulu swung me wildly over the battle. Too bad flying monkeys didn't come with seat belts.

Toto and Dorothy didn't see us until we were almost on top of them. Dorothy had one hand on Toto's neck, and I could see the power pulsing there, flowing directly from her body into his. Her eyes were sunken into huge, dark hollows, and her hair was lank and lifeless. She slumped over on Toto's neck as if she barely had the strength to sit up straight. Turning Toto into the Hulk of house pets was taking a serious toll on her. I thought of my mom, hollow-eyed and worn after a bender. Dorothy looked the same way. Oz's magic was killing her. Nox and the Wicked were right: it would eventually kill me, too. But right now, it was the only way. One set of Toto's jaws snapped shut, and the bottom half of a monkey fell out of the air as Toto gulped down the rest.

"Ready?" Lulu said. I wasn't. I had never been more terrified in my life. But it didn't matter.

Before, when I'd used Oz's magic, it had been like turning on a faucet—like something I could control, even if I didn't always understand it. But something had changed. I remembered what Nox had said to me before Dorothy had pulled us into Kansas: that Oz's magic was coming back, and that it had a will of its own. I could feel it, like some massive, alien awareness behind the flow of power. It was like I'd unleashed a raging torrent. The magic was powerful enough to knock my consciousness out of my body, sending my mind floating upward as Lulu carried me toward Dorothy. I could see everything happening around me at once, like I was watching a movie screen: Nox and the monkeys, fighting side by side; Mombi and Gert fighting toward them, their faces drawn with exhaustion; Glamora and Glinda, evenly matched and still locked in battle, oblivious to everything happening around them—even Dorothy and Toto. I could feel power backing up inside me, and faintly understood that I'd tapped into something that had the potential to destroy me. But there was no stopping this magic. I was like a leaf floating down a raging river. All I could do now was try to survive whatever it was that I'd let loose.

TWENTY-FOUR

I'd tapped into the same dark, dense magic that had transformed me once before. This time, I gave in to it. *Do what you will,* I whispered. I felt my body changing, expanding. Lulu's fingers lengthened and sprouted dark tendrils that wrapped around my shoulders and sank into my flesh. Her arms melded into my back, and I could feel her own wings stretching outward, ribbed and leathery like a dragon's. Horns sprouted from my forehead. Serrated teeth split outward from my gums and I opened my widening mouth in a roar. My fingers were lengthening into claws, my arms and legs rippling with new muscle covered with velvety-soft emerald-green fur. I was changing into a monster. And I liked it. The feeling of unparalleled power. The wings pumping at my shoulders, bringing me closer to my enemy. Dimly, I could hear Lulu's voice at the back of my mind, like a bee buzzing in a glass jar, but I didn't care.

Toto reared up to meet me. A blast of rank, hot breath hit me full in the face as I swung my knife toward the first of his three heads. Time seemed to slow down as my blade met his scaly flesh and sliced through it like a hot knife through butter. His head went spinning to the ground, its mouth still open in a roar and the stump of his neck spurting huge gouts of black blood. I danced away from the snapping jaws of his other two heads, moving as fast and as nimbly through the air as a dragonfly despite my size. Dorothy was clinging to the ribbon tied around Toto's central neck, staring at me with something in her eyes that I realized was fear. In one smooth motion, I cut off the second of Toto's heads. "No!" Dorothy cried as Toto's remaining head roared in pain and rage. She let go of his ribbon and tumbled off his back. I drew back my arm, ready to run her through as she fell, but something stopped me. There was something about killing Dorothy that I couldn't remember. Something important . . .

Toto lunged for me, snarling, and knocked the knife out of my claws. I threw myself at him and sank my fangs into his scaly throat, tearing it open. His hot blood coursed over me and I lapped it up as I clung to his throat. The monkeys swept in for the kill, hacking away at his remaining head. I darted away just in time as Toto crashed to the ground, his eyes already fixing in death. I landed next to his corpse. The monkeys backed away from me, raising their weapons. I could see myself reflected in their eyes, twisted and monstrous. And I loved it. Being a monster felt incredible. I could do anything, kill anyone. I could destroy them all. Oz would be mine. . . . And then something flared to life deep inside me. Something silvery and cool like a mountain stream. Silver strands of light wrapped around me, holding me tightly. *Come back, Amy.* It was as if Dorothy's shoes were speaking to me somehow. Preventing Oz's magic from taking over my body completely.

"Amy!" Nox's voice brought me back to myself. He was running across the battlefield, screaming my name. Amy. I was Amy. I felt the dark magic churning within me, unwilling to let go. *Release me,* I thought. *Please, release me.*

Dorothy's shoes flashed silver. I screamed in agony as my bones cracked and twisted, Lulu's body separating from mine. This time, the transformation wasn't easy. It was so painful I thought I was going to die right next to Toto. I sobbed in pain and fear as my claws retracted and my fangs sank back into my gums. A moment later, Nox's arms were around me. I clung to him like a life raft in an ocean of pain.

"You're okay," he whispered into my hair, rocking me back and forth. "You're okay." Slowly, the agony ebbed away, leaving exhaustion in its wake. "*Never* do that again," Nox said. "Ever. I thought I lost you." The emotion was thick in his voice.

"What the hell was that!" Lulu was yelling. "What the hell did you just do, you little witch?"

"Dorothy," I gasped as Nox helped me to my feet. "Find Dorothy."

Dorothy was lying in the grass next to Toto's body, one leg twisted under his massive carcass. She struggled to sit up, trying feebly to push Toto's body off her as I limped toward her. It felt as though the magic in the diamond-studded boots was the only thing keeping me upright.

"You," she said, her voice more exhausted than angry. "It always comes back to you, doesn't it." She closed her eyes, almost as if she was so tired she couldn't even keep them open. I knew how she felt. She'd given in to the same magic that had almost destroyed me just now. She'd given everything she was to Oz. Even returning to Kansas hadn't undone the damage Oz's magic had caused. I realized that whether or not I was the one to end her, Dorothy was doomed.

"You can't kill me," she said. "And you're not going to win." Her red heels flashed with a pulse of ruby light, and I flung up one hand to protect my eyes from their radiance. "Don't forget about me, Amy," she said with a ghost of a smile, and then she was gone.

"Is it too much to ask that you just kill the bitch?" Lulu grumbled. All around us, the monkeys were still fighting off Dorothy's army, but with Dorothy gone and Toto dead her soldiers began to mill around in confusion. Some of them sat down where they'd been fighting, staring off into the distance like machines whose switches had been flipped off. Others threw down their weapons, or joined the monkeys in battling Glinda's army. Most of Glinda's soldiers seemed dazed and disoriented, no longer sure who they were even supposed to be fighting.

"What just happened to you?" Nox asked in a low voice. I shook my head.

"I don't know. The shoes saved me, I think. I don't know how or why. But listen—something is different. This time, I *could* have killed Dorothy, unlike before. I knew it somehow." I looked down at my sparkling boots. "I think everything is different now, with these."

Before he could respond, the witches suddenly crashed to the ground behind us.

"Glinda," Nox said. "We have to help Glamora fight her." They were so covered in blood it was impossible to tell which witch was which. I knew Glamora wanted this fight to be hers alone, but I couldn't let her die. I gathered my wits, knocking aside Glinda's soldiers and the occasional rogue creation of the Tin Woodman's as I raced toward the two of them.

When I got closer, I saw that Glinda was on her back. Glamora straddled her, her hands wrapped around Glinda's throat. I should have felt elated, but it was like watching a horror movie. There was something about the expression on Glamora's face that gave me chills. She wasn't even using magic anymore, just her fists. "This is for everything—you took—from me," Glamora snarled, punctuating her words by slamming Glinda's head into the ground. She wasn't trying to kill her—she just wanted Glinda to suffer.

"Glamora!" I cried. I don't know what I thought I was going to do. She was winning—and it's not like I wanted to help Glinda. I just wanted Glamora to go back to being the witch I knew—fierce but elegant, beautiful and kind, not this bloody inhuman banshee who was taking so much pleasure in her sister's suffering. But as Glamora looked up at me in surprise, Glinda slapped her across the face. Startled, Glamora let go of her sister's neck and Glinda struggled to get out from under her. Glamora punched her so hard that Glinda's head snapped back and she lay there, completely stunned. And then Glamora sank her fingers to the knuckle in Glinda's eye sockets.

Pink light blazed outward from Glinda's face. Glamora threw her head back, her face fixed in an awful smile. I fell to my knees as Glamora screamed triumphantly—and then her scream changed to something else as the pink light flowed up her arms and chest and reached her face. Her jeweled features twisted.

"Glamora!" I shouted again, scrabbling toward her on my hands and knees.

She was flesh and blood again now, and the face she turned toward me was somehow hers and Glinda's at the same time, the scar on Glamora's cheek transforming into a scar on Glinda's forehead and then switching back again, first Glinda and then Glamora looking out at me from those haunted blue eyes.

TWENTY-FIVE

As I watched helplessly, Glinda's form dissolved into pink light, flowing upward into Glamora's arms. Glamora's body rose slowly into the air, revolving in a pink cloud of power. Her mouth was open in a silent scream, her eyes staring outward sightlessly. "Glamora!" I cried, lunging forward. And then a final flash of pink light exploded outward, knocking me backward with a huge boom.

"Are you okay?" Nox was at my side, helping me to my feet. I nodded, too winded to speak. Only one witch lay crumpled on the ground. The other one was gone.

We started at the inert body curled up on the bloody dirt. I kept my knife at the ready as we tiptoed toward it. Nox gave the body a shove with his foot, and the woman flopped over on her back.

At first, I didn't know *who* I was looking at. Her eyes were closed, but the rise and fall of her chest told us she was still alive.

Her skin was flawless porcelain, with neither Glamora's gaping scar nor Glinda's ugly new wound. Her golden hair tumbled around her, as clean as if she'd just washed it. And she was completely, totally naked.

There was something tragic about seeing her like that. Someone like Glamora, for whom manners were everything.

"Give me your shirt," I ordered Nox.

"My what?"

"Your *shirt*, idiot." I tugged at the garment in question. Slowly, comprehension dawned and he tugged it over his head, his muscles rippling. He cleared his throat and I realized my mouth was hanging open.

Blushing, I grabbed his shirt and threw it over Glamora. If it *was* Glamora.

"We have to figure out what just happened," Nox said. "If that's Glinda . . ."

"I saw Glinda disappear," I said. "At least, I think that's what I saw. It was like they just fused into a single person somehow."

"I'll stand guard over her in case she wakes up," he said. "Why don't you make sure everyone else is safe."

"Already a step ahead of you," Mombi said, coming up behind us with Gert close on her heels. Melindra was behind them. I didn't see Annabel, or most of the other fighters who'd come to the castle with them.

"Annabel?" I asked, and Melindra shook her head, her face full of sorrow. Next to me, Nox caught his breath.

"Annabel and I have known each other since . . ." He trailed off, his voice catching, and bowed his head. I could hear Lulu barking orders somewhere nearby.

"I am so sorry, Nox," I said. There was an extra layer of guilt there because I had never liked her. And now she was gone.

"We've had heavy casualties," Mombi said grimly. "Lost a lot of the monkeys and most of our fighters. But the battle's over now. Most of Glinda's soldiers ran for the hills when Glamora took her out, but the monkeys are rounding up the remaining few."

"What about Dorothy's army?" I asked. Mombi scoffed.

"The survivors are helping the monkeys," Gert said quietly. "They were enslaved by Dorothy's magic, but they aren't evil. Her magic isn't strong enough anymore to control them from a distance. Most of them are just farmers and peasants the Woodman kidnapped and imprisoned before he died." Her voice was full of sorrow. *So much suffering*, I thought. And none of it was necessary.

"No time for tears in a war," Mombi said gruffly, "We'll have to face Dorothy again, but we've got more pressing problems to deal with for the time being." She hunched over the inert witch lying in front of us, holding out her hands to Nox and Gert. "Join the circle," she snapped, and Nox and Gert obeyed, kneeling beside her. The three of them closed their eyes, holding their linked hands over the witch's sleeping body. A soft, golden glow formed a cloud over the three cloaked figures. Mombi murmured a long string of syllables, and the golden cloud seemed to respond to her voice, gently probing the sleeping figure's body and face. At last, Mombi let out a long sigh and released Nox's and Gert's hands, opening her eyes. There was a strange expression on her face that I didn't know how to read.

"It's her," she said. "It's Glamora. She did it. She won." Slowly, the cloud sank into the sleeping witch's chest, until she began to glow with the same yellow light.

"Rejoin us, sister," Gert said. "Rejoin the Order. Rise with the Wicked." The sleeping witch opened her eyes.

"Welcome back, Glamora," Mombi said. "You defeated Glinda."

TWENTY-SIX

After everything that had happened, I'd kind of forgotten about Pete and Ozma. We found them playing a game of checkers that Ozma had improvised out of pebbles and bits of armor in the Tin Woodman's throne room, still in their chains. Nox leapt forward, and for a second I thought he was going to hit Pete in the face. Not that I'd have stopped him—although technically, I was the one who should have been punching Pete. He'd clocked me in the face before he'd summoned Glinda and gotten Polychrome killed.

"Checkers?" Nox growled. "Are you serious? People *died* out there."

"I thought it was a good idea to keep her quiet and hidden," Pete said miserably, glancing at Ozma. We all stood in silence looking at each other while Ozma burbled happily, moving around her rocks and bits of metal. Pete looked haggard and anxious. His green eyes blazed in his thin face and his dark hair was even shaggier. But Ozma looked perfectly serene. As Oz's magic had returned, she'd had more and more flashes of clarity, and in the past there were moments where I had almost been able to reach through to her. I remembered the vision of her that Polychrome had revealed, serene and regal and powerful. But that Ozma was still lost somewhere and we had no idea how to bring her back.

"I'm sorry," Pete said. "I can't ask you to forgive me for what I did. But maybe you can understand. Polychrome was going to kill me. I didn't have a choice."

"You always have a choice," Nox said. He was right. But somehow, I felt my anger dissipating as I saw the guilt and pain on Pete's face. He'd always been a mystery, but he'd helped me so many times in Oz. Was what he'd done really so much worse than anything I'd have done in his place to stay alive?

"Leave him alone," I said. Nox glanced at me, startled.

"Checkmate!" Ozma said happily, sweeping the checkers pieces off the board.

"Checkmate is in chess, Ozma," Pete said gently, stooping to pick up the pieces. He seemed almost brotherly, with a protective note in his voice.

"Can you tell what she's thinking?" I asked. Pete shook his head.

"The connection is completely broken. I don't think she has any idea who I am."

Nox tugged on my arm and leaned into me. "Why are you so

willing to let him off the hook?" Nox asked in a low voice. "He betrayed us."

"Glinda's defeated, so he can't betray us to her again," I pointed out. "And somehow my spell separated Ozma and Pete permanently. If we don't have a reason to kill him, he doesn't have a reason to turn against us."

"You don't have to talk about me like I'm not here," Pete said, standing up as Ozma cheerfully set up the checkers board again. "Look, Amy's right. I shouldn't have summoned Glinda, but it was the only thing I could think of at the time that could have kept me alive. I had no idea she would kill Polychrome or destroy Rainbow Falls."

"You could have done a hundred different things," Nox said coldly. "Instead you got people killed. People like Annabel. Polychrome *would* still be alive."

I sighed. "Nox, I don't trust Pete, but I don't think he can harm us anymore. Even if he could contact Dorothy, he doesn't have any reason to."

"Kindness can be a weakness, too," Nox said, not taking his eyes off Pete.

"That's not what you've been telling me," I said. "All along, you said it was the thing that made me different." I couldn't say why I wanted to spare Pete. Nox was right: so far, kindness had done nothing but get me nearly killed in Oz. But if Oz's magic was changing me into some kind of monster, maybe my willingness to forgive Pete was proof that it hadn't swallowed me up entirely.

Relief flooded Pete's face. "You mean you'll just let me go?"

"Not so fast," I told him. "I might be willing to keep Nox from killing you, but that doesn't mean I want you around. You've been basically nothing but trouble since the day I showed up in Oz."

"I saved you when you were in Dorothy's prison!" he protested.

"That was a *long* time ago," I said. "Anyway, you didn't save me—Mombi did."

At the sound of Mombi's name, Pete grimaced. I knew there was no love lost between him and the witch who'd enchanted him in the first place. Mombi probably had motives of her own when it came to Pete, and I didn't want to deal with them. My life was complicated enough as it is. "I want you to leave," I said. "Like, now. For good. I don't ever want to see you again. Is that clear?"

Pete looked at me for a long time, his dark eyes thoughtful. Once upon a time, I'd felt something for him. But that was long gone. Now he was just trouble.

"It's clear," he said finally.

"Good," I said. I turned to Nox. "I can help you set them free. The shoes will protect me." I sounded a lot more confident than I felt.

Nox looked like he wanted to protest, but he only nodded. He closed his eyes, raising his hands and resting them on Pete and Ozma's chains for a second time. Whatever I'd told Nox, I didn't trust the shoes completely yet. I'd leave the bulk of the magic up to him. But I knew he wasn't strong enough to free Pete and Ozma alone.

Nox grunted with the effort of sustaining the spell. I put my hands over his, concentrating hard on my magic boots. *Help me,* I asked them. *Help me help Nox.* I could feel them respond, the magic within them humming to life. And I could feel Oz's magic, too—the dark, dangerous pull of more power than I could handle, urging me to just let go, reminding me of how good it felt to be consumed by magic, transformed into an unstoppable monster. I concentrated instead on the shoes, willing the darkness to stay back. I could feel its disappointment as if it was a living thing.

Nox gave a final gasp, and Pete and Ozma's chains shattered into harmless pink fragments. I slumped backward in relief. *That was close,* I thought. Maybe too close. Were the shoes on my side? Or was the feeling of safety they gave me some trick of the Nome King's?

Nox saw my face. "Are you okay? What happened? And you said something before about the shoes somehow letting you be able to kill Dorothy?"

"I'm fine," I said. "I was right. The shoes can protect me from the effects of Oz's magic. I don't want to push my luck, but I can use magic if it's necessary. And yeah—whatever was binding me to Dorothy before—the shoes have undone." Nox shook his head, but he didn't reply. I knew he thought I was wrong, that magic was too much of a risk. I knew, too, that there was a strong possibility he was right.

"Get out of here," he said to Pete. "And if I see you again . . ." He trailed off, but the threat was clear.

"Do you want to teleport me away, or should I use the door?" There was no mistaking the note of sarcasm in Pete's voice—or the hurt.

"The door is fine," I said. Pete's eyes met mine, his expression unreadable and his mouth set. I wondered if I'd just made us a new enemy.

Pete turned and hugged Ozma close. Her eyes opened wide, and for a second I saw a spark of clarity. "Checkmate," she murmured, burrowing into his shoulder. Pete closed his eyes, stroking her long dark hair, before pushing her away gently. "Take care of her," Pete said to us. He half raised one hand as if to wave, and then shrugged helplessly and dropped it. Before he turned away I saw that his eyes were filling with tears.

"Good-bye, Pete," I said quietly. I watched his back recede across the long, dusty hall.

"I hope we're not going to regret this," Nox said quietly.

"So do I."

"Checkers?" Ozma asked, pointing to the board.

TWENTY-SEVEN

That night, a mournful group of the Wicked filled the Tin Woodman's palace. Four beat-up, exhausted witches, a handful of battered soldiers, a half-tin girl, an unusually quiet army of monkeys, and me.

I looked out over my friends and companions as Nox and Mombi conjured up a simple meal of bread, cheese, and water. Battle-hardened and weary, we were all filthy, bloody, and bruised. I wasn't even sure if we had won. And Dorothy was still alive somewhere, waiting to strike again. It was too much to think about. I remembered Annabel's smile, her long red hair, and squeezed my eyes against the tears I could feel coming. I wondered if I'd ever see the day where I could leave the war behind. Somehow, the brief moment in Kansas where I'd been able to pretend I was just a normal girl again made everything else worse.

All the witches were subdued. Nox had disappeared soon

after we'd finished eating, and I let him go. Glamora was barely coherent after her battle with Glinda, and sat out the celebration, huddled in a corner of the Tin Woodman's old throne room wrapped in a blanket and nursing a mug of foul-smelling tea that Lulu insisted was restorative (I hoped it wasn't made out of the same stuff as the monkeys' artisanal napalm). The most seriously injured monkeys rested with her.

I was worried about Glamora. She seemed more than just tired—she seemed like a zombie. I thought of the monster I had turned into, and I wondered if the spell Glamora had cast to transform herself had made her lose some piece of her humanity.

"She'll be fine," Gert said, interrupting my thoughts. She was seated next to me at the banquet hall's long table, and she'd been quiet for most of dinner. "She just needs to rest. Glinda was one of the most powerful witches in Oz. It's impossible to fight someone that strong without coming out of the battle a little worse for wear."

As if she could read my mind, too, Mombi waddled over to us. "There's no time to rest," she said. "We have to plan our next move." Gert nodded, and went to get Glamora and Melindra.

I looked around the hall, where monkeys curled up into sleepy balls. Lulu was already snoring loudly at the table. But there was no rest for the Wicked, I thought ruefully. I followed Gert, Mombi, and Glamora upstairs.

This time we found a small chamber with a few unbroken chairs instead of hanging out in the Tin Woodman's bedroom, which made me grateful. Sure, he was dead, and he hadn't lived in this palace since before I'd come to Oz, but it was hard not to see that creepy cabinet where he slept without thinking of all the horrible things he'd done to people I cared about. Starting with Indigo, my very first few hours in Oz, the Munchkin who the Tin Woodman had tortured to death in front of me after we'd helped the wingless monkey Ollie escape. People who helped me out tended to get hurt in Dorothy's Oz, I thought suddenly. By now, the list was long. Indigo. Ollie. Polychrome and Heathcliff. Jellia. Even Pete, although it was harder to feel sorry for him.

Mombi wasn't going to give me any time for moping. She closed her eyes and snapped her fingers as soon as the rest of us sat down, and after a minute Nox shuffled into the room. Being connected to the Quadrant had a lot of drawbacks. Pure power on the one hand, being summoned like a dog when you wanted time alone on the other.

"Let's get down to business," Mombi said gruffly. "The landscape has shifted a little, to say the least. That tends to happen a lot around here, doesn't it?"

"Dorothy's power is eating her alive," Gert answered. "And Glinda is the one who was helping her. But from what Amy discovered in Kansas, it seems more and more possible that the Nome King has been moving against us all along. It's entirely possible that he brought Amy to Oz once he realized that Dorothy would be swallowed up by its magic. And now that Glinda's dead—"

"*Is* Glinda dead?" Nox interrupted, staring at Glamora. "How do we know for sure?"

"The spell I performed on the battlefield would have found any traces of Glinda if she still remained in Glamora," Mombi said.

Glamora smiled gently. "It's me, Nox, I promise. But the final battle with my sister has given me important information that will factor into our plans. I was able to see inside her mind in those last moments, and I know why Dorothy and Glinda's paths diverged." She looked at me. "But I'm not the only one with a connection to our enemies, am I, Amy? You have Dorothy's shoes. You can tap into their power to see what Dorothy's planning next."

"No!" Nox said immediately, jumping to his feet. "It's not safe. We've covered this already. I don't care what Amy says about the shoes protecting her—she can't use magic in Oz."

"I'm right here," I said sharply. "I can speak for myself. I also have news—I can kill Dorothy. The shoes seem to have broken whatever link we had."

Glamora smiled again, her blue eyes glittering. "Why don't I start by telling you what I saw in Glinda's mind," she said.

TWENTY-EIGHT

Glamora stood up, leaning heavily on the back of her chair, as if to emphasize the seriousness of what she was saying.

"There's been trouble between Glinda and Dorothy for a while now," she began. Despite her obvious exhaustion, her voice was clear and unwavering. "My sister has been trying to control the throne of Oz for a long time, and Dorothy is only the most recent of her little . . . plans."

Glamora's knees wobbled and she gripped the chair more tightly for support, taking a deep breath. "But like Ozma, Dorothy proved to have a mind of her own—only in this case, Dorothy was soon so warped by her power that she decided to set herself up as tyrant in chief. Glinda has been looking for a way to quietly get rid of her." She looked at me. "I think Dorothy guessed that Glinda would turn against her, but the Wizard's spell took you both to Kansas before she could do anything about it. Now . . ." She shrugged. "If the Nome King is the one who's been trying to control Dorothy all along, all the more reason to kill her. And if he isn't—well, we all know Oz isn't safe as long as she's alive. I don't like it any more than you do, Nox, but Amy has to use the shoes at least once more."

"It's a huge risk," Mombi said. "We could be playing right into the Nome King's hands."

"I don't think so," I said. All the witches turned to look at me. "I mean, I know he wanted me to find the shoes and come back to Oz. I know he's hoping to use me in the same way he wanted to use Dorothy. But I don't think he realizes that the shoes are *good*."

"What do you mean, good?" Nox asked. "You want to risk your life on a hunch about a pair of shoes we don't know anything about? After you've already seen what the other enchanted shoes did to Dorothy?"

"I can't explain it," I said, knowing how stupid I sounded. "I can just tell. The shoes are trying to help me."

"Help you do what, though?" Mombi asked. No one answered for a long time.

"Anything we try will come with risks," Glamora said finally. "I think we should let Amy use the shoes." Mombi glanced at Glamora, her expression unreadable. *There's something Mombi knows that she isn't telling us,* I thought suddenly. Something about the Nome King? Or about what Glinda had been planning? I sighed. Secrets on top of secrets. Whatever. I'd had one job in Oz—to kill Dorothy. I might as well do my best to make sure the job got done.

"It's your decision," Gert said, reading my mind.

"We don't have a choice," I said.

"There's *always* a choice," Melindra said sharply, drumming her tin fingers against the table.

"I don't have *much* of a choice, then," I amended.

"We can use our power to try and protect you," Mombi said, gesturing to the other witches. I nodded and they stood up, forming a circle around me. I could feel the current of power running between them, creating a bubble around me like a shield.

"Let us guide you," Gert said. I could sense each of them in their magic: Nox's felt blue and cool, like a stream in fall. Mombi's was thicker, denser, like a gnarled old oak tree. Gert's was warm and comforting, but with a hint of steel underneath the softness. And Glamora's was a little too sweet, like overripe fruit. I let their magic flow into me and course through my body before settling into my feet. Dorothy's shoes blazed with a white light and I staggered, only held in place by the Quadrant's net of magic. "Concentrate, Amy!" Glamora cried.

The room around me faded away, the way the battlefield had when I'd used the shoes. I was in a cavern underground; I could feel dank, stagnant air on my face. Somewhere in the dark, a thundering ticking reverberated through the cavern. And the air was full of magic, so thick I could touch it with my fingers. The Quadrant's power was keeping me tethered to my body like a lifeline, but I knew if they faltered I'd be swept away. And something was wrong, I could feel it. There was something that wasn't supposed to be there. The pale thread of their combined magic thickened and began to turn darker, as if poison was running through it. Faintly, I could hear Nox and Gert screaming my name.

Let go, something seemed to be saying to me. *Let go.* It would be so easy to give in. To let myself sink into it. Finally, I'd be able to rest.

Dorothy's shoes glowed even more brightly and suddenly I thought of Nox's sandalwood smell, Gert's comforting hug, Mombi's gruffness. Even Melindra's bitchy, disdainful attitude. Lulu's snores. Ozma's huge green eyes. I thought of everyone I cared about in Oz, and I threw myself toward them with everything I had.

The cavern vanished around me and I crashed through the circle of the witches' arms, hitting the floor with a thump that jarred my bones. Gert and Nox were at my side in an instant, helping me up.

"What happened?" Nox asked. "Are you okay?"

"I'm fine, but I didn't see Dorothy. I saw some kind of cavern. And I could hear this crazy ticking sound, but I don't know what it was."

"The Great Clock," Mombi said. "Dorothy's trying to tap into its magic."

"What's the big deal? Wasn't she already using it to make the days as long as she wants them?" I asked.

"The Great Clock is connected to the oldest, deepest magic of Oz," Gert said slowly. "Even the fairies, the true rulers of Oz, have never understood how it works. Dorothy's been siphoning its magic off a little at a time. But if she's trying to unleash the full power of the clock . . ." She trailed off into silence.

"So what happens if she tries?" I asked. No one answered. Gert stared at Glamora. Glamora stared at the ground. Mombi stared at Nox. Nox stared at the door. None of this seemed like a very good sign. Nox sighed and looked at me.

"If Dorothy somehow taps into the magic of the Great Clock, it's pretty likely she'll destroy all of us. Oz, the Other Place—"

"Wait, you mean *Kansas*? How can Dorothy destroy Kansas with a giant stopwatch?"

"Oz and your world are intertwined," Gert said. "You know that, Amy." I remembered what the Wizard had said about Kansas and Oz being two sides of the same place. The strange ways in which Dorothy and I were linked. And the way that magic-crazed Dorothy was tied to the innocent farm girl she'd been in Kansas.

"Oz is layered over the Other Place like another dimension," Mombi said. "The two worlds don't interact, but they're dependent on each other to survive. No one's ever tried to tap into the magic of the Great Clock before. If Dorothy does, the power will be uncontrollable."

I'd never really missed Kansas much, but the idea of it being wiped off the map was a totally different prospect from the idea of just never having to go back. I thought of my mom, totally oblivious to the fact that Dorothy was about to drop doom on the whole universe like she'd dropped a house on a witch all those years ago. Dustin and Madison and their baby. Even bitchy old

Amber and dopey Mr. Stone. I put my head in my hands as if I could shut out reality myself by covering my eyes.

"Can I stop her?"

Gert looked at Mombi, who shrugged. "You're connected to the same power she is. You have her shoes. You're connected to *her*. I'm pretty sure you're the only one who can."

"You or the Nome King," Glamora added. "But I don't think we can exactly count on him to help us."

"He can't possibly mean for Dorothy to destroy Oz," Gert protested.

"We still don't know *what* he wants," Nox said. "And if he's still in the Other Place, we don't know if he even knows what Dorothy's doing. Maybe he thinks she's too powerless now to do any harm." He shook his head. "But I don't like it. You keep saying Dorothy's shoes are protecting you, but how do we know for sure that's true? What if this is all a trap? I don't think it's safe for you to go after Dorothy. We have to think of another way."

"There is no other way," Glamora said sharply.

"Amy's risking her life!" Nox protested.

"We're *all* risking our lives," Mombi pointed out drily.

"I won't let you just use her!" Nox said fiercely. "You took my life away—fine. I don't have anything left to lose. But Amy can still go back to Kansas someday. She has a family out there. People who love her. It's not right for us to ask her to risk this much for a place where she doesn't even belong."

That *stung*. Was that how Nox saw me? After everything we'd been through together? "Don't I get to decide for myself?"

I snapped. "My life will be a hell of a lot better without Dorothy in it, too, remember?"

"You have a family to go back to," he said softly. "You have a life, Amy. And you're not strong enough to fight Oz's magic alone."

"You don't get to make that decision for me!" I said sharply. "This is everything I've trained for, everything *you* taught me to do!"

"I know," he said brokenly. "Believe me, I know."

"Joining the Quadrant requires we set our *personal* feelings aside," Glamora interrupted smoothly. Nox looked like he was about to hit her, but he only shook his head in anger. I almost laughed. The Quadrant's rules wouldn't let me be with Nox, but they couldn't stop me from volunteering for a suicide mission to save him.

"I'm going," I said.

"You make me sick," Nox said to Glamora, his voice cold. "All of you. You ask too much. You use people up and throw them away. I might be bound to you, but I don't have to agree with what you're doing." He turned on his heel and walked out of the room.

"Well," Mombi said after a short, uncomfortable silence. "If we're leaving for the Emerald City in the morning to save the world, we should all probably get some rest."

TWENTY-NINE

There weren't really enough blankets to go around, and the monkeys had already nabbed most of the palace stock. Ozma was sleeping peacefully with her head pillowed on Lulu's back, and I paused for a moment to look at them both. Lulu was still snoring gently with her mouth open, looking a far cry from the fierce warrior I'd so recently seen in battle. And Ozma—was she really still in there somewhere? I'd seen her moments of clarity, but none of them ever lasted long enough to give me faith that she'd be back to normal anytime soon. I'd been fighting Dorothy for so long now that I'd never given much thought to what would happen once she was finally defeated. If Ozma was still loopy, who'd take over? The Nome King wanted it to be me. But I was tired of being a pawn in someone else's story. Nox was right. I didn't belong here. If Dorothy's shoes had taken her back to Kansas, they might work a second time for me, too. Once I'd defeated her for good, I was going home, Nome King or no

Nome King. Oz would have to solve its own problems.

Gert, Glamora, and Mombi had drifted off—to find private chambers of their own, probably. But as tired as I was, I didn't want to go to sleep. Instead, I walked out into what had once been the Tin Woodman's gardens.

The gardens were probably well-kept when he lived here, but they'd long since become overgrown and gone to seed. Still, as broken down as they were, most of the worst of the fighting had been far enough away from the palace that they weren't any worse for wear than they already had been—save for some trampled patches and a scattered spot of blood here and there.

But elsewhere, flowers bloomed in the moonlight: huge, nodding blossoms that reminded me a little of dahlias, sighing on the wind and releasing little puffs of perfume into the cool air. A swarm of big-winged butterflies drifted past, flapping velvety-soft wings and singing a tiny, almost inaudible lullaby. A big yellow moon hung in the sky, so low that I thought I could touch it if I climbed up high enough. Like the moon at home, this one had a face; only Oz's moon was a gently smiling woman who reminded me a little bit of Gert.

I wasn't sure how long I had been standing there when I realized Nox was next to me.

"You should go to sleep," he said. "Tomorrow will be . . ." He didn't need to say it. We both knew. But sleep was the last thing I could think about. Suddenly, he grabbed my hand. I startled at the warmth of his touch. The feeling of his skin against mine.

"Look," he breathed. "Night-blooming tirium."

"What's that?"

He held a finger to his lips and beckoned me to follow him, tiptoeing toward a tall plant the size of a sunflower. "Be totally quiet," he said into my ear, his voice sending a thrill through me. "If you frighten it, it won't bloom." He settled down on his haunches to wait and I squatted next to him.

He was watching the tall plant as intently as a cat guarding a mouse hole. The seconds stretched into minutes. I fidgeted. He put one hand on my knee to caution me and left it there. All my senses felt totally alive. His sandalwood smell. The heat of his body. The movement of his breath. He smiled, but he wasn't looking at me. He was looking at the plant.

A single pale tendril was unfurling from the top of the stalk, as slow and elegant as a ballet dancer pirouetting across a stage. Another delicate frond followed, and then another, waving gently in the night breeze. The tendrils sent out shoots of their own, like a silken spiderweb weaving itself in front of our eyes. Slowly, the strands knitted themselves together into a huge, white flower, sparkling with moonlight and moving back and forth almost as though it had a will of its own. I realized I was holding my breath and let it out in a long, slow exhale. The tirium flower was beautiful and impossibly fragile—a reminder that no matter how comfortable I got here Oz would always be an alien land, governed by rules I didn't fully understand.

The tirium blossom turned toward me and then exploded silently into a starburst of tiny white lights, like fireflies, that swirled around us and drifted away across the grass. Where they caught on leaves or branches they hung glowing until the soft white light finally faded away. The flower was so gorgeous—and so fragile. Like everything good in this crazy world. Like hope. Like whatever had started between me and Nox that we weren't allowed to finish. I felt my eyes filling with tears, and Nox reached up to brush them away.

"I forgot Dorothy didn't destroy everything beautiful in Oz," I said.

"She didn't destroy you."

"Not for lack of trying," I said, and then realized the implication of what he was saying and blushed. I was grateful for the darkness that hid my flaming cheeks.

"My mom would have loved to see something like this. I wish I could've said good-bye to her, at least," I said quietly.

"You're not going to die," he said fiercely. "Not tomorrow anyway."

"I hope not. But I meant when we came back to Oz. I want to go home somehow. But let's face it, I'll probably never see her again. I just wish there was some way I could have told her I love her."

"You can see her," Nox said. He pointed to a puddle of water at the base of the tirium plant, closing his eyes. I remembered the scrying spell Gert had used to show me an image of my mom back in the caverns of the Wicked. I bent down for a closer look as power flowed from Nox's hands into the clear water. At first, all I could see was grass and leaves. But then the surface of the water shimmered and grew opaque, and I was looking into the living room of my mom's new apartment. She was sitting on the couch, her eyes red as though she'd been crying. Jake was sitting on one side with his arms around her. And on the other—

"Dustin and Madison?" I breathed in surprise. Dustin was saying something while Madison nodded, bouncing Dustin Jr. on her knee. And over them all loomed Assistant Principal Strachan.

There was something in my mom's lap, I realized. Something they were all looking at. A leatherbound book with charred edges. "Dorothy's journal!" I exclaimed. "My mom must have gone through my room after the tornado and found it. But if they realize what it is—"

"They might figure out Oz is real," Nox breathed.

"They couldn't," I argued. "You don't understand how hard it is for people from my world to believe in this stuff without seeing it with their own eyes. If they realize what the journal is, they'll probably just think it proves that Dorothy was a real person—who was totally bonkers." A strange feeling crept down my spine—warm, heavy, and itchy, like a drop of molten metal rolling along my vertebrae.

"But I thought . . . ," I said, trailing off as I leaned forward. Assistant Principal Strachan looked up, as though he could sense me. And then, impossibly, his eyes met mine.

And they weren't Assistant Principal Strachan's angry eyes. They were the silvery-pale eyes of the Nome King. I gasped. He smiled at me and put one hand on my mom's shoulder and the other on Madison's as they turned the pages of Dorothy's journal.

Do not forget, Miss Gumm, how much you have to lose.

His voice slid into my thoughts and I flinched.

Remove our little friend Dorothy or do not; it is no matter to me either way. But I will come for you very soon. And then, Miss Gumm, what you do will matter very much to me indeed.

I gasped aloud as his thoughts pushed into my mind as if he was just trying to show off how easy it would be to control me. *No!* I thought fiercely. The boots sent a warm pulse of magic through my body and the Nome King's grip loosened.

Do not think your shoes are enough to keep me at bay for long, Miss Gumm, he hissed. As suddenly as it had come, his hold on my mind was gone. The vision of my mom's living room burst like a bubble popping and the puddle evaporated with a steaming hiss, knocking me back to the ground.

"Amy?" Nox was shaking me. "What happened? What did you see?" I was groggy and my thoughts were sluggish as if I'd just woken up from a long, bad dream.

"The Nome King," I said thickly. "He's with my mom. He said he's coming for me."

Nox breathed in sharply. "Coming for you to do what?"

"I don't know. He doesn't care if we kill Dorothy. He's got something else in mind."

Nox was silent, thinking. "I don't like this," he said finally.

I laughed. "You think I do? But we have to kill Dorothy, even if it's part of the Nome King's plan."

"I think you should give me the shoes."

I shook my head fiercely. "So far they've protected me. They helped me fight off the Nome King just now. I don't want to give them up."

"Don't want to? Or can't?"

We both knew what he meant. Dorothy's red stilettos, fused to her feet, had transformed her into a monster. I had nothing but my intuition to tell me that my boots wouldn't do the same thing. It was entirely possible they were transforming me already. That giving me a feeling of protection was just a trick. But I couldn't use magic and stay myself any other way. And there was no way I was going up against Dorothy without the ability to use my power.

"Promise me something," I said, not taking my eyes off his. "Just in case."

"Depends on the promise," he said. He was standing so close to me I could feel the heat from his skin. I had to bite my lip to keep from kissing him.

"These shoes," I said, gesturing to my feet. "After tomorrow, if they turn me into . . . you know. Her. If I try to take them off and I can't. I want you to promise me you'll do whatever you have to to get them off."

His eyes widened. "It won't come to that."

"Nox, don't lie to me. It *can* come to that. So promise me. You'll get the shoes off no matter what. Even if you"—I took a deep breath—"even if you have to cut off my feet. Even if you have to kill me."

"Amy, that's crazy."

"It's not crazy, and you know it."

"I never wanted this for you. I'm so sorry that you—that this—" He made a helpless gesture.

"I know. Promise me, Nox," I said. He opened his eyes and looked deeply into mine, as if he was trying to drink me in.

"I promise," he said.

"Whatever it takes."

"Whatever it takes."

We looked at each other for a long time. "Good luck tomorrow," he said gruffly, glancing away. I wanted him to say something else. To find just the right words to tell me everything was going to be okay. To tell me that he'd find a way to be with me. That he'd find a way to help me get home. But instead he turned around and walked away from me, back into the Woodman's palace. I followed, telling myself the pain in my ribs was just exhaustion and not my heart breaking into a million little pieces inside my chest.

THIRTY

The next morning we assembled in the courtyard. Lulu wanted to come with us, but agreed to stay at the Woodman's palace with her monkeys in case any of Glinda's army returned. Ozma was too much of a liability in the Emerald City, and Lulu was only too happy to look after her. We were all trying to make up for our pasts in one way or another, I guess. Except for Ozma, who couldn't remember hers. Suddenly, having your memory wiped seemed more like a blessing than a curse.

So in the end it was just Nox, Gert, Mombi, Glamora, and me who prepared to teleport to Dorothy's palace in the Emerald City.

The last I'd seen it, it had been a scary place. The city had been leveled as if it was hit with a bomb and the palace itself had seemed to be growing like a living thing, like it had been possessed by some kind of demonic force.

It had been the Wizard's doing, and he was gone now. But

knowing Oz, and knowing what I knew now, I thought it was unlikely that things had improved much, even without him. If there was one thing Oz had taught me, it was to prepare for the worst.

So the five of us joined hands, and Mombi began to mumble the familiar words of the teleportation spell that would take us all there.

I was an old hand at flying by now, but it still didn't lose its thrill. I felt the familiar jerk of magic lifting me up into the air, and the sensation of the bottom of my stomach dropping out as we rose into the sky, our hands still linked. Far off on the horizon, I could see the pale stripe of the Deadly Desert; in the opposite direction, the tall peaks of the mountains. For just a moment, in that glorious weightless space, I could pretend that I wasn't going back into battle—just flying over the jewel-bright landscape of Oz with the wind in my hair and the sun on my back. I could see the same joy in Nox's face. Even Mombi, who hated heights, was smiling as we hurtled toward our destination.

Then Nox's expression changed. I turned my head to follow his gaze and gasped out loud.

We were flying into a storm. Out of nowhere, dark clouds gathered into a churning inferno before us, looming directly over the ruined Emerald City.

I'd seen the changes in the city on the ground, and that had been bad enough. But from the air, it was terrifying: the bombed-out buildings, the empty streets scattered with broken gems. From here I could see there were bodies in the ruins, too—twisted and broken like the buildings around them. I swallowed hard. At the center of it all, the twisted spires of the Emerald Palace stabbed upward into the dark, oily-looking clouds. The palace seemed to radiate a tangible sense of menace. Dark, serpentine vines twined up its twisted towers, and smoke boiled out of some of its broken windows. What had once been orderly gardens looked more like a jungle, thick with thorny plants I didn't recognize. The air was filled with a deep ticking noise, like the world's biggest grandfather clock was somewhere inside the palace. "The Great Clock," Gert said grimly. "She's already trying to use it."

"Hold on!" Mombi yelled, her grip tightening on my hand. As we drew closer to the storm, gusts of wind began to buffet us, hard and insistent as fists. One blast was so strong it almost pulled me out of Mombi's grip. On my other side, Gert squeezed harder, too. The witches began to chant.

"Don't let go, Amy!" Gert yelled over the rising wind. She didn't have to tell me twice. I held on for dear life as Gert and Mombi's chanting rose in strength to meet the force of the storm. We were almost on top of the palace now. Suddenly, I could make out a teeming mass of figures in the overgrown and tangled gardens surrounding the palace.

"There's still an army there!" Nox shouted. The ground was rushing toward us at a terrifying speed. The plants in the garden reached up with spiky branches, and a long vine uncoiled from one of the palace's towers and whipped at us furiously.

"Look out!" I screamed, but the vine lashed across Mombi's

arm before she could move, leaving a broad, ugly gash. She yelped in pain and let go of me. I felt my other hand slipping out of Gert's grasp.

"The plants are attacking!" Glamora shrieked. "They're defending the palace!"

"Amy!" Nox yelled frantically on Mombi's other side. The vine wrapped around Gert's legs and yanked her away from me. Glamora cried out as I plummeted toward the waiting thorns. Just as I was about to slam into the ground, a huge gust of air picked me up and sent me spinning gently. *Nox,* I thought, struggling to get my bearings. Nox had saved me.

Gert sent a blast of fire at the vine still tangled around her legs, severing it in midair, and it reared back as she crumpled to the ground. I ran over to her. "I'm fine!" she gasped. "No time! You must hurry!" On the ground, the ticking noise was even louder and more incessant. I felt like it was trying to crawl inside my head, and had to resist the impulse to cover my ears.

"Soldiers!" Nox yelled. I reached for my knife and whirled into a battle crouch. My reflexes were back, and none too soon. These soldiers were different from the ones who'd attacked us back at the Woodman's palace. They were entirely mechanical, whirring and buzzing like a clockwork army. Some of them stood on two legs and looked almost human; others had wheels, or tons of jointed legs like a centipede. Some carried weapons in metal claws, and others had swords and spears embedded in their tin torsos.

Nox flickered in and out of sight, teleporting himself back

and forth between the soldiers as he hacked at them with his knife. A terrifying howl split the air, and I saw a line of three-headed miniature clockwork Totos descending on us from the direction of the palace. Their eyes glowed with an eerie red light that reminded me of Dorothy's shoes. Each head's jaws bristled with dripping, serrated fangs as long as my forearm, and the mechanical dogs' tails were edged with jagged steel plates that they whipped back and forth. I readied myself to fight.

A fireball sailed over my head and landed among the tin soldiers, sending several of them flying. Glamora leapt to my side. "We'll hold them off!" she yelled, sending another spray of flame into the oncoming army. "You and Nox find Dorothy!"

I ducked a stray blow and came up swinging, cutting a soldier in half on my upswing. "How will we get to the palace?"

"Nox can take you into the palace. We can only hold them for so long—you have to move as fast as you can."

Behind her, Mombi threw fireball after fireball into Dorothy's clockwork army; though each one landed, there were always more soldiers to rush in and fill the gaps she made. Nox was moving so fast behind me he was just a dark blur. Gert's face was pale, but she was hovering over the battlefield, lashing out with a glowing blue whip she'd fashioned out of magic. I couldn't just leave them out here to die.

"No thinking!" Glamora yelled. "Just go!" I knew she was right. This might be our last chance. If I couldn't kill Dorothy now, this was it. The witches couldn't last long out here.

I grabbed Nox's hand. Dorothy's shoes blazed to life on my

feet, and I felt the answering stir of Oz's magic. *Not yet,* I told it. I squeezed my eyes shut.

When I opened them, Nox and I were standing inside Dorothy's banquet hall, although it was ruined almost beyond recognition. What furniture was left was splintered and broken. The windows were shattered, letting more of those sinewy vines creep in, and a mossy-green slime covered the walls. The carpet squelched underfoot. I didn't want to know what it was soaked with. Inside the palace, the ticking was so powerful that the walls shivered with each stroke. It was like standing right next to a speaker at a concert. I could feel the noise like a physical force moving through me.

Nox squeezed my hand, and we raced through the palace, following the sound of the clock. As loud as it was, it was still stronger in some directions than others. But the farther we went, the more the palace twisted and turned. New corridors sprang up in front of us, and when we turned around the hallways we'd just been running down had been replaced by stone walls. I hadn't spent enough time in the Emerald Palace to memorize its layout, but even I could tell this was like a fun-house mirror version of the real thing, all nightmarish hallways and unexpected turns. Sometimes a hallway seemed familiar, and I realized we'd already gone down it.

"The palace is leading us in circles!" Nox said behind me. "We have to figure something else out."

"Keep running!" I argued, tugging him down another hall. We ran through a doorway into a huge room I didn't recognize, a wooden door slamming shut behind us. The room was a perfect circle, studded with identical doors every few feet. The ticking of the Great Clock thundered through the chamber. Nox tried every one of the doors in turn, but they were all locked. The Emerald Palace had sent us to a dead end.

"You're right," I said. "The palace is moving against us." It was time to use magic. "Don't let go of me," I told Nox. He nodded and tightened his grip on my hand.

I closed my eyes, sending feelers of magic out through the palace. The more I tuned in to my magical senses, the more I could see and feel. The rats running through the palace cellars. The whirring and clicking of the soldiers as they battled the witches outside. The few remaining living inhabitants of the palace, creeping in terror through the halls and hiding in forgotten rooms. The evil in the palace was so strong it made my skin itch, as though a million ants were crawling all over me. I steeled myself and kept looking.

And then I felt her. A malevolent mass at the heart of the palace, like a fattened spider at the center of its web. I shuddered involuntarily. Nox's fingers tightened through mine. "Where is she?" he panted in my ear. I knew what we had to do.

"This way," I said. Instead of trying to open one of the doors, I turned and led him directly into the wall. But instead of slamming into solid stone, we hit something firm but yielding. At first it resisted us, as though we were walking into a wall of butter, and then dissolved. There was a rushing noise, and everything went dark and very, very cold. Nox was holding my hand so tightly I thought I might lose circulation in my fingers—but I was squeezing his back just as hard.

“Amy Gumm,” said a familiar voice. “You found me. I had a feeling you would.”

THIRTY-ONE

A red spark lit the darkness and slowly spread outward. Nox and I were standing side by side on the rough stone floor of a cavern so huge its ceiling was lost in darkness. In front of us, a dark pool of water reflected the low red light, and on the far side a familiar figure hunched over an ornate, old-fashioned clock. I'd been expecting something huge, monstrous—but it just looked like an ordinary antique you might see in your grandparents' house, except for the fact that it was made out of solid gold and studded with dozens of pebble-sized emeralds. In the red light, Dorothy's face looked hideous and twisted, like a monster's. The clock shook, and a low boom echoed through the dark chamber.

"I knew it was just a matter of time before we met again, Amy," Dorothy said. Her voice was raspy and low, like she'd suddenly taken up a pack-a-day habit. She coughed, and the clock boomed again. I realized the sound was the same ticking, but slowed down somehow. Dorothy smiled. "No pun intended," she continued. "Time *is* what matters, when you get right down to it. For everything there is a season, right? I learned a few things in the Other Place, Amy. I learned that things don't get any more fun there for girls as special as me. I learned that magic really is the best way to do things. And what better source of magic than the heart of Oz?"

"Lurline's pool," Nox said. He was still squeezing my hand, but his voice was steady.

"You're smarter than you look," Dorothy said coquettishly. "Between the Great Clock and Lurline's little puddle"—she gestured to the dark pool—"I have enough magic to keep me going for as long as I want. Which is, of course, forever. I thought the Wizard was on my side. I thought Glinda was my friend. But the only person you can *really* rely on is yourself."

"You can't do this," I said, keeping my voice as steady as I could. "Using the Great Clock will let loose all of Oz's magic. And Oz and Kansas are two sides of the same place. You know that. You'll destroy them both."

"I don't care about *Kansas*," Dorothy snapped, but for the first time she sounded uncertain, as if she hadn't thought her plan through.

"That much magic will tear you apart," Nox jumped in. "You can't survive it."

For a second, Dorothy almost looked to be on the verge of changing her mind. As impossible as it seemed, I thought we might have convinced her to abandon her crazy plan. But then she scowled.

"You've taken away everything I cared about, Amy Gumm," Dorothy said. "You killed my friends. You ruined my city and made Oz impossible for me to rule. You even killed my *dog*. I'm not going to do *anything* you tell me. And I'm *not* going to let you take away Oz."

In one sudden motion, she picked up the clock and threw it hard into the pool. "No!" Nox shouted. The clock disappeared noiselessly into the black water without even making a splash. For a second, everything held completely still.

And then the water of the pool began to bubble violently. A black cloud formed over it, whirling faster and faster in the red light of Dorothy's shoes. She raised both arms over her head, and the cloud above us split open. I could see through it—straight through to Dusty Acres, still as abandoned and sad-looking as the day the Wizard had pulled me and Dorothy through to the Other Place. Arcing sparks of red light shot from Dorothy's fingers into the black mass, landing on the ground in Kansas and flaring up into fires that quickly caught in the dead grass. Huge fissures cracked open and spread through the parched earth. I had to do something. I had to stop her, before she destroyed Oz and Kansas both. But how?

The shoes. Dorothy's shoes. They'd had the power to take Dorothy back to Kansas. Maybe they had the power to save it. It was a stretch, but the connection was there, and right now it was the only idea I had. I had to save my mom and I had to save Nox. I couldn't let Dorothy take them away from me. "I love you!" I yelled at Nox, yanking my hand from his grip.

"Amy, stop! What are you doing?" He threw himself at me but I dodged his arms. Maybe I could get the clock back. Maybe the shoes would help me. Maybe I was about to die. There was only one way to find out. I took a deep breath, got a running start, and jumped.

"No!" Dorothy and Nox screamed at the same time as I plunged into darkness and everything went black.

THIRTY-TWO

When I opened my eyes, I was standing on a golden road in the middle of a jungle. Dorothy and Nox were gone. The sun filtered down through a green canopy of leaves. Birds sang in the branches, and the trees around me dripped frothy masses of green moss. The air was as warm as bathwater. The road beneath my feet looked like the perfect version of the Road of Yellow Brick; it was smooth and seamless, made out of some translucent material that caught and held the sunlight that made it down through the trees to the forest floor.

"Welcome, Amy," someone said behind me. Startled, I turned around.

"Ozma?" I asked in surprise. But I quickly realized the creature in front of me, though she looked almost exactly like the fairy queen, was someone else. Her face was Ozma's, youthful and pretty. Her bearing was Ozma's, too, in her clear moments: regal and serene and confident. A pair of golden wings fluttered from her back. But her eyes were a stranger's. Unlike Ozma's green eyes, hers were the same pale gold as the road and far, far more ancient than her face suggested. The depths of wisdom and compassion in that unearthly golden gaze were startling. She practically radiated peace. For a while, my mom had been really into Amma, a Hindu guru who could transform people's lives by hugging them. I got the same feeling from the fairy in front of me.

"Ozma is my great-great-great-granddaughter," she said, holding out one hand to me. "I am Lurline, the creator of Oz. Come, Amy. Let us walk a little while."

Bemused, I took her hand, and she led me down the golden path. "But Dorothy—" I began.

Lurline smiled. "Dorothy will still be there when you return, child. We are in a time outside of time now. She cannot touch you here." Ahead of us, water glinted through the trees and as we approached, I realized that it was a spring. Like the road, it was somehow a more beautiful version of the pool I'd jumped into. The water was clear and pure and depthless. On the far side of the pool, two trees had grown together to form a kind of bench carpeted in soft green moss. Lurline indicated for me to sit, and then tucked in her golden wings and sat down next to me.

I leaned back into the warm embrace of the branches that supported my back. The moss smelled delicious, warm and earthy. The bench was unbelievably comfortable. I could have fallen asleep in the dappled sunlight and stayed there for a hundred years.

Lurline picked up a wooden cup that rested on the ground beside the bench, scooped a cupful of water directly out of the spring, and handed it to me. "Drink," she said.

I didn't realize how thirsty I was until she said the word. I took a cautious sip of water. It was delicious: cool and crisp and incredibly refreshing. A soothing feeling spread through me as I drained the cup. My aches and pains faded away, and my thoughts cleared. I felt as sharp and fresh as if I'd slept for a week.

"Are we in heaven?" I asked.

Lurline laughed. Her laughter was like the sound of the wind in the trees, beautiful and wild. "No, child. You are in a place between your world and Oz. After I brought magic to the Deadly Desert and created the land of Oz, I traveled to this place. All fairies come here when they are ready to move on from the mortal world. But I look in on Oz from time to time." She gestured toward the pool. "My spring is a window between worlds."

I frowned and looked down at my feet, still battered and bloody in my new magic boots. "Did Dorothy's old shoes bring me here?"

She raised her eyebrows, like she thought I was being very silly. "You brought yourself here, didn't you?"

"Yes, but . . ."

She raised a slender finger. As she touched it to her red lips, I found that I had been silenced. As hard as I tried to speak, I couldn't.

"The spring has judged you," Lurline said. "And it has

judged you worthy of standing here before me. I cannot interfere directly in the matters of your kind. I did not say you were without flaws," she added with a smile, as if she could read my thoughts.

She looked troubled. "I am afraid you cannot rest here long, Amy. But I want you to listen well."

I nodded.

"The magic of Oz is not safe for people from your world. It has driven Dorothy mad, as you know."

She nodded in response to my unasked question. "It will drive you mad, too, if you let it," she said with a sigh. "All things will continue in their own way, but if Dorothy succeeds in tearing everything apart, the creatures of Oz *and* the Other Place will perish. I do not wish this to come to pass. And you have more to worry about than just Dorothy." Her voice was still gentle, but it was terrifying, too. I had the feeling that anybody who tried to make something come to pass against Lurline's wishes didn't fare well.

She laughed her musical laugh again, and I realized she *could* read my thoughts.

"You mean the Nome King," I said, suddenly able to speak again. She nodded.

"I do. Even I cannot entirely guess at the game he plays, but I know he wishes to use you and Dorothy as its pieces. And very likely Ozma, too. I'm afraid your work in Oz is not yet done. I can see the pain in your heart, child, and I am sorry to ask more of you. So much rests on your shoulders. Especially when not all of your companions wish the same healing for Oz that you do."

"What do you mean?"

She shook her head. "I cannot see that far; only that you must be careful. Trust in yourself, but do not place your trust easily in others. You are very strong, Amy—strong enough to defeat Dorothy, possibly strong enough to defeat even the Nome King. But not in the way that you think. The most obvious way is not always the right path."

She was making about as much sense as Ozma. I wondered if anyone in Oz had ever given any question a straight answer. She put a hand on my shoulder.

"I know this is difficult for you," she said. "You have suffered much, already, and you still have not learned to know yourself. Dorothy is blinded by her own pain and anger. Take care that you do not walk down the road that she has chosen. I cannot promise you a future without harm, but know that I am watching over you. You have drunk of my spring, and that is no small trifle. And you have my shoes." She gestured at the diamond-studded boots with one elegant hand.

"*Your* shoes?" I gasped. "But I thought they belonged to Dorothy."

She smiled. "Dorothy had them for a while, yes. But they belong to the fairies. They are made from our magic. They will serve you well if you trust in their power."

I had so many questions. But she shook her head and held a finger to her lips. "All in good time," she said. "The way is cloudy now, but soon I think we will be able to see the path again."

She reached up to her neck and undid a thin silver chain, drawing a pendant out of her dress and handing it to me. "This, too, you will find useful," she said.

I looked at the necklace. The pendant was a pale golden jewel, made of the same material as the road. The harder I looked at it, the more I thought I could see movement in its translucent depths, as if it were filling with smoke. I felt as though I were falling down a long, golden tunnel.

"Be careful," Lurline said at my side, and I snapped back to the present. I made as if to fasten the necklace around my neck, and she shook her head. "It is not for you, but for another. You will know when the time is right to put it into the proper hands."

I tucked the necklace into my pocket instead. Lurline stood up and held out her hands to me. "And now I must send you home, dear child."

"To Dorothy," I said, standing up.

"To Dorothy," she agreed. "But to many brighter and wonderful things as well. To the living, breathing world. To a boy who loves you, if I am not mistaken." I turned bright red and she giggled. But then a look of longing flashed across her face. "There is a part of me that envies you, to be returning to the living, breathing world. Think of me when you go into the mountains," she said softly, her gaze far away. "When you look out over the blue valleys to the far horizon, say my name that I might see them, too, through your eyes. And remember as in all of us, it is only your capacity for wickedness that makes selflessness possible."

"But you still haven't told me how to defeat Dorothy."

"Dorothy is connected to you, Amy. To find that answer, you must look within yourself."

I almost rolled my eyes, and then I remembered Lurline could read my thoughts.

She smiled again. "I have faith in you, Amy. You have done well. I will help you as much as I can. I will hear you when you call me. Be strong. There is more power aiding you than you know."

She let go of my hands, and the world around me began to fade. As if I was switching between TV stations, Lurline's world tuned out and Oz tuned back in. Nox's outline, shadowy at first, solidified. There was a roaring noise in my ears that I soon realized was Dorothy's storm. I was dripping wet. And Dorothy, still glowing with that terrifying red light and hovering off the ground with her arms outstretched, was screaming into the howling wind.

THIRTY-THREE

I could still see Dusty Acres through the swirling clouds; Dorothy's magic was tearing up the earth as giant cracks spread across the landscape. A huge strip of ground peeled up and was sucked up into the maelstrom.

Nox was trying to distract her with fireball after fireball to no effect. "Welcome back," he said grimly, dropping his hands in exhaustion. Another chunk of earth flew up through the rent in the floor and hit the ceiling of the cave with a thud, showering us with dirt and rocks. Dorothy cackled in delight. I grabbed Nox's hand, calling on the power of my silver boots. Nox caught on immediately, slowly feeding his magic into mine. I leaned into our combined strength and opened myself up, deciding to just let the magic of the shoes flow through me.

I could somehow see through the dark water of Lurline's pool to the other side, where Lurline waited. I could see the clock, suspended between Oz and her world, drawing her magic into itself and funneling it to Dorothy. I could see Kansas as Dorothy tore it apart. I could see Lulu, back at the Woodman's palace, holding Ozma's hand as they walked through the ruined gardens. Melindra, digging a grave for Annabel as tears rolled down her face. I could see my mom, holding Jake's hand and crying. I could see Mombi, Gert, and Glamora, fighting desperately outside the Emerald Palace. Mombi was badly wounded, and Gert was pale with exhaustion. I knew instinctively that they couldn't hold out for much longer. I could see the end of everything I cared about, everyone I loved.

And I could see Dorothy, connected to the clock with a thick line of magic that fed her more and more power, like a leech bloated on the blood of its unsuspecting victim. She was pulling all the magic out of Oz and into her own body. But it was too much for her. She hung suspended in the current, her skin beginning to smoke and blacken, her eyes wide in pain and fear, the red heels pulsing with awful red light. Her mouth opened in a silent scream, magic pouring out in a torrent of sparks. Any second now the power of Oz would tear her—and us—apart.

You know what to do. This time it was Lurline's voice instead of the Nome King's that I heard inside my head. And I did—I did know what to do.

Nox and I reached forward, moving as though our two bodies were combined into one. I felt Lurline's magic surging through us, giving us strength. We took hold of the cord binding Dorothy to the Great Clock and I staggered backward as the full force of Oz's magic lashed out at me. It was like trying to hold on to a lightning bolt. The diamonds on my boots glowed white-hot, anchoring me to the stone floor.

NOW, Lurline shouted, her voice echoing through my head and ringing out across the cavern. With all the strength we had, Nox and I yanked backward. The cord of magic snapped loose from Dorothy's body, whipping around the cave. The clock pulsed with emerald-green light. And then, as if it could no longer contain its own power, it exploded into a shower of glittering fragments.

The shock wave rocked the cavern and sent Nox and me crashing to the floor. The window to Kansas shut with the sound of a thousand doors slamming. Dorothy fell to the ground with a sick thud and lay there unmoving.

"Now!" Nox gasped, doubled over in pain. "Do it now!" Without thinking, I reached for my knife and immediately felt its reassuring solidity in my hand. I sprinted past the pool to where Dorothy had fallen. Her body looked as though she'd been burned alive. Her flesh was charred and smoking. Her hair had been seared away on one side of her head and her eye had melted in its socket, running down the bubbling, raw meat of her cheek. I almost gagged.

And then she stirred. Incredibly, horribly, she was still alive. She groaned, her fingers twitching.

It was time for Dorothy to die. I raised the knife over my head.

THIRTY-FOUR

Take care that you do not walk down the same road that she has chosen. Lurline's words flashed across my vision like a subtitle from a foreign movie. Suddenly, I remembered my first friend in Oz—Indigo, the goth Munchkin who the Tin Woodman had tortured to death in front of me. That had been my introduction to Oz: loss and murder. And I'd taken those lessons to heart. I'd learned to kill without remorse to protect myself and the people I loved.

But where had it gotten me? What had it done for me? I remembered what it had felt like to kill the Lion, to find myself covered in his blood. The way the monkeys looked at me in fear. Glinda's dead-eyed girl soldiers. All the life I'd taken wasn't saving Oz, or even myself. Killing the vulnerable was Dorothy's way.

But it didn't have to be mine. I was done with murder. I wouldn't turn into Dorothy. I wouldn't let the power of Oz make me into a monster. I was stronger than that.

I threw my knife to the cavern floor and it vanished in a puff of oily smoke.

"Amy?" Nox said, coming up behind me. He was looking at Dorothy in horror.

"She used to be just like me," I said, walking away from her. Nox followed me to the other side of the cavern. I thought of her aunt Em and uncle Henry. Dead now, like so many other people. "Someone's niece, someone's friend. She was just a farm girl from Kansas before Glinda got hold of her." I looked him in the eye. "I don't want to become her, Nox. I can't kill her."

Saying it out loud almost took my breath away, but suddenly, I felt a huge, incredible sense of relief. I'd admitted it. I didn't want to kill her. I didn't want to kill *anyone* anymore. I was done. Nox's eyes widened, and then his face softened and he reached forward and took my hand.

"Look at her," he said quietly. "You *don't* have to kill her. Oz's magic took care of it for you. She's defenseless and she can't hurt anyone anymore. It's over."

We'd done it. We'd defeated her. I sank to the ground in exhaustion. And then with a deep, terrible groan, the walls of the cavern began to ripple and crack.

Nox reacted instantly. "The palace is coming down!" he shouted, pulling me to my feet. I looked at Dorothy's motionless, rag doll body. Now that I'd decided not to actually kill her, I didn't know what to do with her.

"What about her? We can't just leave her here!" I cried.

A section of the roof collapsed with a roar directly in front of us, sending a shower of dust billowing in our faces. Coughing and choking, I looked across the cavern to where Dorothy had fallen—but the floor was covered with towering piles of broken rock.

"We can't save her!" Nox said, grabbing my arm. "She can't have survived that, there's nothing we can do."

I let Nox pull me out of the room just as a giant piece of ceiling fell right where we'd been standing. In the hallway, I stumbled, almost bringing both of us to the ground.

"You have to keep going!" Nox urged, dragging me along. "We stop, we die."

"I can't," I gasped, tripping again.

"You have to," Nox said grimly, refusing to let me go. The walls were crumbling around us as we ran down corridor after corridor. Beams crashed to the floor. The Emerald Palace was even bigger than I remembered. But Nox wouldn't let me stop. He wasn't going to leave me behind, no matter what—and I wasn't going to be responsible for his death, too.

Finally, we turned one last corner and I saw daylight. We'd come out into the front hallway of the palace, where big windows let in a view of the crazy sky. It was like all of Oz had gone insane.

A huge storm was raging, like nothing I'd ever seen before. Bolts of red lightning struck the earth with earsplitting cracks. Thunder boomed and orange sparks rained down from the violent yellow-green sky. With one last, desperate push, Nox and I ran for the front door and tumbled out to safety as the ceiling of the main hall fell in with a crash of stone and timber. But Nox didn't stop.

"Keep going!" he yelled. "The whole thing is coming down! We have to get clear!"

The ground itself was heaving under our feet. Nox still refused to let go of me. I struggled after him, trying to keep my footing, and then made the mistake of looking back.

Towers were swaying back and forth, listing drunkenly as the Emerald Palace collapsed in on itself. Widening cracks radiated outward as the earth around it split apart. All around us Dorothy's overgrown gardens were wilting and turning gray before dissolving into dust. As I watched in terror, the cracks ran together into a single chasm, impossibly deep. "Nox!" I screamed.

"I see it!" With one final effort, Nox pulled me to safety as the Emerald Palace crumbled into the gaping abyss. The rift shuddered and then sealed itself. The rain of fire dissipated and the lightning stopped. A gentle breeze sprang up, pushing the gray-green clouds across the sky and scrubbing it clear. With a last, almost sheepish clap of thunder, the storm vanished, leaving behind a clear blue sky and a cheerful yellow sun. Behind us, a bird chirped tentatively and then burst into full-fledged song. My knees buckled and finally, mercifully, I collapsed. Nox fell beside me in the grass, still holding my hand.

Groaning, he propped himself up on one elbow and looked down at me. His dark hair was thick with dust, his face smeared with a mask of blood and dirt. His clothes were filthy. He'd never seemed so beautiful. "You know what?" he said. "Never mind the Order. I'm falling in love with you, too." He leaned in to kiss me.

And that, of course, was when Lulu showed up.

"Well, this is a hell of a bunch of bananas," groused the monkey's all-too-familiar voice. "I always said the Emerald Palace could use a good redecorating, but nobody was suggesting razing it to the ground."

Nox groaned aloud and flopped over on his back. "Hi, Lulu," I said tiredly, sitting up.

"And what have you done to yourself? You look like a monkey's hind end," she continued, looming over me. Ozma was standing behind her, gnawing meditatively on her thumb. Lulu was decked to the nines in true Lulu form, sporting her cat's-eye rhinestone glasses, a sequined motorcycle jacket, and a leather miniskirt decorated with appliqués of tropical fruits.

"What are you doing here, Lulu?" I asked.

"Helping, obviously. And let me tell you, you need it. I was just twiddling my thumbs in the Woodman's palace, playing checkers with Ozma and watching Melindra mope around. Nothing restores the spirits like a little action, I tell you what. Grabbed some of my monkeys and flew us all over here while you were sitting around on your heinies, apparently. Or did you actually do anything besides demolish the heart of Oz?"

"Nothing much," Nox said, still prone on the grass. "Just defeated Dorothy, restored order to Oz, and survived the collapse of the Emerald Palace. How does the city look?"

"Terrible, what do you think?" Lulu snapped. "It's been in ruins for weeks. There are bodies everywhere." And then she stopped short. "Did you say you defeated Dorothy?"

"The one and only," I confirmed.

"The bitch is *dead*?" Lulu's jaw was literally hanging open. "Oz is free? You did it? You really did it? You killed her?" She hopped up and down excitedly. "Why, we're going to have a party to end all parties! The ball of the century! A banquet for the ages!"

"Party," Ozma agreed happily. "Monkey party!"

"I didn't kill her," I said. "But she can't possibly have survived the collapse of the palace."

Lulu stopped short. "What do you mean, you didn't kill her? Did you defeat her or not?"

"I defeated her," I said. "*We* defeated her. She tried to unleash the magic of the Great Clock but it almost destroyed her. There was no point in killing her. She's buried now under the entire Emerald Palace."

"Are furless freaks all as stupid as you look? You didn't make sure she was kaput? Do you know how many of my monkeys are dead because of that little princess? Do you have any idea how much suffering she's caused? You had a chance to rid Oz of evil for good and you just *left* her there?"

"Lulu, the palace came down on top of her."

Lulu shook her head. "You think that's gonna stop a bitch like her? That was probably our only chance, and you blew it." She snorted in disgust. "Trust a human to screw up the most important job in the kingdom. You should have let the monkeys handle it. I know how to finish what I start, even if you don't."

"Lulu, there's no way—" I began, but Lulu's face shut down. There was no arguing with her. She was too angry, and I couldn't really blame her. But I knew I'd done the right thing.

"Worthless," Lulu muttered, turning away in disgust. I stood up, about to go after her, but stopped in shock at the landscape in front of me. Where the Emerald Palace had stood, an angry slash like a scar cut across the earth. Around it, everything was wasteland. The gardens were gone. Rubble was strewn across what had been the palace grounds. And as for the palace itself, there was nothing left. It was as if it had never been there at all.

Gert, Glamora, and Mombi were walking toward us, looking seriously the worse for wear. Like me and Nox, they were filthy and bloodied, but their faces were bright with triumph. "Gert!" I exclaimed happily, and she folded me up in an enormous hug.

"My dear," she said. "I was worried I'd never see you again. But you've done it. You've killed her."

"I didn't kill her," I said, and explained all over again what had happened. Mombi raised an eyebrow. Gert was silent. And Glamora just looked at us with a strange, unreadable expression on her face.

"She's defeated," I said. I was starting to feel like a broken record. Why did no one think I'd done the right thing? Was Nox doubting me, too?

"For now, at least," Mombi said.

"She has to be dead," I protested.

"Not if you didn't kill her, she doesn't," Mombi said. But then she relented. "You're right, though. She's not going anywhere for now, at least."

"We guessed you'd won because the tin soldiers stopped working all at once," Glamora added. "Dorothy's power was the only thing animating them."

"And a good thing, too," Mombi added. "Our geese were just about cooked. Another minute of fighting, and we'd have been done. Even *we* aren't strong enough to hold off a clockwork army forever."

"Same thing in the city," Lulu said. "All the buildings are leveled. Your work?"

"I'm guessing Dorothy's," Nox said. "Or, more accurately, the power from the Great Clock. She set it loose without being able to control it."

"And I destroyed it," I said.

But Nox shook his head. "The Great Clock is at the heart of Oz. It can't be destroyed any more than Lurline's pool can. It'll turn up again."

"Lurline!" Lulu scoffed. "That's just a kiddie story. Nobody believes in that claptrap anymore." Ozma looked startled, and I wondered if she'd understood that Lulu had just dismissed the existence of her ancestor.

"Hardly," I said. "I met her. In fact, she gave me something." I pulled the amulet she'd given me out of my pocket. Glamora's eyes lit up and she reached for it. Something about her look was so greedy that I snatched my hand away instinctively. "It's not mine. She said I'd know when the time was right to give it to someone," I said defensively, and then my gaze fell on Ozma.

She was looking at the amulet with her head cocked to one side, like a cat waiting outside a mouse hole. "Pool," she said distinctly. The smoke-filled stone began to glow. *Of course,* I thought. Lurline's gift wasn't for me. It was for her great-great-great-granddaughter. Without a word, I handed the amulet to Ozma. She looped the chain over her head and the amulet settled on her chest.

"We should wait—" Glamora began, but it was too late. The amulet flashed once, and a glow in Ozma's green eyes matched its brilliant light. Her long dark hair whipped around her as if stirred by an invisible breeze, and her big gold-edged wings unfurled from her back, crackling with magic. She stretched her arms out as if she'd just come to the end of the world's most excellent yoga class and gave a huge sigh of satisfaction. When the light faded from her eyes, they were clear.

"Oh my," she said with a sigh of relief. "That's *much* better."

"Princess," Lulu breathed. "You've returned." She sank to one knee in a sweeping, courtly bow. After a second, Mombi knelt, too. Then Gert, and then Nox, who elbowed me in the ribs. I yelped and then took the hint, curtsying before Ozma, who nodded regally. Only Glamora didn't bow. Ozma looked her dead in the eye, and finally, she knelt, never taking her eyes off the princess.

"You do not think I am myself," Ozma said, bemused.

Glamora looked away at last, unable to meet her gaze any longer. "I don't think we should be hasty," she said, almost sullenly, like a teenager scolded for not cleaning her room.

"Of course it's her," Lulu barked, jumping to feet and brandishing a little pistol she seemed to have pulled out of nowhere. "Why, you—"

Ozma laughed merrily. "My dear champion! Lulu, what would we do without you? I don't blame Glamora for doubting me." Her expression grew sober. "I've been gone for a long time. But I promise you, Glamora, it's me. And with Dorothy gone, I can at last regain my rightful place as the ruler of Oz."

Lulu cheered, dancing around the princess in what looked suspiciously like an actual jig. I stifled a laugh. Even Nox cracked a grin. He stood up and helped me to my feet. Gert and Mombi soon followed. But Glamora remained on her knees.

"Forgive me, Princess, for being suspicious," she murmured, her eyes downcast. "As you said, it's been a long time."

"There is nothing to forgive." Ozma sighed and looked out over the ruins of what had once been the Emerald City. "I hope too much has not been lost for the glory of Oz to be restored," she said sadly.

Mombi cleared her throat. "Come now, Princess, that's no way to talk," she said gruffly. To my astonishment, I saw that her eyes were filling with tears. "Oh, never mind this old bag," she grumbled, embarrassed, as she dashed them away with the heel of her hand. "I never thought this day would come."

But I remembered what Lurline had told me. "We're not done yet," I said. "We still have to deal with the Nome King."

"If we've defeated Dorothy, he'll be planning his next move. We're safe for the time being," Glamora said.

"But he's with my mom. I have to get back to Kansas somehow. I think I can use the shoes to—"

"You're not going anywhere with those shoes," Mombi said sharply. "They belong to Oz. Their magic stays here."

"But—"

"We all make sacrifices, Amy," Glamora said silkily. Mombi was nodding in agreement.

Nox stepped forward, taking my hand. "Listen to them, Amy," he said. "They know what's best." Had he lost his mind? I opened my mouth to protest. He winked at me, too quickly for the other witches to catch, and I understood. There was no point in fighting all three of them now. He was right. We could figure out a better plan later. And the fact that he was on my side made everything suddenly seem more bearable.

"A coronation!" Gert exclaimed, straightening up, as if we hadn't just been arguing about the fate of Oz. "That's just what we need. Bring the country back together, give people something to look forward to. Oz loves a new monarch. Even if she's a monarch we've already had."

Ozma laughed. "I've already *had* a coronation, Gert," she said, but Gert waved a hand dismissively.

"That was ages ago," she said. "Besides, we had that whole unfortunate interlude with Dorothy the Usurper. We want to reassure the whole country that the right person is back in charge for good. A coronation is what the people will want."

"We don't even have a *palace*," Mombi pointed out.

"We'll host it in the land of monkeys," Lulu said excitedly. "Boy, do monkeys know how to throw a party. Why, the last time we—"

"No, no," Ozma interrupted. "Of course I appreciate your offer, dear Lulu, but the coronations of Oz have always been in the Emerald Palace. If there's no palace, we'll have to build something. The heart of Oz is here and always has been, even if the palace is no longer standing."

I was pretty close to no longer standing myself. I didn't realize I'd said it out loud until Nox shot me a funny look. Ozma laughed again and clapped her hands.

"What am I thinking?" she exclaimed. "First, my brave Wicked must rest. You've been through so much. We can hardly plan a party if you're all starving and exhausted."

As soon as she said it, I realized I *was* starving. I might have even been more hungry than tired.. Without waiting for another word, Ozma brought her hands together, and they began to glow with power. There was something almost alien about her magic; the light she created shimmered with an oily, rainbow sheen, like gasoline leaking across water. It arced upward, drawing the outline of a structure that slowly took shape under her direction. In just a few minutes, Ozma created a big, silk-walled pavilion stretched over a delicate golden frame with wrought filigree at every joint. Gems winked here and there in the framework, and a beautiful flag fluttered from a pole that sprang from the pavilion's highest point.

Inside, a long table was laid with more kinds of food than I'd ever seen in one place in my life—even at one of Dorothy's banquets. An entire roast pig with an apple in its mouth. Platters of fruits, most of which I didn't recognize, and some of which were talking to each other. Baskets of steaming rolls. Tureens of soup, under which tiny fires burned, stoked by tiny figures who carried tiny logs. An enormous platter of desserts: rainbow-frosted cupcakes dusted with glitter that made me think sadly of Polychrome. A miniature Emerald City, rendered in chocolate, studded with emeralds made out of sugar. A cake in the shape of a dragon that breathed fire. Ozma's post-maybe-defeating-Dorothy banquet was enough food to feed an army.

Which turned out to be a good thing, since Lulu put two fingers between her lips and emitted a piercing whistle. Monkeys bounded up out of nowhere. Lulu had brought her army—or at least, all its surviving members. Ozma giggled as the monkeys flung themselves at the amazing spread with glee. Even Nox and Mombi were laughing.

"Oh dear," she said, waving her hand, and bunches of bananas popped up at one end of the table. "You'd better eat something fast. They're not going to leave leftovers."

I didn't need to be told twice. Nox and I waded in among the gleeful monkeys, who were devouring the feast like an army of locusts. I found a plate and began to fill it. I didn't even look to see what I was grabbing. At that point, I would have eaten pretty much anything.

Nox and I took our plates to one corner of the pavilion, where a little table and two comfy chairs appeared with a pop just as we were looking for somewhere to sit.

"Ozma's hospitality sure beats Dorothy's," I said, sinking gratefully into one of the chairs. A napkin materialized out of thin air and tucked itself discreetly into my collar.

"She doesn't think much of your table manners, apparently," Nox said with a smirk. I was too tired to do anything about it.

"I don't blame her," I said. "The way I feel right now, I'll be lucky if I can get half this stuff into my mouth."

Nox had already dug in, and I followed suit. Everything was delicious. Some things tasted how they looked, and others changed into something else in my mouth. The flavors were all different, but subtly harmonized. It was like eating a symphony.

Ozma hadn't touched the food, and I wondered if fairies had some weird eating disorder or if they just didn't need to eat. I couldn't remember if I'd ever had a meal with her when she was the spaced-out version of herself. After the feast, Ozma snapped her fingers. Table and dishes vanished, and the pavilion began to reconfigure itself into a long hall with dozens of silk-walled rooms flanking it.

"And now, my dear soldiers, it's time to rest," she said gently. "Tomorrow we work, but tonight we sleep."

When Ozma had walked away, I leaned in closer to Nox. "We have to figure out a way for me to get back to Kansas and stop the Nome King," I said in a low voice. He shook his head at me.

"Not here," he whispered. "It's not safe to talk anywhere near them." I nodded to show I understood. "Anyway, you need rest," he said in a normal tone of voice. "We all do." He took my hand and I rested my forehead on his shoulder. From across the tent, Mombi cleared her throat, and I jerked backward. Nox dropped my hand like it was a hot coal.

"They're watching us," he said so quietly I almost missed it. I sighed. Nothing was ever simple in Oz.

"Good night," I said loudly as I stood up and walked away

from him. More than anything, I wanted him to be able to follow me. To let my guard down, just for a night. To fall asleep in someone's arms. But I pushed those thoughts out of my head. I couldn't let the witches suspect that I was going to try to get back to Kansas on my own—or that Nox and I had feelings for each other that went directly against the Quadrant's demands. I was pretty sure Gert couldn't read my thoughts unless I was next to her, but there was no sense in trumpeting my feelings. And Nox was right. More than anything else right now, I needed to sleep.

Pushing aside the curtains and entering one of the little rooms, I saw that it contained a soft, thick mattress piled with pillows and blankets. The magic boots glittered on my feet, but I didn't have any choice but to sleep in them. Besides, I was so tired it didn't matter. I didn't lie down so much as face-plant directly onto the bed. And I'm pretty sure I was fast asleep before my cheek even hit the pillow. Thankfully, I didn't dream.

THIRTY-SIX

Late-morning light filtered through the silken tent walls. I stretched and yelped aloud as every battered muscle in my body twinged in protest. My feet were sore and swollen. Despite how deeply I'd slept, I was still exhausted. I could feel the shoes tugging at me, like a house cat butting its head against my palm demanding to be petted.

Nox stuck his head through the curtain that closed off my room. "Hey," he said softly. "The Quadrant wants to see you." He crossed the room and sat next to me on the bed. He'd cleaned himself up that morning and I caught a whiff of the rich, sandalwood scent of his skin. Suddenly, I was acutely conscious of my messy hair and unbrushed teeth. But Nox was looking at me like—well, like I was beautiful. I blushed furiously.

"Hi," I said stupidly.

"Hi." He smiled.

"Are you ready? I'll take you to them." I stared up at him,

as dopey as a new puppy. Not letting Gert know how badly I wanted to jump Nox's bones was definitely going to be a serious challenge.

"I—can you—I don't want to risk using the shoes—" Flushing, I pointed to my greasy hair and unwashed face. A look of comprehension dawned on Nox's face. He touched my cheek, and my hair untangled itself into a sleek curtain. The wrinkles fell away from the clothes I'd slept in, the bloodstains vanished, and the tears mended themselves. A minty-fresh taste filled my mouth.

"Thanks," I said. I followed Nox to where the rest of the Quadrant was waiting in a clearing near Ozma's tent palace.

"We have to talk about the shoes," Gert said without preamble. "As long as they're on your feet, you're in danger."

"We're *all* in danger," Glamora added.

"Their magic belongs with Oz," Mombi added.

Gert nodded, her warm face creased with worry. "You haven't had them that long. The shoes are too powerful for you to remove them yourself, but we should be able to help you take them off."

I didn't like the sound of that "should." And there was something about their faces that sent a sliver of unease through me. I trusted them—more or less—but that didn't mean they weren't working from their own agenda. I'd always known there were limits to how much they told me. Gert, I knew, could hear my doubts, and so I tried to think about something else. Flowers. Kittens. Mochas.

"Lurline told me the shoes would serve me well if I trusted

in their power," I said. "Without them, I don't think I can use magic at all."

"Amy, we can't trust anything that came to you from the Nome King," Glamora said. "The risk is too huge."

"Maybe Amy's right," Nox said. I knew he'd had no idea what the witches wanted, or he'd have warned me back in the tent.

"You're not disagreeing with a Quadrant decision, are you?" Glamora snapped.

For a second, none of us spoke. The air was full of tension. I wanted to fight them, but even with the boots I doubted I'd be strong enough. Maybe I could steal the boots back again. Maybe I could find some other way to get home. I didn't like it, but I couldn't stop them if they wanted to overpower me—and I had no doubt they'd do it.

"Will it hurt?" I asked. "When you take them off, I mean."

"It might," Mombi said. Glamora shot her a look. "What?" the old witch grumbled. "She should know what she's getting into." Unexpectedly, she looked at me with sympathy. "We know you've been through a lot, Amy. I'm sorry to ask one more thing of you. We wouldn't do it if we didn't think the shoes could end up hurting you."

"Ready for us to try?" Gert asked. I nodded. Nox gave me an anxious look, but he joined hands with the rest of the Quadrant.

The witches closed their eyes and began to chant softly. At first, nothing changed. And then my feet started to feel warm. The boots' glow intensified into a radiant white light that hurt my eyes. The heat got more and more excruciating, and

I squeezed my eyes shut, willing myself not to cry. I could feel myself floating into the air and hovering a few inches above the ground.

The chanting grew louder and then stopped. The witches' magic surrounded me, probing at my feet and legs like dozens of strong arms poking and prodding me. When Mombi had said this might hurt, she wasn't kidding. I'd had to go to the dentist when I was a kid to get three cavities filled at once, and I had the same powerless feeling. Knowing that what was happening was supposed to be good for me didn't make it feel any better. Anger flooded through me. I couldn't help it. I was *tired*. Tired of fighting, tired of hurting, tired of all this pain and death and doing the right thing for the wrong people. I wanted to be left alone. I wanted to go the hell back to bed. I could feel the tidal wave of fury rising up in me, the same anger that had turned me into a literal monster once before. My feet were on fire.

"I want it to stop!" I yelled, and a wave of power burst out of me like water crashing through a dam. Mombi, Gert, Glamora, and Nox were thrown backward across the clearing. My fingernails lengthened into claws, my arms rippled with muscle. "Leave me ALONE!" I roared through a mouthful of jagged teeth. And then I felt a gentle, cooling surge of magic from the boots. Reminding me of who I was. Not a monster. Not under Oz's control. Just Amy Gumm, a girl trying to save her family. The monster's talons retracted back into my fingers. I pushed myself upright from where I'd crouched on all fours as the witches picked themselves up and brushed themselves off. Nox looked stunned. Glamora looked thoughtful.

"Well, then," she said. "I guess we'll have to find a different way to free you from the shoes."

Mombi was looking at me with an unmistakable expression of worry. I knew they thought I was dangerous. I didn't blame them. But they wouldn't do anything to hurt me. Not yet anyway. I wished I could talk to Nox, but there was no safe way to do it.

"Fine," I said. Let them think I'd given in. Let them think I was willing to give up the shoes as soon as they found a way to get them off my feet. I'd figure something out. I always did. "I'm going back to bed." I didn't look back at the witches when I left.

The next few days were a bustle of activity. When Ozma had insisted the coronation be held on the site of the Emerald Palace, I'd been pretty dubious. Why not start over somewhere that wasn't a former battleground? The scarred wasteland looked worse than post-tornado Dusty Acres, and the city itself was in even more terrible shape. But the land had significance for her. And for Oz. And Ozma, with the help of the Wicked, went immediately into full cleanup mode. First, she deputized a handful of Lulu's monkeys as messengers and sent them out to all the corners of Oz with the news that Dorothy had been defeated and the coronation was coming. Joyful citizens of Oz came pouring into the city, eager to help rebuild. At all hours of the day and night the streets were full of Munchkins, Winkies, Pixies, and talking animals industriously carting wheelbarrows of debris back and forth, carefully repaving the streets with salvaged gemstones, and repairing the buildings that were still standing. Ozma and the Wicked—Nox included—devoted their energy to constructing an elaborate tent city where the palace had stood and carefully coaxing the ruined gardens back to life. The monkeys busied themselves in the remaining trees, hanging streamers and lights and an elaborate network of bridges and platforms, with Lulu barking orders from the ground like a drill sergeant.

I helped where I could, but I couldn't shake the feeling that something was wrong. It had all happened so suddenly that Dorothy's defeat hadn't really sunk in, but everyone else in Oz seemed to think it was totally normal that a tyrant had been defeated, the old queen had been reinstated, and the Emerald Palace had been completely destroyed.

The morning of the coronation was as sunny and clear as every other day had been since Dorothy's defeat. Ozma herself was directing the final touches: a small army of Munchkins was busy cooking an enormous feast. Pixies fluttered about from tree to tree, hanging streamers and long strands of glass balls that must have been some kind of decoration. Mombi, Gert, Glamora, and Nox were busy putting the last details on the newly planted, magic-enhanced gardens. They were still a far cry from the splendor that had once surrounded the Emerald Palace, but they were a lot better than the wasteland they replaced.

Dorothy's surviving ex-soldiers had shown up for the party, too. At first I was startled to see the mangled, mechanized figures as they wheeled and creaked around, and the other Ozians gave them a wide berth, too. But they made themselves indispensable, helping with heavy lifting and the most unglamorous tasks, like doing dishes and cleaning up. They, at least, had been through even worse than me. I remembered the Scarecrow's laboratory, and shuddered.

Finally, it was time to get ready. Ozma had set up a bathing tent that was as luxurious as a fancy spa. Big, claw-foot bathtubs were curtained off with walls of pale, billowing silk. As soon as I entered one of the rooms, invisible hands turned on the taps, and the tub filled with steaming, scented water as a pile of thick towels materialized next to me. I'd no sooner taken off my clothes and climbed into the tub than the same invisible presence began to briskly lather my scalp with a floral shampoo. "No thanks," I told it. "I think I'd rather do it myself." I thought I heard a sulky little sigh, but the hands withdrew, and I knew I was alone.

I stayed in the bathtub for a long time, magic boots and all (turns out they were waterproof), dreading the night ahead. I'd never been much for parties, and big banquets still reminded me of those awful days when I'd pretended to be one of Dorothy's maids. I remembered what she'd done to Jellia, and a chill ran through me despite the hot bathwater. I was going to have to get a grip if I wanted to make it through the night, but I couldn't let go of all the pain and suffering I'd seen. Maybe people in Oz were more used to it and that was why they could get over it so quickly, but before I'd come here Madison Pendleton had been about the worst thing I'd experienced. Well, that and my mom's addiction. I splashed my face angrily with hot water and stood up, sloshing bathwater over the sides of the tub. A towel floated into the air and wrapped itself around me. "Oh, fine," I sighed, stepping out of the tub. If it was possible for an invisible handmaid to towel me off smugly, mine did.

While I'd dozed in the tub, a rich, embroidered dress had been laid out on a chair next to the rack of towels. I looked at it in dismay. I'd feel like an idiot in a ball gown, even at Ozma's coronation. I hadn't worn a dress in months. "Maybe something else, please?" I said politely to the air. There was a frosty silence, and then the elaborately beaded and sewn dress disappeared and was replaced with a maid's uniform. I laughed. "No, come on," I said aloud. The maid's uniform vanished, and finally a plain but pretty dress appeared. I picked it up. It was made of a soft, gray material that felt like clouds, and it was simply cut and unembellished. "That's perfect," I said. "Thank you." I heard a little sniff of disapproval, and hid a smile.

Outside, twilight had fallen. I gasped when I saw the open space at the heart of the tent city where Ozma would be crowned. The glass globes the Pixies had hung were filled with tiny, glowing insects that cast a beautiful amber light over the new gardens. Tendrilly vines, heavy with sweet-smelling white flowers, reached up into the warm air and climbed around a canopy the monkeys had erected, creating a high, broad pavilion of blossoms. The citizens of Oz were already beginning to assemble in respectful rows, looking solemn and happy. Lulu's ball gown was so heavy with rhinestones I saw her as a dazzling blur from a hundred yards away. The rest of the monkeys all wore neatly cut suits—surprisingly dignified, I thought. Even Dorothy's former soldiers had done their best to dress up. Their metal parts were polished to a blinding glow that reflected the lamplight, and their furry bodies were brushed to a shine.

"You look beautiful, Amy." Nox was walking toward me. He looked amazing; he'd let Ozma's invisible handmaidens deck him out in a well-cut and closely fitted suit that looked equal parts James Bond and millionaire, like he was headed to a super-fancy dinner but wasn't too overdressed to take out a couple of villains if he had to—which, actually, was true. Instead of looking silly, the purple cloak on top made him look like a prince. His longish dark hair was slicked back, which only emphasized his high cheekbones. He'd even found dress shoes.

"Thanks," I mumbled, looking at my own diamond-studded boots. They were out of place in Oz, but they felt exactly right to me. Besides, with my cool gray granny dress the whole effect was kind of nineties. All I needed was a velvet choker.

And then I realized it: now was our chance. Finally, we were alone. But as soon as I opened my mouth, I saw Glamora swooping down on us, grinning like she'd PermaSmiled herself. "Nox! Amy! Are you ready?" she cooed.

From behind her came a voice I hadn't heard in what felt like years. "You clean up nice, Amy." Ollie! And his sister, Maude, was at his side. I swooped in and gave them both hugs. I hadn't seen them since Mombi had made me leave them behind in the Queendom of the Wingless Ones.

But there was no time now for catching up. The sound of

trumpets cut through the air, and Nox gave me a helpless look. I followed him and Glamora across the newly planted lawn.

Ozma stood at the far end of the canopy of flowers, dressed in a simple white silk shift that spilled in shimmering waves to her feet. Her long black hair was bound up with more of the huge, fragrant white blossoms. Her glorious gold-veined wings fluttered behind her. She looked tall, and beautiful, and radiant, and wise. She looked every inch a queen. Tiny Pixies buzzed through the air, carrying more of the luminous glass globes. A line of monkeys holding sunfruit lamps was arranged on either side of a long, richly decorated carpet that unrolled to Ozma's feet. At its opposite end, Lulu stood in her amazingly jewel-encrusted dress, holding a delicate golden crown with the word *OZ* spelled out in a curlicued font. I found a place next to Nox at the back of the audience. The trumpets sounded their final notes, and the crowd fell into an expectant hush.

"My dear, brave citizens of Oz," Ozma began, her clear voice carrying without effort. "Long have you waited for this moment, and much have you suffered." It was still a shock to hear her speak like this—to see infinite wisdom flickering in her deep green eyes. "I am so happy to return to you, and to promise you that Oz is ours again—a free kingdom, with liberty and justice for all its subjects."

A spontaneous cheer rose up from the happy crowd at her words, and the full impact of what I was witnessing hit me. For now, anyway, Oz was *free*. Dorothy was gone. We'd done it. All that fighting, all that loss and sacrifice—I'd never actually thought we would *win*. Without thinking, I reached for Nox's hand. He looked at me, surprised, and then squeezed mine back. I put my head on his shoulder. He was just the right height for us to fit perfectly together. After a minute, he put his arm around me, and I relaxed into the warmth of his body, closing my eyes as Ozma's words washed over us.

"As many of you know," she continued, "we owe much of this victory to a very special warrior who has risked much to help us, though when she began this fight she was not even one of us. She believed in the freedom of Oz, even though it was not her world. She has shown extraordinary courage in the face of great danger, and she was the one who set me free from the prison of my own mind." Nox elbowed me in the ribs and my eyes flew open. Everyone in the tent was looking at me.

"Amy Gumm," Ozma said in that beautiful, rich voice. "We owe you our lives and our freedom. We will never be able to repay our debt to you, but you will always have a home among us." And then, to my total astonishment, she moved through the crowd until she was standing right before me, and went down on her knee. After a second, everyone else knelt, too. To me. Like I was a queen. To my absolute horror, Nox knelt, too. I had no idea what to do or say. I wasn't a ruler. I was just a teenager from a trailer park in Kansas.

"I can't—" I stammered frantically. "I mean I didn't—I didn't do anything special. Anyone in my place would have done what I did."

Ozma remained kneeling for what felt like a million years but was probably just a few seconds, and then she stood with that same effortless grace and held out her hands to me. "Stand beside me, dear Amy," she said. "It would be an honor to be crowned at your side. I owe this—all of this—to you." The crowd around me, also rising to its feet, parted wordlessly. I stood frozen to the ground in terror until Nox gave me a gentle shove.

"Dorothy was way scarier than this," he whispered. "You're fine."

"Easy for you to say," I muttered under my breath, but I stepped forward. I was glad I'd gone with the dress after all, now that what seemed like every eye in Oz was on me. My heart was pounding so hard I almost laughed at myself. Nox was right; I'd faced down Dorothy, but couldn't handle an appreciative audience?

Ozma beamed at me as I joined her at her side. She took my hand in one of hers, and gestured to Lulu with the other. The little monkey should have looked ridiculous in her bedazzled dress, which was over the top even for her. But instead she looked perfect. Sort of like a really dignified chandelier, but in a good way. She was weeping openly as she slowly carried the crown toward us.

When she reached us, Ozma curtsied deeply, dipping her head low enough for Lulu to set the crown on her dark hair. Everyone around us breathed out a sigh of combined relief and awe.

"At last, our queen is returned to us," Lulu proclaimed, holding Ozma's hand aloft as they turned to face the crowd. There was a brief second of complete stillness, and then the pavilion erupted. Everyone was hugging and shrieking and clapping and cheering. Munchkins jumped up and down, waving their arms. Winkies high-fived each other. Even Gert and Mombi were hugging and dancing around like little kids. Nox ran up to me, picked me up off my feet, and twirled me around while I giggled with delight. Lulu had her arms wrapped around Ozma's midsection and was sobbing noisily. Only Ozma remained calm and collected, smiling down at Lulu and at all the other citizens of Oz who tried to touch her dress or embrace her.

Finally, the mayhem died down enough for Ozma to call out, "And now we feast!" Another enormous cheer erupted from the crowd, and everyone surged toward the banquet.

THIRTY-SEVEN

Nox and I were swept up in the tide of people and carried along with them to where long tables had been set up. Sunfruit hung in the air, casting a warm, gentle light over the piles and piles of food.

Nobody had to be told twice to eat, including me. Ozma had decided on an informal party, given the circumstances—no servants, no seats, just banquet tables piled high with food and heaps of cushions and bright woven carpets scattered around the floors of the tent city. Most people elected to take their food outside, finding spots in the grass or under the trees. But I noticed as I filled my plate that people were getting out of my way, or even bowing to me. It was a strange feeling, one I didn't really like. I tried to make myself as unobtrusive as possible as I carried my plate outside and found a place far from the crowd.

That was when Nox found me. At last, we'd gotten away from the rest of the Quadrant. For how long, I didn't know.

"You don't have to tell me," he said in a low voice. "I know. There's something wrong, but I can't figure out what it is."

I set my plate in the grass, my appetite gone. "I have to find a way to get back to Kansas," I said. "If the Nome King has my mom . . ."

"The Quadrant will try and stop you. And I don't know if I can stop them."

"Because you're bound to them?"

He nodded. "I can try to undo the spell that binds us together, but I might not be strong enough to do it on my own."

"I can help."

"Even with the shoes, Gert and Mombi are more powerful than you are. I don't know." He shook his head, his expression bleak. "I want to help you, but I don't know how to get away from them."

"Come with me," I said impulsively. "If we find a way back. Just come with me. We'll defeat the Nome King somehow. We'll prevent him from coming back to Oz. We can stay there together and forget about all this war."

"Come with you to the Other Place?" he asked, startled. "For good?"

I realized what I'd asked of him as soon as the words were out of my mouth. "You're right," I said. "I'm sorry. That's totally unfair. I can't ask that of you, any more than I can stay here."

"I didn't say no, Amy." His dark eyes searched mine. "What's left for me here?"

"Uh, everything? Your entire life?"

He shrugged. "My family is dead. My home is gone. But I can't leave Oz until I know it's truly safe. In a perfect world—"

"We don't live in a perfect world," I finished. If I left Oz now, Nox wasn't coming with me. And I wasn't sure, deep down, if that was a sacrifice I was willing to make.

He looked at me and I knew he saw everything I was feeling in my eyes. Without speaking he leaned in and kissed me. He slid his hands down the side of my waist as I ran my fingers through his thick, soft hair. I knew I'd be smelling sandalwood in my dreams for the rest of my life. Nox fumbled with the buttons on my dress, sliding it down one shoulder and kissing the curve of my neck. A shudder ran through me—like magic, but something completely new. I felt the lean, rippling muscles of his back through the soft fabric of his jacket.

"Nox," I whispered.

"Shhhh," he said, kissing the words away. "We've earned this. Just this once, forget—" Footsteps crunched across the gravel and we both sat bolt upright. I could hear the murmur of familiar voices. Nox grabbed my hand and tugged me upward—into the air. We floated into the branches of a gnarled old tree and hovered there, hidden by the foliage.

". . . think you're worrying too much," Mombi was saying. "Ozma defeated the Nome King once. She's strong enough to keep us safe now."

"In the past she might have been," Glamora argued. Her voice had a strange, harsh echo to it. "But the Nome King is stronger now than he's ever been. If he finds a way to control Amy, we're all in danger. He could easily turn her against us. And Glinda will have made Ozma more cautious. United, we're as powerful as she is. She won't trust us. The Quadrant is in danger."

"Amy's in love with the boy," Mombi said dismissively. "And the shoes protect her. Nox is tied to the Quadrant. He'll keep Amy under control." Despite the situation, I blushed furiously. Was it really *that* obvious?

"And you saw what happened when we tried to control him," Glamora snapped. Nox and I exchanged glances. What was she talking about?

"What exactly are you suggesting, Glamora?" Mombi's voice was cool and distant. "Treason?"

"Of course not," Glamora said. "Nothing done for the good of Oz is treason."

"The good of Oz, of course, being dependent on our control of it," Mombi said drily.

"Whatever you think of Ozma, we have to gain control of Amy," Glamora stated. "She's a danger to all of us."

"She won't use magic again," Mombi said.

"Can you guarantee that?" Glamora asked.

"I'd bet my life on it," Mombi said. For the briefest second, her eyes flicked upward. *She knows we're here*, I thought. So why wasn't she revealing us?

Glamora looked as though she was about to object, but she bit down on the words and smiled, yielding unexpectedly. "Very well, dear sister. I'm sure you know what's best. Shall we return to the celebration?"

"You go ahead," Mombi said. "I'm going to enjoy the peace and quiet a little longer." Glamora gave Mombi a searching look, but she nodded and turned back toward the clamor of Ozma's celebration.

Mombi waited until I could barely make out Glamora's slender figure. "All right," she said, looking up at us. "You can come down now."

THIRTY-EIGHT

Warily, Nox and I eyed Mombi. Whose side was she on? What about what we'd just overheard?

"You're going to tell me you think Glamora is Glinda," she said gruffly. My jaw dropped, but Nox nodded. Mombi sighed. "It's more complicated than that. She's still Glamora, but Glinda's a part of her now. I think they're still battling it out in there. Glamora is keeping Glinda in check for now, but who knows how long that will last."

"When did you guess?"

"Right after the battle. Gert should have known, too, but Glamora is using Gert's ability to read minds to cloud her thinking. The connection runs both ways if you're powerful enough. It wasn't safe to move openly against her. But now, with all this talk of controlling Amy . . ." Mombi shook her head. "She's going to do something soon and we have to be ready to stop her. Glamora might still triumph but Glinda is incredibly powerful.

And if she wins, she can use the Quadrant magic that binds us together to control us."

"Why didn't you *tell* me?" Nox asked.

Mombi shot him a sympathetic look. "Sorry, sonny, but it wasn't safe. And no offense, but Gert and I are stronger than you, Quadrant or no Quadrant." Mombi sighed. "The Nome King in the Other Place, Dorothy who knows where, Glinda trying to defeat Glamora and take control of the Quadrant . . . Not good, not good at all. And if the barriers between Oz and Ev are as malleable as the barriers between Oz and the Other Place, we're in trouble. The Nome King has a whole host of nasty creatures at his disposal." She shook her head. "Never a dull moment in Oz," she said.

"I have to go back to Kansas," I said urgently. "I have to help my mom against the Nome King."

"Not a chance," Mombi said dismissively. "Even if we knew how to send you back—which we don't—you wouldn't last for a second against the Nome King without magic. He's already shown that his power isn't limited in the Other Place. He'll crush you like a bug."

"But the shoes—"

"No buts. First things first: it's time we figure out how to stop Glinda and get Glamora back."

"Well, well," said a voice from the darkness. "We certainly do learn a lot when we eavesdrop, don't we?"

Glamora stepped out of the shadows. "It's not very nice of you to run around behind my back, dear sister," she said. I recognized Glinda's menacing, sickly sweet syrupiness in her voice. Mombi met her gaze steadily. She didn't look too surprised that Glamora had been spying on us.

"I didn't think you'd be stupid enough to try anything before now, but apparently I was wrong," Mombi said. "You know that even as strong as you are you can't defeat the rest of the Quadrant and Amy combined."

"Oh, I don't need to be," Glamora said with a smile. "I have help." The air beside her began to glow with an all-too-familiar silver light. A twisted metal wand appeared in Glamora's hand and she held it aloft. More silver light ran down its length like mercury, dripping to the ground and spreading outward into a flat pool of molten metal.

"Get back," Mombi said urgently. She didn't have to tell me twice. The pool's surface shimmered and grew transparent. I could see through it as if it were a window to another world—and it was. Below us was the main hallway of Dwight D. Eisenhower Senior High. I recognized the worn tiles and watery fluorescent lights immediately. A perfect square of less-faded linoleum marked where the diorama had once stood. The windows were boarded up where the Nome King's storm had broken the glass but the rubble had been cleared away. The hall was empty, but daylight filtered in through the few unbroken windows. Class must be in session. Nox grabbed my arm as if to restrain me and I realized I was leaning toward the pool as though I wanted to jump through it to the other side. "You can't, Amy," he said urgently. "It's not a portal."

"Not for you it isn't," Glamora said. "But for some of us it works quite nicely." She smiled and waved her wand. "It's time," she said. At first, I had no idea who she was talking to. And then Assistant Principal Strachan strode into view in the deserted hallway. And he wasn't alone. He had Madison by the shoulders. Dustin Jr. was held tightly in her arms. Dustin Sr. ran behind them. His mouth was open as if he was shouting something but I couldn't hear him.

"Get out of there!" I yelled, but it was obvious he couldn't hear me either. Whatever window Glinda had created, it only let us see into Kansas.

"Oh, it's no use," Glamora said. "They can't hear you. But *he* can. And if I were you, I wouldn't upset him. Just because he thinks he can put you to good use doesn't mean he won't punish you if you provoke his temper. Our friend is very old—and don't tell him I said so, but sometimes he's *awfully* grumpy."

Assistant Principal Strachan looked up, his eyes meeting mine through Glamora's window. And then he smiled. Silver smoke billowed up from his feet. His body began to ripple and his skin peeled away in long strips that dissolved into silvery ooze. Madison's mouth opened in a silent scream of terror as Assistant Principal Strachan dissolved, revealing the Nome King.

"Now it's time to finish the work the Wizard started," Glamora said. Her tone was almost cheerful but her eyes sparkled with an insane light. I wondered if the struggle between Glinda and Glamora had resulted in something that was a combination of the two. Something more than a little crazy.

"I thought the Wizard wanted to rule Oz," I said.

"Oh, his vision was limited, make no mistake," Glamora said. "But he had the right idea. After all, two worlds are better than one. In exchange for unlimited access to Oz's power, my new friend has offered to help me rule this world—and yours."

"You can't do that," Mombi growled. She was edging almost imperceptibly toward Glamora as if being closer to the deranged witch would somehow make it easier to stop her. At my side, Nox was tense, his eyes flicking back and forth between the two.

"I can do whatever I *want*, you old bat," Glamora snapped in a little girl's petulant tone. "I can smash Oz into *smithereens* if I feel like it. But for now, I'm just going to throw a little welcome party. I hate to overshadow Ozma's big day, but this can't wait." She dodged away from Mombi and pointed her wand at the silver pool. The Nome King reached upward, still keeping his grip on Madison. His body began to stretch and lengthen as he rose to meet Glamora's outstretched arm. It was like watching sand move through an hourglass in reverse. Madison's face was filled with absolute terror as the Nome King pulled her toward Glamora's window. I watched in horror as the baby slipped from her arms. Nox gasped and Mombi jerked forward as if she could somehow catch him. But we were too late. The baby tumbled toward the ground.

And then, incredibly, Dustin dove for the baby. In that second I understood exactly what it was that had made him Dwight D. Eisenhower Senior High's biggest football star. He moved with almost superhuman speed, reaching for Dustin Jr. as if he was going for the biggest touchdown of his life. He caught the baby seconds before he hit the ground. At the exact same moment, the Nome King burst out of Glamora's window, sending drops of molten silver flying. I screamed in pain as the hot liquid burned through my dress and seared my arms and legs. Next to me, Nox slapped at his smoking clothes. Glamora giggled in triumph. And Madison Pendleton, still in the Nome King's bony clutches, was screaming bloody murder.

"That's quite enough," the Nome King said curtly, letting go of her long enough to slap her. Madison shut up immediately. Her eyes were huge, darting around the clearing, and she gasped in shock when she saw me. She was shaking so hard I thought she would fall over.

"Now then," the Nome King said. "Miss Gumm, I believe you have something that belongs to me. I'd like it back."

THIRTY-NINE

I glanced involuntarily down at my boots. I knew exactly what he wanted and I had no intention of giving them to him.

"The shoes don't belong to you," Mombi snapped. "They belong to Oz."

"Oz will shortly belong to me, you impertinent old fool," he said. He flicked his fingers at her and a ball of black smoke sent her flying across the clearing. She hit a tree with a thump and crashed to the ground.

"You can't take them from me," I said with more confidence than I felt. Out of the corner of my eye, I saw Mombi stir. At least the old witch was still alive.

"I do realize that," the Nome King said. "Which is why I'll take you *and* the shoes. I could use magic to control you, of course, but you're much more powerful if you're using the shoes of your own free will."

"I won't help you," I said.

"I thought you'd say that. Which is why I brought along a guarantee of your cooperation." His grip tightened on Madison's arm and she screamed in pain. I heard bones cracking as the Nome King stared at me.

"Stop it!" I cried, unable to bear the sound. "Leave her alone! Fine, I'll do what you want!"

"Amy!" Nox hissed next to me. "You can't!" But too many people had already gotten hurt because of me. The Nome King had pulled her out of Kansas because of me. For all I knew, she was stuck in Oz now for the rest of her life, away from her baby and her family and everything she knew. I wasn't going to watch the Nome King torture her on top of it all. There had to be another way to stop him.

"I'm so glad you've decided to cooperate," the Nome King said in a pleasant tone. "And now, you'll just—"

That was when Mombi hit him. Not with magic. With a branch. The old witch had crept up behind him and swung with all her might. He roared in outrage, loosening his grip on Madison's arm for the barest instant. Glamora launched herself at Mombi, magic sparking from her fingertips. And I dove for Madison, knocking her out of the Nome King's arms.

"Run!" Mombi screamed. "Amy, run!" She raised her branch to hit the Nome King a second time but he threw a sticky net of molten silver at her that tangled in her arms and legs. Mombi stumbled as the net tightened its grip around her. Glamora pointed the wand at her and the Nome King raised his hands. They were going to kill her. I knew it. I had to stop them. Mombi looked directly at me. Her face was suffused with an eerie calm. As if she was finally at peace. "Go, Amy," she said. And then Glamora was on her.

"No!" I yelled, but Nox grabbed my arm. The Nome King was already turning toward us. My boots came to life, blazing with white light, and he threw up one hand to shield his eyes. I didn't waste a second. I grabbed Madison's hand, pulling her after me, and ran. "Take my other hand!" I screamed, reaching for Nox. The Nome King was right behind us. I could feel his magic moving toward us like a silver wave. But the shoes carried me faster and faster, and Madison and Nox with me. Madison was sobbing in fear. "Trust me!" I yelled to her. "I'll keep you safe!" I had no idea if I could keep that promise but I knew I would do my best.

And then I tripped over something glinting in the grass and fell, sprawling, onto the Road of Yellow Brick. Nox tumbled next to me. Madison crashed into me from behind. The road heaved and buckled under us, tearing away from the grass with a huge ripping sound just as the Nome King reached its edge, but he was too late. The road lifted us up into the air and he dwindled to a tiny speck below us.

We were flying toward the stars. I ducked as they came rushing toward us, but just before we ran into them the road stopped and hung, hovering, in the sky. I could have sworn it wiggled a little, like an impatient puppy.

"It's helping us," Nox said in disbelief. He climbed slowly, painfully, to his feet, and then helped me and Madison up, too.

"Amy?" Madison whispered. Her cheeks were streaked with tears and her voice was shaking. "What—what is this? What's going on? Who was—what was Assistant Principal Strachan? Where's Dustin?"

"It's kind of a long story," I said. She still looked terrified but determination was creeping into her expression, too. Madison was tough as nails. She'd do just fine in Oz.

"Why would the road help us?" I asked Nox.

"I don't know." Nox reached up and flicked the nearest star, sending it spinning. Its light refracted around us like sunlight through a prism. My boots sparkled as if in answer. "I don't know where it's taking us either."

The road was pulsing with a strange, golden energy, stretching ahead of us until it dwindled to a point on the horizon. I took a deep breath and grabbed Nox's hand.

"Well," I said. "I guess there's only one way to find out."

Together, we took the first step.